A Necessary Compromise

The Billionaires' Reunion, Volume 3

Rose Fresquez

Published by Rose Fresquez, 2024.

Join my Insider Group and get an exclusive Novella, THE THERAPIST'S NEIGHBOR [1]

---

1. https://dl.bookfunnel.com/pucr7p3use

ACKNOWLEDGEMENTS

I want to thank the Lord, my Savior. Without you, Father, there's no point in trying to do anything at all. It's my prayer that I can honor you with my words. I thank you for connecting me with an amazing group of people who helped support me in accomplishing this novel.

To my husband Joel, who works so hard to provide for our family, so that I can stay home and take care of the kids. I'm so blessed that we get to journey through life together.

To my children Isaiah, Caleb, Abigail and Micah, you fill my heart with joy. Thanks for the giggles, laughter and encouragement.

To my insider team, thanks for always suggesting the coolest ideas.

To my Street Team. Thank you from the bottom of my heart.

To my editor, Deirdre Lockhart. You're a true blessing from God. Your insights and wisdom have helped shape this story.

CHAPTER 1

Fear wasn't standing in the way of Vanessa Douglas's dreams.

However, unforeseen circumstances repeatedly hindered her pursuit of becoming a teacher, casting a shadow over her future. On numerous occasions she'd felt compelled to abandon her goals, to slump on the sofa, and idly wait for opportunities to arise. But that approach wasn't the solution. Life was full of surprises, and she'd had to learn to handle them—even when it meant leaping over the obstacles until she steered her life back onto the path she wanted.

She pondered that this morning as she drove her BBQ food truck and took in San Francisco's charming shops and cafés, each with its unique character. Fog now obscured her view of the towering skyscrapers looming above the Victorian-style homes. But on a clear day, she'd see Alcatraz Island rising from the Bay, and the gray scenery could transform in a matter of hours, much like her temporary food business.

She pulled into the parking lot where the restaurant construction workers wearing lime-green vests and orange hats were already lined up for lunch. She couldn't help but grin. The smell of the sea, the sight of colorful sailboats and yachts in the Bay's blue-green waters, and the rustle of the palm trees above the lush grassy area lifted her spirits.

After she parked, she hurried out, avoiding eye contact with her customers so she could focus on firing up the generator.

Ava, her colleague, walked in, radiating energy and carrying brown bags filled with vegetables. She unpacked lettuce and tomatoes. "This is going to be the best day ever."

"I hope so." Vanessa handed her assistant a purple apron, stamped with the words *Mama Dee's BBQ Queen* above a crown. The smells of grilled meats and chicken skewers in the oven filled the truck. She moved to the pinboard to double-check her list. She'd already checked everything on the pinned paper, but she could never be too confident—especially after this morning. "It sure had a slow start."

"Uh-oh. That doesn't sound good." Ava nudged her.

"My fault. I was late showing up, and the taco truck claimed my designated spot this morning." Vanessa cringed again. She knew better than to show up thirty minutes late. Torn between pursuing her passion and facing reality, she still kept a schedule of some sort. But how was she supposed to keep up with a routine on the day she volunteered at the special needs school? Autistic children were unpredictable, and she'd had to stay to tend to Henry when he had a meltdown after they'd stopped him from taking another child's ball. Henry had then darted out of the classroom, and she'd chased him and brought him back.

Some autistic kids loved running, which could be dangerous when they outran the adult tending to them. She'd done her best to calm him down using the minimal tactics Mom found worked for Vanessa's deceased autistic sister, Ola.

Ava scowled. "You should have spoken to Juanita and claimed your rightful spot for the truck. After all, you've got the permit for it."

Right. Two months ago, Vanessa shelled out a fortune for the permit so she could avoid parallel parking between other cars. But since then, she'd learned the certified paper didn't guarantee the spot. Anyone with a permit could park in any of the designated truck spots. "After how my argument with the deli truck owner escalated last time?"

She'd cited evidence and asserted herself as the spot's rightful owner, but...

"Not everyone has a psycho daughter who's gonna spray paint your menu board and your truck's sign."

The crazy woman had smirked. "No one messes with my mom and gets away with it!"

Shuddering, Vanessa heated the grill. "True enough, but lately, my prayers include far too much asking God for forgiveness for losing my temper and being edgy." The Bible story about turning the other cheek always came to mind, an answer from God, no doubt. But when the food business got the best of her, she lost all sense of reason.

As if her truck's brownish-purple paint wasn't gaudy enough, now the thing had neon-pink and green spray paint. Add her duct-taped menus—the ones she'd replace as soon as she could afford to—and the truck didn't give the most appealing first impression.

"I'm trying to respond to conflicts peacefully by leaving, like today, even though every fiber of my being wanted to stay and fight."

"That's so not fair." Ava shook her head, her dyed-purple ponytail swinging side to side since she hadn't put on a hairnet yet. "It took forever to obtain that permit, and you paid a hefty price for it."

"It's still worth it to avoid the hassle of waiting for weekend events."

After selling her food at weekend events that didn't require street permits for seven years, Vanessa had realized she'd never reach her goal of opening a restaurant—her mother's dream and one Vanessa intended to fulfill ever since Mom passed away eight years ago.

The mouthwatering aroma of broiled meats, barbecue, and sausage lingered in the truck. "Anyway, the morning's prepared menu didn't go to waste. After driving around for nearly an hour, I found a gas station where the manager agreed to let me use the space for five percent of my profits. I sold all my sausage sliders, and I can give the leftover breakfast bowls to the homeless people on the sidewalk near my apartment. But seriously, Ava, I don't know what I'll do without this space. It's my bread and butter."

One of her regular customers from the farmers market had enjoyed her food, and since he couldn't find her in one place, he suggested she park before his waterfront music store here in Sausalito from noon to six. The fantastic offer gave her a place where she didn't have to compete with other food trucks. Plus, the stunning views of the Bay and San Francisco skyline made up for the hard work. She loved this city she'd called home for fifteen years.

But now, this venue presented a new set of challenges. The building was under reconstruction to become a five-star restaurant, and the restaurant manager had informed her she needed to vacate by the end of March. She tried to negotiate a longer stay, but the manager wouldn't accommodate her request.

Despite the setback, she held onto the permit and her agreement with the former owner. Even though the new management voided the agreement, she'd fight for her business. As April progressed, anxiety about her uncertain future consumed her. She needed to meet with the restaurant owner to convince him to let her stay longer. Growing up with a single mom taught her the importance of resilience and perseverance, values that helped her endure the challenges with her business.

Time to focus on the now. "I hope we don't run out of barbecue sauce today. It's one of the favorites, and I hate letting down our customers."

"I've never seen that happen before." Ava crossed to the sink and turned on the water. "Not sure why you always stress about the sauce."

Vanessa always made more sauce than they needed, but she could never be too sure. After washing their hands, they put on gloves and hairnets and began spreading out disposable paper baskets.

"Our lines keep getting longer and longer each day," Ava commented, her light skin contrasting Vanessa's brown complexion. She usually wore short jeans over leggings, while Vanessa preferred to wear leggings by themselves. Ava loved dying her hair with exotic colors, but Vanessa kept hers natural and only styled it when not working. Despite their differences, Ava was the perfect assistant.

Vanessa slid steaming pans of pulled pork, sliced chicken, and prime rib from the mini-oven and set them on a separate counter where Ava was preparing buns. Early morning preparations in the commercial kitchen gave her a jump start to keep up with the day's demand.

"Ready to rock this day?" she asked her assistant.

"I was born ready," Ava replied, giving a fist pump.

Vanessa swung open the truck's serving window and greeted repeat customers by name as she took their orders. Her voice rose above the chatter and the generator's hum as she called out orders to Ava, who then passed the food through the window.

"Number 2," she bellowed to Ava while searching for change in the metal box below the lever. Most customers paid by cash, so to avoid dealing with coins, she charged an even price. Those who paid by credit card used Vanessa's touchless credit card machine and scanned over the screen to pay.

She moved quickly, slapping meat onto the bread for those who wanted sandwiches or chicken and roasted potatoes. Meat was one less step to prepare than sandwiches.

"My mouth is watering." A short man with a Hispanic accent accepted his basket of chicken and roasted potatoes.

She beamed. "Enjoy."

"Number 3," another customer shouted. "Extra BBQ for me, please!"

Vanessa bellowed the order to Ava and snatched two mini plastic cups of sauce for her customer, then winked at him as she handed over his prime rib sandwich. "The sauce is the boss."

The construction workers enjoyed her food the most. They usually returned to buy seconds after the lunch rush died down. They also ate most of her dinner. Staying here, she was helping the crew, and they were helping her. She'd use that in her pitch to the restaurant owner if she could get an audience with him.

She could use a third employee handing out sodas and water and emptying the trash can, but she couldn't afford it while she was saving every penny. Other than the construction workers, most of her customers were employees from the charming buildings with unique architectural styles across the manicured lawn. Quaint clapboard storefronts to sleek modern structures and boutiques drew in tourists, some of whom stopped by her truck. And the area offered the added blessing of two benches in front of the fountain where people sat while others lounged on the grass underneath the palms. Many nearby shops also had outdoor seating areas where her customers could sit and eat while watching the boats go by.

More people trickled in, smiling as they interacted. Although it wasn't her passion, she enjoyed talking to people. By almost three, the rush died down, and she swept the floor and cleaned the dishes before she and Ava sat in the truck to eat.

Through the back window by the small table, she could see the earlier fog had vanished, and a sweet breeze stirred from the back and front serving window. The truck was always warm, but she resisted plugging in the fan. The fewer appliances plugged in, the better.

"Thank you for your hard work." Vanessa forked her roasted potato.

Across the table, Ava saluted her with a bottled water. "This is our year to claim our dreams."

It wasn't Vanessa's place to judge anyone's aspirations, but she never wanted Ava's talent to go to waste. "Are you sure I'm not holding you back from your dream job?"

Ava swallowed the prime rib she'd been chewing and gestured toward the corner counter where a framed photo of Vanessa's mom and sister hung. "*You* may have changed your mind about starting a restaurant and teaching, but *I'm* counting on having this truck come October."

In case Ava assumed Vanessa would have her mom's restaurant in October, she'd better clarify. "October is my deadline to get the money. Starting a business requires planning." The cost of rent, even in her cheaper Hunters Point neighborhood, was frightening, and that would be the only place she could afford if she ever reached her financial goal. But Ava didn't need to know all those details as long as she had her hopes in the food business. "The truck will be yours, as promised."

Surprisingly, some people were passionate about the street-food business. Vanessa had met Ava through the special needs school.

"My mom thinks I should go after my dream." Ava eyed her water bottle. Then, with her index finger, she drew the three letters of her name on the condensation amassing on its sides. Her ten-year-old son, Malcolm, had Asperger's and sensory sensitivities of all sorts. Blessedly, her parents lived with them, giving her some much-needed family support.

Vanessa reached over and grasped her friend's hand. "Your mom is a smart woman."

A male voice at the window interrupted their conversation.

Vanessa stood up.

"It's that man," Ava muttered under her breath.

Vanessa's heart rate picked up when she faced the restaurant manager. Wiping her hands over her apron, she took a deep breath before walking to the window and forcing a smile. "Xenon, hi."

He half smiled back, his pointed beard and mustache making him look like an anchor. "You're still here, I see."

Her gaze drifted to the flashing lights of heavy equipment and machinery and the orange cones and barricades marking off the work area. She needed to be careful with her words this time. "I'm grateful you haven't called the city council on me."

His thick eyebrows drew together, and he put on his business persona. "My assistant is working on that. Are you really looking for that kind of battle?"

If only he would understand! She shook her head. She'd explained before how she needed a space with foot traffic, not that it was his concern.

As she gripped the window, she drew in a deep breath. "As soon as I can speak to your boss." She'd requested this before. "If he kicks me out, I'll go."

Despite her permit not expiring until December, she understood the new owners had the right to possess their space after the previous landlord sold it. Unlike the shops across the street, the restaurant was the only building on this side, visible to all the tourists walking up and down the street.

"I'm sure you're nice," he began, and she suppressed a chuckle as his stomach growled. Undeterred, he continued with his business speech, moving his hands to emphasize his point. "In another world, we could even be friends, but—"

"Hold that thought," she interrupted, realizing he hadn't even bothered to summon the owner to meet with her. She hurried to the oven, swung it open, and pulled out one of the pans with sliced brisket.

"What's the plan?" Ava whispered across the counter as she restocked the woven basket with disposable utensils.

"A man's heart, you know," Vanessa replied. Using tongs, she scooped a generous amount of sliced prime rib into the serving basket, then added the roasted potatoes. She was out of salad. Her mother used to say the way to a man's heart was through his stomach, which never made sense because the two men in Mom's life had left her. But it couldn't hurt to try.

"Here." Ava handed her the set of utensils and a mini cup of BBQ sauce. "The sauce is the boss."

"Thanks." Vanessa returned to the window and held out the plate.

The man's brows scrunched further as he eyed the food, then her.

"I know you probably ate, but just in case you hadn't, I figured I'd..."

He moved closer and snatched the basket from her. "My boss is a busy man."

She ripped open the utensils and handed him the fork. At least, he was now talking about his boss.

He forked the meat and lifted it to his mouth, letting out a satisfied moan. "This is good stuff."

Bouncing her foot on the smooth surface, she let him enjoy his food before she gave him a napkin. *Please, God, soften his heart so he can be reasonable today.*

"What if he refuses to meet with you?" Xenon asked halfway through his meal.

"Then I'll ask you for his number, perhaps." She shrugged.

Pointing his fork at her, he gave a slight smile. "That's not how I operate."

"Just try to convince him to meet with me, please." Would that involve traveling out of state? "I can travel too if it's what it takes for me to see him."

She'd prefer not to spend money on a plane ticket, but if she could keep her truck in this location for a few more months, it'd be worth it.

"Everything tastes good when you're starving," Xenon remarked after swallowing.

"So?" She tried to refocus him on the main subject. "Is it a deal?"

"I'll see what I can do." He shook his head before lifting the basket with his half-eaten food. "Was this a bribe?"

She grinned, folding her hands together as if praying. "Did it work?"

"For now." He forked another piece of meat.

For now was all she could cling to.

She was thirty-four, and if she didn't succeed with the food business soon, she'd have to abandon her dreams altogether. Even if his boss agreed to meet with her, she couldn't be certain everything would work out. What would she do then?

CHAPTER 2

Nate Stone's footsteps echoed on the pavement as he paced, each labored breath muffled by the helmet encasing his head. Around him, his crew buzzed with energy, tearing down and rebuilding the Number 62 Chevrolet with surgical precision. Time was slipping away, and with it, his chances of clinching victory at the Geico 500—one of NASCAR's most prestigious races.

Though racing had once been a beloved hobby, the burden of earning a living through it now drained him. His pulse hammered in his ears, drowning out the hum of rival engines and the distant murmur of the crowd. He sent a silent plea to the heavens, seeking solace in his faith on race days like these.

The clear sky offered a small consolation, but his desperation to rejoin the race clawed at him. Fingers trembling in their gloves, he fought to keep his fear of losing from showing. This high-speed track had already bested him once. Now, another defeat gnawed at him, and the unblinking gaze of the TV cameras followed him, scrutinizing each move.

Heat seeped through his fireproof jumpsuit. He considered hydrating but balked at the idea of another pit stop for a bathroom break. Fanning himself with gloved fingers did little to alleviate the swelter.

"Never let them see you sweat," a distant memory whispered, though its origin eluded him—a line from an action film or a recent deodorant shoot, perhaps.

If it had been a simple issue like refueling or changing a tire, he wouldn't have had to leave the car. His disappointing Daytona 500 performance loomed in his mind. Now, the Geico 500 victory slipped further out of reach, and the mounting pressure threatened to crush him.

"Let's get you back out there." Doyle's voice came through the headset, a soothing balm for Nate's frayed nerves.

He nodded his appreciation and clambered back into the compact car. After securing himself in the driver's seat, he grasped the steering wheel, and adrenaline surged through him as the engine vibrated.

The crowd's cheers swelled, their excitement palpable. He inhaled, zeroing in on the race. His heartbeat thundered as he sped down the track, navigating through the other cars.

"Only five cars separate you from the lead."

At the news his spotter relayed, a glimmer of hope ignited. Small as the victory was, it fueled his determination. Clenching his jaw, he pushed harder to close the gap and give his fans a performance to remember.

He concentrated, the heat and din of competing engines fading as he wove through the pack. He could see drivers tailing him in his rearview mirror, but he remained composed.

"Twenty-five to go. He's eating your lunch, getting off the corner," his spotter instructed.

Nate braced against the intense g-forces as he navigated each turn to seize the lead.

"Hold that line," his spotter continued. "Coming up on the white flag. You got a good spot. Don't give it up."

Forty-eight seconds later, Nate found himself choking on the fumes and exhaust of his newest rival, Guy Damon. In a split-second decision, Nate swerved to avoid the noxious cloud and the car ahead. But in doing so, he collided with another vehicle.

Nate's car slowed, the accelerator sticking as he pressed down. His brakes screeched, and a shallow angle sent him careening into a collision with another car. His heart plummeted while the impact jerked his body, his car spinning out and getting rammed on both sides.

Emerging from the wreckage, he grimaced, his left arm, wrist, and muscles aching. His intense workout routine had conditioned his body to endure such punishment, but it didn't stop the impact hurting. Two cars sped ahead, leaving him to assess the damage.

"You're okay, chief?" Doyle's concerned voice came through the headset.

"Lost at the kink. But I'm okay. Got hit hard." Nate strove for steadiness. A sinking feeling weighed down his gut. This race was over for him.

Something had disrupted the accelerator pedal mechanism—possibly a faulty throttle or an external factor. He'd have to wait for the team's analysis to uncover the cause of his devastating loss.

"Let's get her fixed up. This race isn't over yet."

Doyle's hopeful voice couldn't dispel the sinking in Nate's gut as he steered toward the pit stop. Guilt gnawed at him. How could he disappoint his hardworking team like this? In a flurry of motion, the crew surrounded the car, tightened bolts, and replaced damaged parts.

"You've got this, chief." Doyle's warm smile and unwavering faith as he set Nate off gave him a needed boost. With renewed focus, Nate wove through several cars, the track stretching out before him. The rest of the race blurred into a high-speed whirlwind of close calls and sheer determination.

When the checkered flag waved, Nate claimed sixth place, his car battered but running. From his decade-long career, he knew even brand-new cars could encounter unexpected issues, but he was alive and finished in the top ten, though his pride and ego had taken a hit.

As Guy Damon basked in the winner's spotlight, Nate climbed out of his car to the sound of fans chanting his name. He forced a smile and waved to shake off his disappointment. Freed from the confines of his helmet, he took a deep breath and allowed himself a moment of happiness for his competitor. Guy, a rookie driver, had just claimed his first NASCAR win in his hometown.

Ultimately, only one driver could win each race, and every victory brought more sponsors and opportunities. Exhausted and aching from hours on the track, Nate needed rest before facing the next challenge. If he wanted to reach the series championship, each race would now count more than ever.

As he huddled with his crew, they reassured him not to dwell on the loss. A moderator approached, microphone in hand. "Nate, tough race out there today. How are you feeling?"

A sixth-place finish rarely warranted attention, but his position in the All-Time NASCAR Cup Series Wins list meant his performance was always in the spotlight. He had to be prepared to explain lousy results.

He took a deep breath and faced her, ready to put a positive spin on things. "I'm feeling pretty good, actually. It was a tough race, but I gave it my all." His response didn't reflect his true feelings, but he wasn't about to admit otherwise.

She seemed to expect more. "Can you talk us through what happened during the race?"

Feeling the pressure, he focused on the positives and praised his crew and sponsors for providing a great car. He then addressed the obvious setbacks.

"Any final thoughts for your fans?" the interviewer prompted.

"I can't express how grateful I am for my fans' unwavering support. I promise to continue giving my all, but that all couldn't be given without my fantastic team. In truth, much of my success is due to their outstanding performances." He faced the camera head-on, sure his eyes shone with the hope and determination pulsing through him. "I can't wait to see what the future holds."

His impressive record had attracted numerous sponsors over the past six years, diversifying his income. But every poor performance threatened his career. As the owner of Vrimix Tech approached, the man's bald head gleamed in the sun. "Don't worry." He gave Nate a reassuring smile and a pat on the back, but disappointment dulled his eyes. "We'll get 'em next time, chief."

At thirty-five, Nate had to keep winning to satisfy his sponsors and maintain his career. Still, each race risked his life—a sobering reminder that his career was temporary and he needed to seize every opportunity he could.

Beyond racing, he was expanding his drag strips in other states, opening steakhouses, and investing in automotive dealerships and racing teams that competed worldwide. These ventures provided a safety net should his career end due to injury.

Win or lose, his supportive family was his rock. They couldn't attend every race, but they watched replays and teased him about his mistakes. His parents called after each race, his mother asking about his retirement plans and his father offering performance tips.

Having spent many of his first eight years in foster care, he cherished his family. Kyle and Regina Stone had adopted him and nine other children. His siblings each brought vital elements that crafted who he was, but Iris, the Stones' biological child and the youngest of their group, was the glue that held their family together.

Later that night, he joined a group FaceTime call with his parents and some siblings. Since his mother's worry was evident, he reassured her he was fine. His father, sharing Nate's blue eyes despite not being blood-related, voiced his concerns about the car's condition.

"Dad," Wade interrupted, his brown hair tousled and shiny as if he had just come out of the shower. "Before you blame the crew, look at the stats. Nate's license was suspended within the first year of acquiring it."

Nate had spent the following summer taking driver's ed classes for the second time to earn his license back, but he couldn't admit Wade was right. The banter continued with Theo chiming in about Nate's practice hours. As the siblings teased him about his driving skills, it was clear they were worried about his safety.

Theo's face popped up on the screen, and his olive skin glowed in the dim light. He spent most of his time in South America, particularly in Brazil, where he ran a multibillion-dollar media company. "Why did you hit the wall? I thought you spent endless hours practicing?"

"Boys." Mom spoke up. "Your brother almost died...."

"What your mother is saying"—Dad filled in when her voice wavered—"is we need to get together more often. We should all try to make it to Nate's home track race next month."

"Ha!" Nate joked. "These two are the last people you want watching my race."

Later, he received calls from three more siblings, each expressing their concern. His sister Iris echoed their mother's worries and asked about his retirement plans. He deflected her questions, discussing her upcoming wedding instead. Despite her persistence, his spirits remained high.

By the time he went to bed, he was beaming from his family's support. Stowing their love and encouragement in his heart, he didn't dwell on the race as he surrendered to sleep.

Grateful for a break the next day, Nate posed for an Edez sunscreen lotion photo shoot on the beach. He'd never used Edez, but the corporate executives who sponsored his car insisted on authenticity. So, after being slathered with the cream, he stood shirtless for hours, but the executives didn't count on him being allergic to the product, which caused his chest to become inflamed, itchy, and red.

Good thing he didn't have a race the next day when he was still feeling itchy during the photo shoot for a car manufacturing company. This time, he was promoting their latest model and highlighting its performance features while dressed in a jumpsuit. However, the shoot took longer than two hours because he kept scratching his chest, leaving him exhausted and irritated by the time he left Alabama for his home in North Carolina.

His hometown was in Colorado, the only childhood home he remembered, but he'd moved to North Carolina. Closer to the NASCAR tracks so he could practice and compete. After dinner, when his house staff left for their quarters for the night, he settled on the leather bench behind the piano in the sunroom.

This was his favorite place to relax and where he chose not to think about racing or anything else that reminded him each day could be his last. Beyond the floor-to-ceiling windows, the sun began to dip below the horizon, casting a golden glow across the nearby foothills.

He ran his fingers over the smooth piano keys, relishing the feeling beneath his fingertips. As he took a deep breath, peace soothed him, and he glanced out to the nature garden beyond his property. A tranquil lake reflected the warm hues of the setting sun as it cast an orangey-pink glow over the distant Blue Ridge Mountains.

With the music of "Lean on Me" playing in the back of his mind, his fingers began to dance across the keys. He'd been practicing the song for a month and had the sheet music open. Now, the piano notes frolicked into the space around him, echoing out into the surrounding landscape. The wind rustling through the trees and the distant calls of birds settling in for the night blended with the melody, creating a harmonious symphony of nature and music.

He'd always wanted a house nestled in the mountains, despite their smaller size compared to his hometown, to remind him of the natural beauty of home. As the day's tension seeped away, he couldn't help but think of his family and the annual reunion he was responsible for planning this year.

He intended to host it at Thanksgiving and had started planning in January during his two months off. But he'd ended up spending that time skiing and racing snowmobiles with his siblings instead. He grinned at the blown-up photo on the beige wall, which featured him, his family, and their chef who was now dating Nate's youngest sister, Iris. Their family had expanded since the photo was taken. One of his sisters was engaged, two of his brothers were married, and one of them had children.

Despite his desire to start a family, he feared getting involved in a serious relationship. How could he risk that when he might die in a race and leave his loved ones to fend for themselves? He wasn't afraid of death itself, but the thought of leaving his family behind was unbearable. He shook his head, trying to shake off the crazy thought, and refocused on playing the piano, correcting himself after striking a sour note.

His phone vibrated, and he slid it from atop the piano. Before he swiped to answer, the contact flashed for the manager who oversaw his many restaurants.

"Xenon, what's up?"

"Great job on the race, by the way."

"Gloating is overrated, you know." Nate spoke lightheartedly. Xenon had become a good friend, one Nate trusted to manage thirty-three restaurants across the big cities in North America. Despite Xenon's disinterest in motorsports, he watched most of Nate's races on TV.

"Why didn't you tell the moderator your car wasn't cooperative?"

He might've said something of the sort. He couldn't even remember his interview anymore. "I blamed the several pit stops." Or something like that.

"I'll give you some advice." Xenon then offered his opinion on how Nate should handle postrace interviews when the race didn't go as the team hoped.

Nate chuckled, then steered the conversation to the food business. "I might become a chef if this career crashes."

"Speaking of chefs." Xenon's voice now turned to his usual business tone. "We've run into a small dilemma in the Bay."

"Don't tell me you need to wait for another permit for something else." The stool scraped against the tile when Nate stood and walked toward the window. The last rays of sunlight had disappeared below the horizon, and the automatic lights had already turned on over the porch.

They'd encountered several obstacles during the restaurant's construction, hence pushing back the grand opening date from July to September. But Xenon wouldn't seek a solution from Nate while the manager was the expert.

"It's the woman who keeps parking a food truck in the lot."

"There's a food truck in the parking lot?" He hadn't seen one the last two times he visited the construction site.

"She's there in the afternoons. The previous owner let her park there. I told her she had until the end of March—"

"We're almost at the end of April." If she'd already been asked to leave, by common courtesy, she should have done as asked.

"It's complicated."

Nate barely registered Xenon's explanation to the Bay Area food vendors. Xenon always dealt with contractors and oversaw the details. Nate's only contribution was having his sister draw the restaurant plans to match the theme of a given city. Iris probably knew more about the restaurant's recent updates than he did. "What's the problem, and how does it involve me?"

"She wants to meet with you. Otherwise, she's in no hurry to make an exodus."

"What?" A strained laugh escaped his lungs. Who did she think she was? He walked toward the seating area, the cozy rug soft beneath his bare feet as he paced between the plush sofas and back to the window. "If she can't be reasoned with, shouldn't you notify the city council or whoever handles such matters?"

A silence passed before Xenon spoke in a low voice as if he was conceding to the woman's request. "My assistant called the city council and left a message last week. I now regret rushing that decision."

"Why?"

"It might move things faster if you meet with her before the restaurant's film and photo shoot next Wednesday." Xenon had a knack for generating buzz and hype about the restaurant long before its official opening day.

Nate needed to focus on practicing for the next race, not juggling a business he had no clue how to handle. He ground his teeth. "I don't have time for this."

"There's no better time to use your new chopper than this short trip."

"I can't believe you want me to do this."

"Let me text you some photos of her truck." Xenon ignored Nate's protests. "You'll see why we need it out of the way for the photo shoot."

Drawing out a frustrated grunt, Nate threaded his hands through his hair. He didn't need to stress about anything other than winning his next race.

Perhaps stopping by his restaurant wouldn't be an inconvenience, though. He did have a couple of meetings in San Francisco early next week. Logan and Serafina would be back from their honeymoon by then too. He'd enjoy another opportunity to see his brother.

"I'll handle it." But how could he have a better approach than Xenon's?

After hanging up, Nate received a text with pictures of a browny-purple food truck covered in neon-pink and green spray-painted food and words. The dingy truck couldn't be further from the image he wanted of his restaurant. How could the vendor convince customers to buy food from such an atrocity?

Why had she summoned him to his property? Was she looking for a fight? Dealing with conflict wasn't his forte, especially with everything else going on in his life. However, his agreeable personality and the peacemaking traits his mother instilled made him flexible, a necessity in his line of work.

So he'd take a diplomatic approach. He'd befriend the vendor and resolve the issue peacefully. After all, he used the same tactic in his businesses to win over investors, and it worked so far. He'd get the vendor to leave his property without causing a scene.

CHAPTER 3

Vanessa's mornings followed a routine when she wasn't volunteering at the local school. She rose at four thirty, spent time in prayer, and engaged in a fifteen-minute Zumba workout via YouTube before leaving at five thirty. She then drove to the commercial kitchen and arrived by six to meet her meat delivery person.

Finding overnight parking for her truck created an ongoing concern. Due to limited space in the city, she often parked outside of Hunters Point. Sometimes, she parked at a gas station and compensated the owner for the privilege while accepting the risk of a break-in. It typically took her twenty minutes to reach her minivan parked nearby before driving her truck to work. If she took the bus, she had to wake up an hour earlier.

Today, she'd taken the bus, and the early start paid off as she secured a prime morning spot on the street. She sold all her breakfast bowls and sliders and even prepared BBQ prime rib and pork sliders for those who wanted them. Some customers ordered chicken and potatoes for breakfast. Simply grateful for the patronage at any hour, she no longer questioned the appeal of BBQ meals in the morning.

Soon, she was off to Sausalito with Ava, serving lunch by the oceanfront. Adrenaline surged through her as she attended to customers. Noticing a bandage on Connor's nose, she inquired what happened as she handed him a plate of chicken and roasted potatoes.

"I wish I could blame it on work." The burly man accepted the food. "My son's toy truck fell from the top bunk while I was stripping his bedsheets."

Vanessa winced, empathizing. "Who knew toys could be so dangerous?"

"You obviously don't have kids." Connor squeezed ketchup onto his potatoes before returning the bottle to the window. "You'd understand if you did."

Although she longed to find a special someone to start a family with, that idea remained distant from her current goals. She'd dated a few men in the past two years, but the relationships hadn't progressed the moment they expressed disapproval of her food-truck business. Maybe she'd never truly fall in love—experiencing such profound affection for someone that life without them would be unthinkable.

"I'll have a Number 2, please," Marnie, the owner of the boutique across the street, called out, interrupting Vanessa's reverie. The line of customers grew longer, spilling from the pavement onto the grass.

Ava was quick, handing Vanessa prepared meals as she called out the menu numbers corresponding to the customers' orders. Crafting dishes in under five minutes was a skill they'd honed together.

As the lunch rush subsided, Vanessa exhaled and tossed the empty baking trays into the sink. She glanced at the microwave clock. Hmm, three ten. Sometimes, they were so swamped they forgot to eat until the day's end. "How about we grab some lunch soon?"

"I'll eat whatever's left," Ava, who was now sweeping the floor, responded.

Vanessa inspected the glass door of the portable ovens. The chicken had turned a golden hue, and the prime rib was undoubtedly ready as well. She kept meat skewering in the ovens to stay ahead of demand. By now, she had a good grasp of their daily sales. If there were leftovers, she distributed them to the homeless outside her apartment.

"Let me refill the condiments and clean that while you prepare our lunch," Ava suggested.

Some barbecue pork remained in a baking dish in one of the ovens, and the asparagus and mixed vegetables would be enough to see them through the evening rush.

Four thirty to five thirty was their busiest time as people got off work, and those still at work had their dinner around then.

"Do you know what I'll do when I run a food truck?" Ava asked from the window.

"You mean doing better than I am?" Vanessa spoke over the whirring noise of the electric knife as she sliced the prime rib.

"Exactly." The humming generator outside their truck and the high-pitched whine of power tools seemed louder when they didn't have customers. "I'll work smarter, not harder."

"Are you trying to say I'm not working smart?" Vanessa slid off her greasy gloves and tossed them in the trash before jamming her hands on her hips.

"I admire that you like to cook everything, but..." Ava wiped down the window, obviously choosing her words carefully.

"Just say I'm a control freak." Vanessa jerked a finger Ava's way, acknowledging her attachment to her mother's recipes. "I won't be mad at you."

Ava chuckled. "I'll hire people to work for me while I collect the big bucks." Ava's purple ponytail shimmered beneath her hairnet as she shook her head. "The whole point of being my own boss is so that I can spend time with my son."

Her lips, also outlined in purple, thinned with sadness. "I want Malcolm to know he's loved. Just because I fell in love with his loser dad doesn't mean my son should pay for my mistakes."

Vanessa's chest tightened. Ava's husband had abandoned her and their son, shirking the responsibility of caring for their special-needs child, a smart and tenderhearted ten-year-old with a whole future ahead of him.

"Your son is perfect," Vanessa repeated the words she told Ava whenever she discussed her fears of raising a special-needs child alone. "He's blessed to have you in his life."

Ava gave a gentle roll of her now-glossy eyes and swung the washcloth toward Vanessa. "You and your blessings."

"What's wrong with blessings?" Vanessa transferred the sliced meat from the cutting board into the pan, leaving some for their lunch. She covered the pan with foil and returned the meat to the oven.

"Oh my!" Ava's exclamation caused Vanessa to close the oven and spin to her friend. Ava was in a daze, her hand frozen with the washcloth on the window. "Who. Is. That. Hottie?"

Vanessa rushed to the window in two long strides.

As she approached, her mouth dropped open. Striding through the grass in a perfectly fitted navy suit and a crisp white shirt was none other than... "Nate Stone."

She hadn't realized she said his name out loud until Ava asked, "You know him?"

Vanessa nodded, struggling to tear her gaze away from him. Tall and lean with dark, slightly curly hair, he was undoubtedly coming from another *GQ* modeling photo shoot. As he approached, she snatched the washcloth from Ava to wipe the already-clean window.

"I already cleaned that," Ava whispered. "But that's one handsome man."

"Tell me about it," Vanessa breathed.

"How do you know him?" Ava clattered serving spoons into the sink. "What are we going to feed him? Do you think he'll like anything from the menu?"

With a multitude of questions, Ava kept dropping things. "I'm going to get a plate of prime rib ready, in case he wants to sample our food."

Vanessa felt hot, but she kept wiping the surface, afraid any movement would cause her to look at Nate.

"We should have had the graffiti removed. Now we may lose an investor for life."

Vanessa winced, remembering the spray paint, but seriously, what a laugh. Where did Ava get such a crazy idea?

"Oh no!" Ava continued. "Why didn't we make your kale salad today?"

Kale salad was one of Vanessa's best dishes, but they'd discussed this earlier when Ava had shown up with vegetables and announced kale hadn't been in the market that morning. Her friend must be as frazzled as Vanessa was.

Vanessa's chest rose and fell, and she concentrated on the construction noise and her chugging generator. Why was Nate here? Then she sensed his nearness because his intoxicating scent, eucalyptus mingled with something pricey, now diffused the smell of smoke and food. Against her will, her head lifted, and there he was, standing in front of her window. In front of *her*.

Her knees felt weak as she looked into piercing eyes the color of the ocean. She leaned out her serving window, bracing her weight on her elbows for support and confidence.

"Hello." He held out his hand. "I'm Nate Stone."

"Vanessa." She swallowed and kept a smile in place, trying to hide her disappointment that he didn't recognize her. She stepped onto her tiptoes to reach out and shake his hand. It was strong and firm, and her disappointment didn't stop tingles from shooting through her arm. She slid her hand back and gripped both hands on the serving window. "What can I get you today?"

His brows knit as he scratched his immaculately trimmed beard, revealing the fancy watch on his wrist. "Have we met before?"

Her heart jump-started from shame that he didn't recognize her, then to pure rage. She had met him twice before through her best friend, Serafina, who was now his sister-in-law. They'd seen each other at a funeral and a wedding. "Maybe you've seen me at the farmers market."

"We have prime rib with homemade BBQ sauce." Ava's voice sounded as she appeared with two disposable baskets of meat with asparagus on each. "Chicken—"

"I'm not here for food, thanks." Nate raised his hand, cutting off Ava's sales pitch. He glanced up at the truck. No doubt, the duct tape holding the menus over the spray-painted background didn't inspire confidence. Then he looked at her, giving away none of his reaction as he crossed his arms. "My manager said you wanted to talk to me?"

What was he talking about? "Why would I want to talk to you?" That came out wrong and rude. How unexpected.

She stood taller and adjusted her apron straps. "I mean, I want to talk to you." She threw her head back, losing her train of thought. That was the consequence of her constantly ogling the commercials Nate was featured in. "I'm sorry."

Just great. Sweat drenched her armpits. She'd need to change her shirt and reapply deodorant as soon as he left. Squaring her shoulders to compose herself, she managed to sound coherent. "You're the one here. I don't think I know your manager."

"I own the restaurant." He tipped his chin to the unfinished building by the yellow bobcat.

The hammers beat out a steady cadence like a timer, reminding her of her limited days in the parking lot as her mind registered his statement.

"You bought the music store?" What were the odds the buyer had been Nate? Wasn't he busy enough racing cars all year long?

He cleared his throat, his brows knitting tighter. He must be wondering why she was surprised, but he had no idea who she was in the first place.

He was a famous race car driver—not just famous. He was one of the few who held the most wins in a single season. He made a lot of money, but probably not a billionaire, like one of the construction workers had mentioned when he said the restaurant belonged to some billionaire.

Maybe Vanessa didn't know as much about him as she thought.

Just like Serafina mustn't have known where Nate's restaurant was, or her friend would've warned her. But even if Serafina knew, she'd been busy planning a wedding. Come to think of it, Serafina hadn't visited Vanessa's new location yet.

Her heart was racing when she turned around, and Ava was carrying the food baskets back to the counter. If the way to a man's heart was through his stomach... Vanessa snatched the prime rib basket from Ava. Food had worked with Nate's manager. Wasn't that why Xenon summoned Nate? Perhaps God was in on it too.

She moved back to the window and lifted the basket to him. Why were her hands shaking? "Eat something before we talk."

He craned his neck to look at the street. The sleek car parallel parked between the SUV and the suburban had to be his. He probably hadn't wanted to park near the construction zone.

"I only have ten minutes." He faced her again.

"Maybe you can eat while we talk." She shoved the plate out further, insisting he take it, but then the basket slid out of her hand and remnants of food fell past his chest before landing on the concrete.

He stepped back, grinding his teeth as he glared at the food staining his shirt.

"Oh no!" She gasped, covering her mouth as she spun around.

"Here." Ava handed her a handful of napkins.

Vanessa scurried for the door, swung it open, and jumped over the three steps. She tripped over her own feet and fell headfirst onto the concrete. Double humiliation when the napkins flew out of her hand and fluttered along the surface.

She was on her hands and knees, having just dumped food on Nate, the man she had a secret crush on and the man she needed to help her keep her mother's food business afloat. Gentle hands helped her stand, and embarrassment burned her neck. She couldn't even look at him when he asked if she was okay.

"I'm fine." Somehow, she thanked him for helping her off the ground before she rushed to gather the napkins scattered by the breeze. She then tried to clean the BBQ sauce from his shirt, but he stepped back, declining her offer.

"It's okay." Soft and tender, his voice caressed her ear. "Do you need to go to the hospital?"

She shook her head, his concern diffusing her embarrassment.

"I have to go." He eyed the food truck. "Just make sure to keep your truck out of the way when the film crew shows up tomorrow."

"Noted."

He hadn't asked her to leave? She had a catering gig at twelve thirty tomorrow. She'd intended to serve lunch for half an hour before rushing off to the event, but it may have been too tight a shift anyway. Maybe the construction workers would let any customers know about the film crew's arrival.

Despite her embarrassment, she couldn't help her heart flutters. The way he looked at her, his chiseled jaw covered with a neatly groomed beard, made her brain fuzzy. She couldn't deny her crush on him, but now, she'd probably lost any chance she had with him.

He strolled back toward the grass and his sleek black car. As the back door swung open, an Asian woman dressed in a cream blazer and pencil skirt stepped out holding an iPad. Probably Nate's assistant or agent or whoever he had working for him during his spotlight gigs.

Vanessa brushed off the dirt on her apron and gripped the napkins in her other hand. She tried to ignore her uneasy feeling about the woman, grateful for the hours she'd spent with Nate, but wishing she could trade places with his assistant, even for just two hours.

"Does that mean we're going to get kicked out of here?" Ava took the soiled napkins from her.

"Not until I talk to Nate." Vanessa attempted to sound confident.

Ava arched her eyebrows. "You're all flustered. Not the feisty food-truck boss I know."

Vanessa waved her off. "Falling face down in front of someone like—"

"Hottie?" Ava interjected with a playful grin.

Vanessa snorted a laugh, still determined to connect with Nate. "I know him, remember?"

"Didn't seem like he knew you."

And that was the problem. Vanessa was attracted to a man who didn't find her attractive. If he had, he'd have remembered her. She'd left a mark on his clothes, so he couldn't forget her now.

She could get his phone number from Serafina, but he didn't remember her. She'd intended to crawl into his heart by attending his family gatherings, but this changed everything. Now he wasn't just a crush—he was a businessman with a venue she needed to operate her truck.

She had to start teaching in the next year or two. Once she hit thirty-five next year, her dream might be out of reach. The last thing she needed was another distraction. She'd have to stop stalking him on the internet as she had been doing when she watched his races or commercials. She couldn't afford the distraction if she wanted to reach her goals.

CHAPTER 4

Morning runs were a part of Nate's routine whether he was home or not. Running helped him stay in shape and clear his mind of the sheer terror that gripped him on race days when he knew the day could be his last.

However, this dawn was different. He wasn't running alone, nor did he have a race to worry about. Instead, Vanessa occupied his thoughts as she had when she'd kept him up last night.

Around midnight Serafina's friend from the wedding came to mind. Logan's wife had a friend with flawless brown skin, and while Nate only had a vague recollection of what she looked like, he remembered long wavy hair and pearly whites. Now, he and Logan were running along Market Street, which was relatively empty except for the occasional dog walker or passing car. They jogged past a truck delivering to a nearby restaurant, and the fierce and beautiful woman came to mind again.

"Have you decided to stay until Friday?" Logan's question pulled him out of his thoughts.

Nate shook his head to clear his mind. "Gotta hit the track tomorrow." The sooner he worked with his crew to prepare for Talladega Superspeedway on Sunday, the better his chances were to finish in the top three.

"You should stay. We have two extra tickets to *Casablanca*."

"Oh man. What has Serafina done to you, bro?" With the happiness radiating through Logan since he fell for Serafina, it seemed easy for him to make extra sacrifices for his wife. Nate rolled his eyes at his brother's new love for retro movies and the similar décor now brightening his modern penthouse. "You're speaking like a real classic fan."

"I have to make my wife happy."

"Especially during your honeymoon phase."

"I'm hoping we'll stay in the honeymoon phase forever." Logan drew out a breath, matching Nate's steady pace.

Just months apart, they could pass as twins, except Nate was taller now than when they'd been growing up. But although they'd always shared their thoughts, he had yet to ask Logan about Vanessa because his brother would want to know why.

He could still remember the surprise in Vanessa's brown eyes when he announced himself as the property owner. He'd sensed her fear when she dumped food on his shirt—good thing his undershirt protected him from getting scalded. When he helped her up, something in her eyes gave him pause. What was it? Almost a daunting familiarity as if she knew him more than the fans who got pit passes for meet and greets.

He'd wanted to linger and ensure she was okay, but he'd had to change before meeting his San Francisco car dealership business partners. He might've had to cancel the meeting if she hadn't had someone with her.

She'd seemed bothered when he asked if they met before. As much as he wanted to tell her to leave his property though, the words couldn't come out after her panic when she spilled that food. As long as she wasn't there tomorrow, she'd get the message to vacate before the restaurant opened. Right?

Another truck plastered with pictures of food drove past them, and he didn't think twice. "What is Serafina's friend's name?"

Logan slowed, drew out a breath, and raised an eyebrow. "She has a few friends, but I'm going to assume you're asking about Vanessa, Serafina's maid of honor."

How many Vanessas were there? Could it be the same woman? He kept a slow pace as Logan began his question assault.

"Why are you asking about Vanessa all of a sudden? Did you guys connect at the wedding?"

"I wish." He'd be so embarrassed if he hadn't recognized the woman who'd spent those days with his family on the island. In his defense, the woman at the food truck had her hair in a ponytail under a hairnet, and the woman at the wedding had worn her hair down.

But only one person could set him at ease. So he'd have to ask Serafina.

When they returned to Logan's penthouse on the fifty-sixth floor, they cleaned up and dressed for the day, then met at the dining table for breakfast. Spoons and forks clanked as Nate sipped his dandelion and turmeric smoothie. Logan and Serafina sat side by side across the table. Beyond them, floor-to-ceiling windows fronted the dining area adjoining the kitchen and living room, and the rising sun cast a vivid orange glow over jaw-dropping panoramic views of the Bay and the Golden Gate Bridge.

"Are you prepared to sign hundreds of autographs this afternoon?" Serafina poked at her omelet with a fork.

"I'm always ready for the spotlight." Nate flashed a smile to tease his sister-in-law about his love of attention. Today's event was for a cause close to his heart, something that connected him to a blood relative he barely knew—his grandfather who was autistic. Grandpa couldn't take care of him after Nate's dad died. Gramps passed away in a care facility when Nate was only five—too young to know all the details, but Kyle and Regina made a point to know Nate's family history.

Ever since then, Nate had a soft spot for autistim causes. Today, he was hosting a meet-and-greet event for fans. The proceeds would go to the charity.

"Glad the spotlight is such a big part of your career." She winked.

"I'd give anything to have a day like yours," Logan chimed in, setting his half-eaten toast on the plate, reminding Nate of the photo shoots and Q&A sessions he often had with fans.

He did have a good job if racing pressure wasn't part of the equation.

"Will you stay for dinner?" Serafina asked.

"I'll be leaving tonight." He just needed to give his pilot a two-hour notice to get the chopper ready. "I need to test drive."

She nodded. "Just be careful."

Nate then remembered something important. "Before I forget, do you have a photo of your friend, Vanessa?"

"Um... yes." Serafina furrowed her brow as she exchanged a look with her husband before asking Nate. "Don't tell me you're bringing Vanessa into your spotlight world?"

He shook his head. "I just—"

"Vanessa is not your type," Serafina interrupted in a protective tone. She pushed back her chair and stood to leave the room.

Whoa. Did Serafina assume he was a womanizer? Admittedly, he'd brought various companions to galas and fundraisers, but those encounters were always one-time dates. None of those women captured his heart or sparked a desire to pursue a relationship beyond their initial meeting.

"You and Vanessa, huh?" Logan grinned. "I'd say she's gonna be different from all your previous—"

"Whoa!" Nate lifted both hands to stop his brother from finishing the sentence. "I don't even know if she's the woman I ran into yesterday."

He recapped the event in front of his restaurant.

Logan rubbed his jaw. "I didn't realize she moved her truck to Sausalito."

Oh man. So they were talking about the same woman.

Serafina sauntered up with her phone and passed it over, a photo on the screen, and something stirred in his heart as he stared at the woman with a vibrant smile. She was dressed in a party dress, and long wavy hair cascaded over her shoulders.

Serafina swiped the screen to show a photo of her and Vanessa, both of them sporting silly grins, goofy party hats, and overlarge costume sunglasses. As Serafina displayed more pictures, Vanessa seemed like a different person, so fun and upbeat, nothing like the stiff and upset woman at the food truck who'd appeared to have the weight of the world on her shoulders.

He needed to meet with her again since they never got to their meeting, but it would have to wait until after this weekend's race.

***

Warm afternoon light bathed the hotel conference room as Nate sat at a table, signing autographs and fielding questions. As passionately as he enjoyed his charity work and raising awareness about autism, weariness overtook him as the questions veered into race-car-related topics having nothing to do with his cause. Still, he was grateful for his fans' support.

As he smiled for the cameras and posed for photos with hundreds of people, his cheeks began to ache. The overpowering perfume from the women who hugged him made his head spin, and he needed to catch his breath.

Finally, Zeke, the charity's middle-aged cofounder, interrupted the chatter to announce a lunch break. A few people in line groaned, but Zeke reassured everyone they'd all have a chance to connect with Nate.

Nate took a deep breath, his stiff neck relaxing at the prospect of a few moments to himself. Workers set out a delicious-looking spread on three long tables with black linens. Despite his weariness, his stomach rumbled at the savory food scents. Now, he could indulge in the enticing food.

Zeke grinned as Nate stepped off the makeshift stage, banners, cameras, and lights in tow. He clapped Nate on the back. "What a great turnout!"

Grateful to Zeke for all of his support, Nate grinned at the medium-height man with a salt-and-pepper beard dusting his cheeks. "You should take credit for all of this."

They'd met two years ago when Zeke sold Nate his dealership. Over lunch one day, Nate had learned Zeke's twenty-two-year-old son was autistic and had Down syndrome. Nate shared his vision to start a charity, and Zeke offered to partner with him. Together, they created Autism Expression, an organization dedicated to offering support and resources for families with children diagnosed with autism. From counseling services to educational resources and financial assistance, they catered to each family's unique needs.

Thanks to Nate's media platform, they'd raised awareness about their charity, and more people were donating online through his website. Being featured in NASCAR video games and commercials had given them even more exposure.

Zeke eyed Nate up and down. "Next time, we'd better limit the number to two hundred."

Energized by the event's success, Nate waved away Zeke's suggestion. "This isn't bad at all."

"Well then, we'd better start scheduling for our next big event." Zeke elbowed Nate, then suggested various fundraising events, jotting them down to pass on to Nate's assistant. Nate nodded along, impressed by Zeke's dedication.

As the room buzzed, people lined up at the food tables while others wandered over to the corner with drinks. Zeke had done an excellent job organizing the event, including an inviting seating area with tables and chairs by the window overlooking the city. He'd been wise to set aside funds for such events, as it was crucial to have a space where people could gather and learn about their cause. Maybe they were making a lasting impact in the community.

Nate's head jerked as a familiar face appeared in his peripheral vision. Was he jumping to conclusions, or was that Vanessa chatting with a server dressed in black from head to toe near the food tables? He squinted to get a better look. Yep, no doubt about it, that was her. The woman she was talking to had purple hair too, just like the woman working with her at the food truck yesterday.

Vanessa's knee-length floral teal dress elegantly complemented the sleek and sophisticated ponytail now cascading over her shoulders, and a sash cinched in at her waist highlighted her curves. Not that he had any right to notice her curves when he was just as far from the finish line in relationships as his poor racing streak this season. Zeke kept talking, but Nate divided his attention between the conversation and stealing glances at Vanessa.

She smiled at the server as she took the serving tray. Huh. Did she also work at the hotel besides the food truck?

As if sensing someone staring, she turned in his direction. Their gazes locked, and she blinked. Then the empty tray slipped from her grasp and clattered to the tile floor. She bent to retrieve the tray as he winced over possibly making her nervous.

After she picked up the tray, she hurried toward the half-open door behind the table, disappeared through it, and closed it behind her. Although she didn't appear clumsy, she might be, given the food incident from the previous day. Perhaps his presence made her jumpy now that she knew he owned the property where she'd set up. Maybe he intimidated her.

"Let's grab something to eat." Zeke motioned toward the tables, probably noticing Nate's absentmindedness. Food was a good distraction at a moment like this.

They approached the buffet spread, but Nate kept glancing at the door behind the tables, expecting her to emerge. Just what had she wanted to talk to him about? And why had Xenon warned him not to eat her food?

As he savored the kale salad and mouthwatering short ribs that fell off the bone, he realized the answer. Vanessa had cooked this. He scanned the room and spotted her moving from one table to another, laughing and talking as she cleared the dirty dishes. While Zeke and the two women at Nate's table carried on a conversation, Nate barely registered what they were saying until the perky waitress with purple hair showed up.

"Can I, um..." Her voice faltered as she stood next to him, asking if he was done with his plate. "Mr. Stone, right?"

"Just Nate." He handed her his plate and fought the urge to ask about Vanessa. Did she still want to talk to him? "The food was very good."

"I know, right?" The woman tipped her head toward the corner table where Vanessa smiled broadly at whatever the animated man was saying. "That's my boss. She makes everything from scratch."

Nate had already figured that out.

When the woman left, Nate focused on the people at his table before they left to get dessert.

Soft music carried on, barely audible under the chatter.

Vanessa walked out of the door, carrying a handful of serving trays.

Acting on instinct, he stood and strode for the door. When he entered the hallway, she stood waiting by the elevator. It beeped, she stepped in, and he followed.

"Vanessa! Wait!" he called out, his voice echoing against the walls as he lengthened his stride.

Good. She thrust the silver trays out to keep the elevator doors open.

"Mr. Stone." She faced him.

"You mean Nate?" He hated the formality, but she seemed to emphasize it. Was it in his head, or was the stack of trays shaking?

"I'll carry this for you." He reached out to take them, but the elevator doors closed before he could grab the trays. As he leaned in, he caught a whiff of her subtle floral scent.

When the doors enclosed them in the small space, a sudden change electrified the air, especially when their eyes met. She had the biggest brown eyes he'd ever seen. How was it he hadn't recognized her right away?

His stomach fluttered, and he cleared his throat.

"The button." He needed to say something, and the elevator wasn't moving.

She pressed the first-floor button, and they began their descent before she bit her lower lip in an enticing gesture that drew focus to her full lips. "I'm sorry again for spilling food on you."

"Is that why you've been avoiding me?" he blurted out, not sure why he said it. But he *had* expected her to come over and acknowledge him.

She shrugged and leaned against the mirrored elevator wall with her arms crossed.

"Your food. You're an incredible cook."

"Oh." She cocked her head, her curly ponytail swinging over one shoulder. "Aren't you supposed to be at a photo shoot?"

"The shoot is for the restaurant. Seems you weren't planning to be in Sausalito today, after all."

"Glad it worked out for both of us."

The elevator doors opened, and they stepped into the massive lobby where glittery chandeliers oversaw the pleasant seating area. The warm light seemed to breathe life into an extravagant bouquet on the coffee table.

"Thank you for helping me with these." She reached for the trays.

But he lifted them higher out of her reach. "I offered to help. Just tell me where you want these, and I'll deliver."

A smile curled at the corners of those full lips. "I suppose I haven't proven capable of carrying things. I'm usually not clumsy."

"I'm not judging." He continued walking.

She fell into step. "I'm taking these to my car."

Time to steer the conversation back to business. "I was hoping you could tell me why you wanted to meet with me." Perhaps she could tell him as they walked. "I had a meeting to get to yesterday—"

"And I ruined your shirt." She shook her head, her shoulders slumping, her gaze downcast.

"I have way too many shirts to count."

As they walked, her black flats padded against the tiled floor, and the hem of her teal dress swished around her knees, her legs lean and athletic. She drew out a breath, seeming less confident than she must've been with Xenon. "I know you're busy."

It took resilience and persistence to object to leaving when you were kicked out of a place. They both remained silent until they walked into the small parking lot behind the building. It was foggy, but not cold, just different from the sunshine two hours ago.

Vanessa stopped at a dented blue Sienna sandwiched between two delivery trucks. She reached into her dress pocket, and keys jingled when she retrieved them and pressed the fob. Then she opened the back, gritting her teeth with a grunt as she pried open the crooked hood. More than the hood was banged up, and the passenger side was scraped like cars on a racetrack that had hit the walls.

The thing looked like she'd taken it drag racing. Was she a horrible driver, or had she bought it used?

Either way, her business mustn't make enough for her to afford a new car. Did she need start-up costs for her food business? He kept his thoughts to himself, not wanting to offend her.

"Thanks for helping me carry these." She took the trays. Her warm fingertips brushed against his, but he ignored the tingling sensation her touch triggered as she deposited the trays in a flat box in the back.

"How did you carry all the food you brought?"

"I cooked in the hotel kitchen." She slammed the hood shut and brushed her hands together. Surely, she could make more as a hotel chef than she made hustling with the food truck. According to Xenon, location was a big factor for food-truck vendors to make a profit.

Although Nate's oceanfront restaurant in Sausalito attracted tourists, he doubted they truly appreciated the exceptional taste of Vanessa's food. Like him, many would initially judge the quality of her cuisine by the appearance of her food truck.

As they stood in silence, lost in their thoughts, he nodded to her to break the awkwardness. "Where'd you learn to cook?"

She scrunched her face, seeming uncomfortable. "I just follow the recipe."

Sabastian, his sister's fiancé, was a chef, and he probably had days when he didn't follow instructions to cook what he already knew how to prepare.

But time was ticking, and Nate had to get back to work. He lifted his wrist to check his watch. In fifteen minutes, he'd have to attend to the fans and donors in the meeting room. He jammed his hands into his slacks pockets. "Did you still want to meet with me?"

Her shoulders stiffened, and she wrung her hands in front of her. "I was hoping to arrange another meeting."

"In an hour, I'll be done." If he kept his interactions with his fans brief. After all, the event was scheduled to end at three forty-five. "Do you want to meet today?"

She brushed her palms over her dress and ducked her head, her brows furrowing. He'd probably come across as pushy. Maybe he should give her an out.

"If it's not convenient, we can schedule for another time." For some reason, she intrigued him, compelling him to meet with her sooner rather than later. "It might be another two weeks before I return to San Francisco."

She needed a decent venue to present her delicacies. If money was an issue, he could help her find a restaurant to work at or even hire her as the chef for his Sausalito location if she was in love with the area.

After confirming she was available, he suggested they meet at four on the eleventh floor.

She swallowed, then wet her soft lips, and dipped her chin with a nod.

The eleventh-floor restaurant was an exclusive space that offered its guests excellent privacy with only four tables spread well apart from each other. Reservations were required. Nate and Zeke used the venue when they met with executives to present the foundation's mission and vision statement.

On his way back to his function, he'd stop by reception to see if the restaurant space was available. If it wasn't, he'd find Vanessa before she left so they could meet somewhere else.

As they walked toward the sliding door, he reached out on instinct and touched the middle of her back, guiding her inside. The warmth through her dress unexpectedly warmed him as well. He withdrew his hand to be professional. Despite the awkward moment, he could see them being good friends someday. For now, he'd focus on helping her get her business off the ground.

CHAPTER 5

"Hey, boss. You okay?"

"Huh?" Back in the event room, Vanessa glanced up as Ava jostled her with an elbow to the ribs.

"Did you know Hottie was going to be here today? You should have worn a better dress."

Vanessa spun around to see who might overhear Ava. No reason to try to shush her assistant. Ava seemed to try to attract attention as if her life wasn't dramatic enough. Still, Vanessa kept her voice down in her response. "Running into Nate today was as unexpected as all my recent endeavors."

"Figures." Ava clattered utensils together, apparently full of jittery energy. "Today's the first time we catered for this client—you said you snagged the gig through your volunteer work at the school, right?"

Snagged wasn't the word Vanessa had used. "I met Zeke there, yes. I never imagined Nate was involved, though." But Nate likely attended many charity functions and events. After all, two of his siblings ran international charities for orphans and families in need, so fundraising events and galas seemed to be the norm in his lifestyle. "And now, he's at an event supporting a cause I'm passionate about too—*and* he's asked me to meet with him afterward."

Ava squealed and bounced off her toes. "No way!"

Several guests glanced their way, and Vanessa's ears heated. "Shh! Ava, please!"

"You're *so* gone for him." Ava snickered.

Vanessa edged further away. Why was she so drawn to him? They'd only exchanged a few words and barely knew each other, if not counting what she read about him. But that familiar feeling was present all the time.

She tensed now, gripping her serving tray with white-knuckle force at the memory of the last two tabloids she'd seen in the checkout line.

On them, different women, including business owners and models, had been photographed with Nate, clutching his hand.

"If you're meeting with him, you should freshen up first." Ava was crowding her again. "Ruth and I can handle the rest of the cleanup."

Vanessa shooed her away. "Stop acting like I'm trying to catch his attention. He isn't even my type." Okay, the other way around.

"Ha, like you can deny how flustered you've gotten, how clumsy you've been, *or* how you've had trouble forming coherent sentences around him."

No, she couldn't. When he'd looked at her in the room, the softness in his eyes sent her blood rushing. Then when he'd put his hand on her back to let her walk through the door first, she imagined walking into a ballroom or attending a charity event as his date. But she'd just be like all the other women who craned their necks and couldn't stop gawking at him. And no matter what Ava thought, Vanessa *wasn't* like that.

Feeling silly for being bothered by the women now embracing him with lingering hugs before taking photos, she escaped Ava again and tried to focus on her goals, not her silly attraction. After all, like Serafina once told her, Nate had heartbreak written all over him.

"Remember, girl," Vanessa muttered to herself as she stacked used plates, "you're only meeting him to keep your prime position for the food truck."

Yeah right. Maybe her jittery heart would get the memo.

Plates clattered as she moved utensils. At least, the hotel let her use their plates for a minimal fee. Otherwise, when she catered, she stuck with disposal plates to avoid doing the dishes. The extra helper Ava brought came in handy especially now during teardown as they finished cleaning up the lounge room. So Vanessa let Ava send her off.

With her mind spinning and her heart in her throat, she rode the swanky hotel elevator to the eleventh floor where she'd earlier learned the top restaurant was open only to paid reservations. She inspected her reflection in the elevator's glass walls. She preferred her hair loose in such moments, but she had to keep it pulled up while she was in charge of food. Thankfully, the hotel had a private shower and place for her to change after cooking.

Dressing up nicely always relaxed her and made her feel good. At least she'd appeared presentable when she unexpectedly ran into the hottie, as Ava deemed Nate.

Vanessa straightened her dress and fluffed the hair she'd taken down and left flowing over her shoulders. Then the elevator stopped and dinged to open. Her heart started thudding when she stepped out and spotted Nate seated by one of the many big windows toward the end of the expansive room. Wow, he could take her breath away more easily than the stunning city skyline.

His fancy suit still looked fresh-pressed, and the blue shirt perfectly accentuated the color of his eyes. His hair, short on the sides and tall on top, was tousled after the long day. Besides the receptionist, Nate was the only occupant in the room. Thankfully, he was staring at his phone. If he took one look in her direction, her weakening knees might never get her to him.

Knowing how busy he was, she appreciated his willingness to meet with her.

She waved at the man behind the counter, and he waved back. She didn't need to ask where she needed to go, and he didn't ask if she was lost. As she crossed the spacious seating area, the soft cream-toned carpet cushioned her steps beneath her flats, and the plush tan sofas and immaculately arranged bouquets gracing each table and the center of the room screamed luxury. Their rich purple hyacinths and irises and vibrant yellow tulips and lilies added classy spring color to the room.

Nate must have heard her footsteps because he lifted his head and his gaze found hers.

She inhaled the hyacinths' and lilies' subtle fragrance. Butterflies danced in her stomach, and her knees wobbled when he grinned and stood.

"Vanessa." He extended his hand. "Nice to see you again."

At least he remembered her name. Like last time and any time in the past when he shook her hand, tingles shot through her arm. She kept the handshake brief so his hand didn't scorch her.

"Please take a seat." He gestured to the table already offering a spread of delicacies, the decadent appetizers visible through the tray's glass lid.

She sat across from him. With her heart in her throat, she made the mistake of looking at him. Her mind was so ruffled she couldn't remember why they were meeting. All she knew was Nate was within reach, and she was breathing in his fancy cologne.

Her gaze flickered past two bottled waters, one on her side and one on his, to the food—cheese cubes, fruit, lunch meat, and bacon-wrapped skewers of some sort. She'd seen him eat her lunch. Was he still hungry?

As if reading her mind, he gestured to the tray. "Compliments from the hotel. Comes with the restaurant reservations. If you need anything besides this—"

"Water is fine. Thank you, Mr. Stone." What she needed was to keep this meeting as professional as possible.

He eyed her and adjusted his tie. "You don't have to prove a point by calling me Mr. Stone."

"What point?"

"Do I intimidate you?"

He would if he had to be that direct! He more than intimidated her. He made her heart beat faster and made her feel things, she hadn't assumed she was capable of feeling

But she waved her hand to dismiss him. "Phew. I don't scare easily."

"That's what I thought."

Really? She cocked her head. Why had he assumed so? She'd portrayed her inability to function in his presence both yesterday and earlier today when she dropped the tray the moment she saw him across the room.

"How would you know that I don't scare easily?"

"You're selling your food in the parking lot, even after my manager gave you a deadline."

His definition made her seem like an outlaw. "I'm sorry about that. That's what I wanted to talk to you about."

He lifted the lid from the tray, and the savory smell of bacon had her mouthwatering.

Her stomach growled. She'd fed the entire crowd, but she hadn't fed herself before the event. She'd been too busy worrying if she'd made enough food. Then while cleaning up, she'd been anxious about their meeting.

"Have something to eat, please." His sheepish grin made her heart somersault and her fingers twist together in front of her. "I stuffed up on your kale salad and ribs. Very good food."

Her chest warmed. At least, he'd eaten her food and liked it. With shaky hands, she snatched a piece of diced cheese and popped it into her mouth.

While she chewed, she surveyed his cufflinks and fancy Rolex watch. Everything about him screamed money. Then she swallowed the gourmet cheese and pressed her lips together before meeting his gaze. It was time for business. "I was wondering if you can let me stay in your space for a bit longer."

He sat back, relaxed and confident, calculating as if he had something on his mind. "Do you enjoy being a food-truck chef?"

Not exactly, but it was her job. If she appeared stressed yesterday, then she needed to do better. "Why do you ask?"

"I have a proposition."

Apparently, he'd thought about this. Piqued, she sat taller. "What's that?"

"I can talk to Xenon to hire you as a chef."

She tried to listen as Nate continued with his grand proposition that had nothing to do with fulfilling Mama Dee's BBQ dream.

"I can even pay you out... however many days you still want to stay. It would save you from hustling. Just tell me how much you make in the parking lot, and I'll have my accountant get in touch with you."

Her eyelids stretched wide until she felt like she was trying to pop her eyes out of their sockets. Could he hear himself as he spoke like a real snob who'd been adopted into wealth that paved a way for his successful future?

"That should solve both our problems."

Was the man for real? Or did he think he was on a TV commercial?

A moment of silence passed as they stared at each other before she slid the food tray aside. Pressing her lips together, she willed herself to stay silent as she chose the right words.

"What do you think?" His blue eyes radiated a gleam. The man appeared unfazed by her reaction, which was none, given that she easily got ticked off lately.

Maybe this was his polite way of kicking her off his property. And it was working.

She felt her chest rise before she pushed out the slow words. "Wow. I'm very touched."

He must have sensed her sarcasm. He spread out his hands in question. "Xenon told me all the hardships food vendors face. I don't—"

"Please." The word hissed from between her teeth. She ground her teeth, raising her hand to stop him as heat coursed through her blood.

His gaze held hers, his brows furrowing. "Just trying to help."

"You're not helping, Nate!" she snapped, unable to rein in her anger. "I don't need handouts. If I needed help, I wouldn't still be a cook." Logan had offered her plenty of side gigs, most of which she turned down because he was paying her more than necessary, giving her donations, and help she didn't deserve. "You think money solves all the problems?"

"Sometimes." He responded in barely a whisper. "Sometimes."

"It doesn't." Her heart began beating faster. Lately, the sudden occurrences put her on edge. Igniting an anger and temper she didn't use to have. Good thing it was just the two of them in the room, if she didn't count the staff member behind the counter.

"I'm not going to fulfill my mom's legacy if it doesn't cost me anything. If I'm going to honor her, there will be no shortcuts and certainly not ones given because some rich guy who despises the truck paid me off so he could feel good about himself."

As if he hadn't heard an earful, she leaned in closer. "I don't expect you to understand, but did you have to insult me?"

When he opened his mouth to say something, she shut him down by waving her hand. It was her turn to speak, and she had more words to say than she could get out.

His blue eyes had gone wide as he stared at her without responding, which was fine because her emotions were bubbling like hot water and her words spilled out unfiltered. She grasped the arms of her chair and dug her fingernails into the plush fabric, grinding her palms against it to keep from waving her hands.

"What kind of self-absorbed snob hangs out with people for an entire weekend and forgets them the moment an event ends?"

"Not me." A trace of a smile crossed his face. "I remember you from Logan and Serafina's wedding."

What? She slapped the table. "You knew me yesterday, and you pretended not to?"

Unrattled by her outburst, he crossed one leg over the other and gripped the upper knee. "Don't you think you're being hypocritical?"

Huh? "Why?"

"You knew me, and you claimed you saw me in a farmers market."

What was with his twitching lips as if he was holding back a laugh?

She rolled her eyes, rubbing her hands together. She couldn't deny it. "I didn't want to act like one of your groupies."

He shrugged. "Pit lizards."

"What?"

"NASCAR groupies?"

She shook her head, acting uninterested, yet she was probably one of his pit lizards, only she watched him in the comfort of her home. "Whatever—"

"You had your hair in a ponytail." He raised his water bottle and pointed to her head. Even if she may have it down by now, she hadn't wanted him to assume she'd changed her hairstyle for him. "The Vanessa I met at the wedding had her long hair down and wasn't wearing an apron."

He twisted the cap off his water and took a sip. She squirmed as his Adam's apple bobbled with each swallow. How could she be mad at him when he didn't raise his voice in response to her outburst?

She inhaled, then exhaled to get things back to normal. But who was she kidding?

"A soft word turns away wrath..."

Like a gentle whisper, the words stirred in her mind—words she'd read somewhere in the Bible, probably one of the times she'd looked up verses about anger.

"So—"

"Please." She squirmed beneath the heat of embarrassment. She needed to vanish.

Leaving was the best alternative, especially now that she didn't need anything from him anymore.

Was that how he got his way and charmed all the stunning women he took on dates? She wasn't his type, and clearly, he wasn't hers, despite her infatuation this past year.

She pushed back the chair to stand, keeping her shoulders high as if she hadn't lost all her pride the moment her words burst out in rapid fire. "Well, Mr. Stone—"

"Nate," he corrected in his velvety voice.

I don't care whatever your name is! But she'd said enough. So, she reached for her red handbag from the chair next to her. Now, she was more furious over letting herself have a secret crush on him.

"I don't need your space anymore." Even as she said that, fear gripped her like acid reflux. What if she couldn't find a good place to park? "I'll leave by the end of next week. I need to let my customers know."

"I didn't mean to—"

"Goodbye, Mr. Stone." She turned to leave.

"It's Nate."

Ignoring the emotions swirling in her mind and fighting the tears burning in her eyes, she barely registered the man behind the counter when she passed him until he wished her a good afternoon. She sensed Nate's gaze on her though, but she wouldn't dare turn. She pressed the elevator with knuckle force and walked in, keeping her back to the restaurant as she pushed the button for the first floor.

Not until the elevator closed did she wipe the tears from her face.

What was tomorrow going to be like? *God! I know I have to trust You, but could You at least let me in on what tomorrow's gonna be like?*

Like all the other days she'd prayed for clarity, she didn't hear an answer.

CHAPTER 6

A day later, Vanessa got home at eight, much earlier than usual because she'd paid to park her food truck at a nearby gas station. It wasn't the safest place to park, but she had secure locks and a smile-you're-on-camera sign hanging on the door. The gas-station manager suggested the sign when she voiced concerns over her truck's safety.

Still stewing over Nate's conversation, she checked the spreadsheet so she could prepare for when she started scrounging parking spots each day. She shifted in the wooden chair at her dining table for two. The bright fluorescent light flooded through the kitchen dining area as she glared at the laptop screen, studying the digits she'd highlighted in yellow and hoping they'd increase automatically.

Since 50 percent of her customers paid cash, she deposited the money the next business day, but she included it in the day's profits. She needed an overview of what early May might look like financially.

She'd earned slightly more than she had by this day in April. But that would change the moment she started competing for customers and parking with other vendors.

Her phone rang, and she retrieved it from the red handbag she'd left on the vinyl floor by her feet. An unknown number with a different area code lit up the screen, probably a side gig. She swiped to answer.

"Vanessa." The familiar velvety voice tangled her stomach in unexpected knots. "It's Nate."

He must have gotten her number from Logan or Serafina. Even if she wanted to ask, she was too breathless, and the last thing she needed was to let him know how he affected her.

If only she wasn't drawn to him, it would make it so much easier to dislike him. She exhaled heavily, bracing her elbows on the table while resting one hand on her chin and gripping the phone to her ear with her other hand.

"What do you want, Nate?" She kept her tone firm. The sooner she cut ties with him, the better it was for Mama Dee's BBQ. Nate would be one of those men embarrassed by her because of her truck alone. That had been the case with two of her past dates. Mom's boyfriend also always wanted Mom to drop the business because it wasn't "legit."

"I wanted to make sure you're okay after our meeting yesterday."

I'm far from okay, but I still have my pride. Facing the board on the wall, she glanced at the photo of Mom and her sister, then the sticky notes she'd written on last night with all the places she'd take her truck next week. Somehow, she avoided looking at the NASCAR schedule she'd foolishly pinned below the board.

Nate was in South Carolina for the Darlington Raceway this weekend. It would be about eleven p.m. for him. Shouldn't he be in bed?

"Vanessa?" Her name rolled off his tongue so naturally, but she wasn't going to fall for his charm.

"Why wouldn't I be okay?"

"I may have..." He cleared his throat. "I have another proposition for you."

Hadn't he made his plans clear? He wanted her to be done with the food-truck business. Something snapped inside her as adrenaline screamed through her bloodstream.

"I don't need your propositions, Nate." She snapped and ended the call.

She was capable of making her own decisions. He'd turned out to be the opposite of what she'd expected. As her body heated, she tossed the phone on the table and refocused on the computer screen. At least, this week's gross profits were higher than last week's. But the expense column made her shiver. She might be okay as long as the food truck didn't break down.

The reality of the bills and the uncertainty of the next week had her grinding her teeth.

Parallel parking terrified her the most. She couldn't afford to have her insurance go up if she bumped into another food truck. If she left the Oceanfront, could she still afford a commercial kitchen?

Renting the kitchen came with additional costs for fridge space and other fees that amounted to over three thousand a month. Add in parking expenses for the truck, food bills, Ava's salary, and taxes, and the business part alone took 45 percent of the earnings.

Then there were her personal expenses. Rent, even in the basic one-bedroom apartment, cost as high as the commercial kitchen. That was expected when living in San Francisco. Even on the outskirts, rent was astronomical.

A nice outfit usually boosted her spirits, but she'd avoided shopping malls or anywhere clothes and shoes were sold. She worked Saturdays, and now more than ever, she couldn't afford to take one off. That should keep her from shopping.

She should've held her tongue until she reasoned with Nate as to why she didn't need a handout for Mom's business. But once again, she'd let her emotions take over so quickly.

Burying her face in her hands, she called out to God. Perhaps He could help her work on her business tone first. "I know You'll help me in the business part, but You probably want me to work on my emotions."

She knew the right thing to do. She still remembered the verses.

"A gentle word turns away wrath, but a harsh word stirs up anger."

Turning the other cheek... Something along those lines.

"But I can't let Nate talk me into giving up Mom's dreams." Her body tightened at the thought, and she closed the laptop with force. She needed to shower, but first a good Zumba workout, then the shower, and prayers and bedtime. In that order.

When she collapsed on her bed, exhaustion claimed her, and she woke up ready to take Friday in stride. Then Saturday, she worked at the farmers market with several food-truck vendors.

Arriving early and claiming a spot at the end was the perfect solution to her parking—both her poor driving skills and her usual inability to find a good spot. She forgot her problems while she interacted with other food vendors after they set up and before customers got them all busy.

Working in perfect synchronization, Ava bobbed to the music drifting in the air. As she handed Vanessa two more orders, she sang out. "I so love farmers-market days!"

Vanessa laughed. "Here, the neon-spray-painted rig doesn't even seem out of place at all." A certain vibe energized the crowded space, buzzing with food and colorful trucks and tents. Even with all the other food vendors, the farmers market attracted enough people for her to make a decent amount. "Too bad these aren't every day rather than weekends only."

"Still, I'm looking forward to Sunday off." Ava swiped sweat from her forehead with the back of her arm, then passed over a Number 3 order and two mini plastic cups of sauce. "Extra sauce as requested. I'll be taking Malcolm to that art festival—you know how he loves to draw. You have any plans? You and Hottie maybe?"

"I told you how that went, so please stop mentioning him." Vanessa stepped away from the window to help collect two more Number 2 orders. "Nope, no plans this Sunday other than unwinding and making plans for the week—and going to church where you can bet I'll be reflecting on my temper tantrums and my inability to rely on God."

"And maybe praying Hottie comes your way again?" Ava smirked, then feigned ducking as if pretending Vanessa was about to hit her.

Shaking her head, Vanessa returned to the window with the orders.

As Saturday came to an end, she made an agreement with a store manager to park her food truck overnight for the next seven days. With some time to spare that evening, she went supply shopping and planned to transfer all the condiments into medium-sized bottles before going to bed so she could relax on Sunday and have less preparation on Monday.

When she parked her car in her apartment building's dimly lit parking lot, a surge of anticipation spurred her on. It was almost ten p.m., not too late considering she didn't have to work the next day.

She said a silent prayer of gratitude, thanking God for providing a spot at the end of the complex's parking lot next to a rusty Ford truck.

Tonight, she didn't have to worry about squeezing her car in between other vehicles, which could scratch it even more than it already was.

She reached for one of the blue tote bags on the front passenger seat where she had consolidated her purse and grocery items. Then she opened the dented trunk with a grunt and retrieved a foil-wrapped pan along with a bag containing disposable plates and utensils and napkins. She'd need to take several trips to bring everything upstairs.

The parking lot was backed into an alley where a few people exchanged drinks and possibly drugs. She made sure to lock her car before shoving her key into her jeans pocket.

As she approached the building's entrance, she tried to ignore the litter on the ground and the exhaust and smoke in the air. But she couldn't ignore the smell of the food in her hands, and she breathed it in deeply, relishing the aroma.

In his frequent visits to their complex to see Serafina, Logan Stone made it a habit to buy food for the homeless. He'd even paid Vanessa several times to cook for the homeless, but she had refused to take his money. She needed to save every penny, but there were people in worse conditions than she was.

As she approached her building, the familiar group of people huddled around the large planters on the sidewalk, probably trying to find some warmth from the chilly night air. The dim light shining from the building illuminated their faces, and smoke lingered as they exchanged cigarettes or whatever else they had.

"Hello, Mama Dee's BBQ." One of Logan's buddies, Golgal, strode away from the circle and toward her.

It was hard to ignore the smell emanating from him, from either his dreads or his body. Nonetheless, she put on a friendly smile.

"Vanessa, such great timing, girl." Marjio walked over. "I'll be in charge of this to make sure everyone gets a fair share."

Vanessa asked about their day as she handed the woman the foil-covered tray and gave Golgal the bag with disposable plates and utensils. They all had fascinating stories about the park where they hung out during the day. "Enjoy."

"Thanks, BBQ Queen," Golgal said, and the four still in a circle clapped.

"Thanks, Mama Dee," someone else said, and she waved at them before she climbed the three flights of metal stairs to her apartment.

As she walked up, she whispered a prayer to God. "Please tell Mom thank you for the recipes."

Sadness chilled her heart like it had whenever she glanced at the black door across the hall where Serafina used to live. The last month since her friend got married had been lonely here. Before, whenever she needed to talk to someone, she'd just cross and knock on her door. Serafina's apartment was still vacant. No lights inside the room. It would take a while to adjust to the new neighbor once someone moved in.

With her bags at her feet, she turned the key to her apartment. Then she stood at the door to keep it open as she flipped on the light before bending to reach for the bags. She deposited the bags on the kitchen counter and returned to her car for the rest of them.

But, as she approached her car, something was off. The passenger window was shattered, glass shards glinting in the dim light. Her heart sank as she walked closer, looking around for anyone in sight.

She tugged on the locked door, then pressed the fob to open the car.

The bags were gone. What?

Good thing her handbag was in the house, in the bags she'd taken in the first load. Or was it not?

She pressed her hands to her head, and her stomach churned at the possibility that she'd made a mistake and left the handbag in the stolen totes. She'd been so careful locking her car and taking all the necessary precautions, but nothing could keep thieves at bay.

Her mind raced. She needed to call the police, but she also needed to make sure her handbag was in the house.

In a whirl of emotion, she hastened back to her apartment. The homeless people were all but a blur as they ate the food she'd given them. Three steps at a time wasn't fast enough to get her up to her apartment.

There, she almost tore the bags when she yanked at all three and dumped the contents across the vinyl flooring. Ketchup and mustard. Disposable bowls, containers, and utensils.

"No. No. *Noooo!*" Her handbag was missing. How had she not realized she'd brought in the wrong bags?

Her stomach churned. Tossing her hands to her head, she groaned and pulled at her hair.

She didn't even have her phone. It was in her handbag.

She needed to cancel her credit cards and change all her bank passwords. She ran back downstairs, too frazzled even to cry.

"You okay?" Golgal asked, his voice gruff but concerned.

So did Marjio and two others.

Vanessa shook her head, grateful for their kindness. "Someone broke into my c–car." Her voice shook as she wrung her hands together.

"Oh no." Marjio's jaw dropped as she tossed a plate into the trash. A siren wailed, and the police cruiser drove past, its noise screeching over the random engine sounds.

"Did you guys hear anything or see anyone?"

The other two homeless men gathered around her, asking where her car was parked. But as she peered over to the parking lot, she could barely see her Sienna past the truck.

"How can we help?" Marjio asked, and Golgal offered to go scope out the alley.

She told them not to worry. The thief wouldn't be chilling in the alley and rummaging through her handbag.

"Do any of you have a phone? I need to call the police." Filing a police report didn't mean they'd update her on anything or that someone would pay for her stolen items. Still, she'd file one just in case the thief was a wanted criminal and the police found her ID in the wrong place. That could make things more complicated for her.

Marjio held up both hands. "My flip phone got stolen last week."

"It wasn't really stolen. She passed out drunk," Golgal said.

"That's stolen, you idiot," Marjio snapped, but Vanessa didn't stick around to listen to their arguments. She returned to her car, hoping maybe by some chance the thief left her driver's license for her.

But she was wrong. She sat in the passenger seat, closing her eyes and imagining she was just having a bad dream. But it was reality when she opened her eyes, feeling more deflated, violated, and vulnerable.

Through the side mirror, movement caught the corner of her eye. A shadowy figure darted across the alley, disappearing into the darkness. Her heart pounded in her chest as she realized whoever had taken her handbag might still be nearby.

Stepping out of her car, she closed the door and pressed the fob as she peered around and over the other cars in the parking lot. Ridiculous to lock the car with the window broken, but regardless of the minimal activity in the alley, she couldn't shake the feeling that she was being watched. With her mind in a jumble, she rubbed shaky fingers to her temples and tried to think past the fear and anger to figure out what to do next.

It wasn't the first time her car had been broken into. She'd forgotten her gym bag once and learned never to leave valuables in the car. Maybe the strings of her red handbag had been dangling through the tote, and the thief had been parading the parking lot with a flashlight to seek his next treasure.

She needed to call Serafina, but she was probably asleep or relaxing on the sofa with her husband.

First things first. She'd go to the lobby and use the phone at the welcome desk. With her luck lately, the phone was probably dead, and no one else would be around with a phone she could borrow.

She couldn't drive the truck without a license. The DMV required appointments, and no doubt, it could be as long as three to five days before she got an appointment.

She did a mental calculation of what was in the handbag. "The money!" Oh no! The cash they'd made that day—a lucrative day, no less—was all gone. The credit/debit card machine was also in her handbag.

She would need to replace the window, the card machine, and probably more expenses than she could think of right now.

Shaking her head and stifling a mirthless laugh, she walked back to the building with slumped shoulders. She wasn't the first victim of auto theft, and things could've been worse, really.

She still had the food permits in the truck. If they stole those, she'd have to start from scratch.

Was this God's way of answering her prayers for the food business? Give up Mom's legacy so she could pursue her own?

Lord, I hate these kinds of surprises. At this point, Nate's crazy ideas weren't nearly as bad. Maybe he was right. She didn't have to hustle and bustle, and she could get back to teaching as soon as she renewed her license.

That, too, seemed like a hustle right now. Whether she ran a food-truck business or not, she needed a driver's license—and a clear mind. She'd better refocus and strategize tomorrow. Serafina's number was the only one she knew by heart.

Crossing her hands over her chest, she walked into the lobby with a renewed mind to call Serafina. Now more than ever, she needed to talk to her friend.

CHAPTER 7

Postrace interviews proved how Nate thrived in the spotlight. After his dignified finish into victory lane at the Kansas Speedway, adrenaline surged through him as he answered the moderators' questions while the crowd cheered.

"Nate, congratulations on your win today." The interviewer held the microphone toward him.

"Thank you." Excitement raced through Nate's veins. "I can't even put into words how amazing this feels. It's been a long road to get here, but it's all worth it for this moment."

The crowd erupted into cheers, and his smile spread wider.

"Can you walk us through your strategy for the race?" the interviewer asked after she recapped his streak that season. "Then, last weekend, you came in first place."

Nate took a deep breath and ran a hand through his damp hair. God always took center stage for his performances, good or bad. He pointed his index finger to the clear evening sky. "I thank God that I have another chance at this. My team kept everything running smoothly and in position, so that made my job easier. They had to rebuild the engine, and that significantly improved my performance. We had a great car today, and my crew did an amazing job. I just tried to stay focused and give it my all."

As the crowd cheered even louder, their excitement fueled his own.

"Any final thoughts for your fans?"

He waved to the fans. "You guys are the best, and I can't thank you enough for your support."

With people jumping up and down, some waving black-and-white checkered flags, he couldn't spot his family members in their reserved seating in the paddock area.

"Congratulations on your win, Nate Stone!"

While cheers filled the crowded speedway, he basked in the warm glow of the setting sun. He didn't mind interviews after he'd won a race.

Being camera shy or terrible at public speaking wasn't an option in his career. Well-spoken drivers who knew how to make a good impression in front of the camera were important to winning over the publics' hearts and the suits' money. Those public speaking courses he'd taken at Yale Business School paid off now, not only in his career but also in his personal relationships.

Not with Vanessa, though. With the way they'd clashed, she'd become a challenge he intended to take on. Images of her flashed in his mind as he walked back to his motor coach.

No matter how many times he'd tried to wipe her out of his mind in the two weeks since their meeting and phone call, he couldn't. The way she looked, the way she smelled, the way fire lit up her eyes... Not only was she beautiful, smart, and passionate but she was also intriguing.

How had he gotten on her wrong side? He charmed everyone, or at least, no one ever accused him of being self-centered. Maybe he was and needed someone like her to call him out.

Some of her words continued to play in his mind on repeat.

"You think money solves all the problems?"

"I'm not going to fulfill my mom's legacy if it doesn't cost me anything."

"I don't need your propositions."

With adrenaline still coursing through his veins, he walked through the paddock area, the warm glow of the setting sun elongating his silhouette. The sky lit, ablaze with oranges, pinks, and purples, casting a peaceful atmosphere over the busy racetrack. The humming engines and squealing tires had faded to a distant drone, replaced by rustling leaves and chirping birds.

He waved and greeted the people around the motor coaches and the pit crews who'd begun to pack up. The paddock area was emptying out. He refocused on the race, or rather, on Vanessa as their interactions came to mind.

She'd walked away from him in the restaurant. She'd hung up on him before he uttered a compromise to their misunderstanding, but she probably wouldn't have found his advice appealing. She was set on not liking him, which could be what drew him to her. That and the appealing fire and passion she erupted with was sexy to say the least. Women were always drawn to him, not running away from him.

He'd just wanted to resolve the issue so they could move on, but the spitfire wasn't going to make that easy.

For now, he couldn't wait to celebrate his victory with his team and bask in the glory of their win. As his motor coach came into view, his manager, Doyle, approached with a smile.

"You nailed that interview!" Doyle slapped Nate's shoulder with a strong hand. Buff and fit, he looked like a bodybuilder, but like for Nate, workouts were important with the nature of their jobs.

"Makes it easier when you put me on the map." Nate unzipped his jumpsuit to get some fresh air now that he was almost to his coach.

"The hotel has a game room for us." Doyle addressed what Nate's assistant had relayed. "I'll go and take a head count to see who's coming."

"I'm looking forward to it."

The presidential suite with several rooms was already reserved for him and any of his family who showed up. They'd celebrate at the same hotel. Nothing wild, but some good food and hang-out time with his team.

"You got company." Doyle tipped his head toward Nate's motor coach.

The only company he got at his motor home was his immediate family. On rare occasions, some fans had hot passes to meet him before and after the race. A few times when he had past girlfriends, they'd give him surprise visits after the race. But recently, he'd decided not to pursue relationships when he wasn't pursuing long-term plans.

Curious, he raised an eyebrow, then spotted a familiar figure beside his motor coach.

The woman standing there with folded arms wasn't immediate family. Her brown skin was flawless and radiant under the motor home's outdoor lights. When she flashed her pearly whites and waved, his brows squeezed together. Surely, this wasn't the same woman who'd hung up on him last week when he'd called to make amends.

Was she here to give him another piece of her mind?

Dressed in leggings that encased her curves, she'd left her long hair down. It fell in waves over her pink top. With her smiling, he easily recognized her as the cheerful woman he'd seen at Logan and Serafina's wedding.

Intrigue had him slide out of his overalls and pick them up before striding toward her. The heat vanished now that he was in shorts and a T-shirt.

"Your brothers..." Doyle's voice bounced off Nate's back. Whatever his crew chief was saying faded in the night breeze as Vanessa's voice rang loud and clear.

"Hey, Nate." She clutched a green handbag to her chest, appearing timid and friendlier than he expected. She called him Nate. Did he hear her right? The last time she'd called him Nate, she'd all but spat his name and hung up on him.

"Spitfire." He called in response, stopping in front of her and running a hand through his hair. He had no idea why the name just flew off his tongue.

Her chin rose to him, and their eyes locked. For the second time in her presence, his stomach fluttered.

With her smile still in place, she beamed. "How did you come up with my name?"

Man, he'd never seen such a smile! It took over her whole face—spreading up her well-shaped lips, bunching up her round cheeks, curving up her twinkling eyes. "Our past interactions."

The smile wobbled. She bit her lower lip, emphasizing its fullness, and looked down at her black Converse shoes as she moved the toe of her All Stars in a circle on the concrete. "I'm sorry. I wasn't—"

"No need for apologies. We got off to a wrong start, I think."

They stared at each other as the air sparked between them.

"You're—"

"I didn't—"

They both spoke at the same time.

Nate chuckled, then realized she was laughing. She had a nice laugh too. Like the way her smile took over her face, her laugh seemed to claim her whole body.

"You go first." He put out his hand, gesturing her on.

"Great race out there."

His neck heated. "Thanks. It was intense."

With the VIP badge clipped to her blouse, she'd probably had Logan initiate her back pass entrance.

"I wouldn't have guessed you to be a motorsports fan."

She tilted her chin as her big brown eyes widened. "You'd be surprised by all the things you don't know about me."

He wanted to know the passion behind the fire.

"Sorry if I caught you off guard when you were just getting into your, um, coach."

"Your visit was a surprise, but I'm not complaining." He tried not to let anything dampen his mood, but today, he had good reason to be in a good mood. He'd won!

"I tried catching you before the race. But you were busy talking to your crew, and I was told I couldn't interfere."

Nate nodded. "Meeting with my crew before the race is critical."

Crickets sang, laughter boomed somewhere, and the TV droned in his motor coach. He'd turned it off, but Doyle must have watched the postrace interview in there and forgotten to shut it off.

They needed a fresh start, so maybe he should invite her into his motor home. But they barely knew each other. Plus, it would feel too tight, even if the space was big enough for four people to sit comfortably.

"I was wondering if you had some time to meet with me tomorrow." She grimaced as if the request embarrassed her.

"You could've called. I might even be in San Francisco next week."

She swung her green purse, still clutching it with both hands. "I didn't think you'd listen to me. I figured you'd hang up like I did on you."

"I may appear intimidating." To her, perhaps he did. He crossed his arms and relaxed his stance. "But for my well-being, I don't hold grudges. Life's too short to make enemies."

"I should know that." Ducking her head, she fumbled with her purse straps. "I'm sorry."

"It's all behind us." He waved away her apology. He hadn't intended to make her feel regretful. "As for tomorrow, my schedule's all over the place. One never knows how long the performance car photo shoots will take. Are you free to meet with me tonight?"

She blinked her widening eyes. "Aren't you tired?"

"Nah. I'm always pumped after a win." He swung his arms free and clapped once as if starting a pep rally. "As long as you don't mind joining my friends or any of my family members who show up—you've already met the family at the wedding." He'd work in a private meeting with her, but starting with a group might take the edge off their bumpy relationship.

Mom and Dad hadn't made it to the race. If they had, Mom would've greeted him by the pit area to congratulate him. He'd have to check his phone and see who had come.

"You want to meet me at the Power Hotel in an hour?"

She pulled out her phone. "Can you give me the address?"

Great. He was going for another hotel meeting. "It's the only Power Hotel in town."

She cleared her throat and turned the phone his way, flashing a photo of the hotel. "Is this it?" At his nod, her full lips quirked. "You really like fancy hotels."

"I like being comfortable after a race." After a race, he stayed in a hotel to recoup and give the driver time to move his coach to the next race field. He winked now. "Plus, this time if you walk away from me, I can retreat to my room in no time."

She winced. "I shouldn't have done that. It won't happen again." She thrust her hand into her handbag, pulled out a maroon T-shirt, then unfolded its graphics—his number, a black-and-white checkered flag, and the word *Impulse*, the nickname of his car. A smile twitched at her mouth when she turned the shirt around to display the back graphics—a pit crew and a crown encased with the words *Mama Dee's BBQ for Nate Stone*. "Since I stained your shirt, I thought this would work as a replacement."

His chest warmed over her effort to make him something.

"That's so nice of you." Fighting the odd urge to pull her into an embrace, he slung his jumpsuit under his armpit to accept the shirt. "Thanks."

She retrieved something else, then handed him a clear zip-top bag. "I made you some almonds."

As she jiggled the coated nuts, he eyed them as if they'd bite him. While her reaction during their past interactions should have him suspecting her sudden niceness, surely, she wasn't malicious. "What did you do to the almonds?"

"I glazed them."

"Did you season them with passion or poison?" When her nose scrunched, her expression fascinating him, he relaxed his stance. "Scratch the poison. Let me rephrase." He leaned against the coach, close enough to smell a floral scent wafting off her. "Did you make the nuts with love and season them with passion?"

She twirled a long tress between her fingers.

"Xenon warned me about your food. He claims your prime rib diffused his urgency to get you off my property." After tasting her salad and ribs, Nate understood what his manager meant. She was a good cook. But she'd made it clear she wasn't interested in anything he had to offer.

"Sometimes I gotta do what I gotta do. Who knows? I might win you over after all."

"Win me?" He cocked his head. *She* was the one who was hard to impress.

She brushed him off with a wave. "I mean, trying to make you forget my temper tantrums."

He tossed the T-shirt to his shoulder, then took her offered nuts. "See you at eight thirty?"

"I'll be there."

A meeting with a softer version of Vanessa Douglas! Now, this night just got better.

When he entered the motor coach, clapping in the seating area startled him.

"Bravo!" Theo's olive skin shone under the dim lighting where he stood by the sink, his phone tucked under his armpit. Theo didn't look like a media mogul in South America. He looked still a child, Nate's brother who liked to play pranks.

Nate tossed his race suit and T-shirt on the sofa. One look at the tinted window, and he doubted his brothers had been watching NASCAR replays on the now-muted TV.

"Thumbs-up, man!" Wade grinned, lifting a thumb. With his brown hair slicked to the side and his crisp button-up immaculate, he stood beside the window by the dining table.

Nate's siblings often showed up for a race and made themselves comfortable in his motor coach. That must've been what his manager was trying to tell him when he'd brought up Nate's brothers before Nate's attention moved to Vanessa.

He dropped the nuts on the table and flopped onto the chair next to the sofa, stretching his long legs out before him.

"You should've told me you'd be in town." He addressed Theo, who was scratching his buzz cut and oozing guilt that he'd been caught spying on Nate and Vanessa. If Theo was going to fly clear from Brazil, Nate would prefer to plan things to do with him and their brothers. But at such short notice, he couldn't he couldn't arrange anything for tomorrow. "We spoke two days ago, and you didn't mention you'd be coming."

Ignoring Nate's comment, Theo smirked. "Spitfire, huh?"

"Since when did you get on a nickname basis with Serafina's friend?" Wade brought a bottle of water to his mouth. Great, even Wade recognized her right away? But then Vanessa had her luxurious hair down today and that glorious smile in place.

"I can't believe you guys eavesdropped."

"Wade put me up to it." Theo plunked his phone onto the counter, then swung open the fridge, and pitched a water bottle to Nate.

While Nate caught it midair, Wade shrugged. "I had to make sure you weren't being stalked by tabloids."

Theo twisted the cap off his water. "Since you don't have a bodyguard and stuff."

"Doyle is my bodyguard on race days."

Unless it was family, Nate's crew manager knew which days Nate could handle guests with pit and hot passes.

"Mom's been worried about you since your Geico incident." Theo sank onto the sofa and spread his arms across its leather back.

"From now on, one of us has to be present at your races, in case you get hurt." Wade sauntered over and sat next to Theo. "Why didn't you invite Vanessa in?"

"You know her name?" Nate uncapped the water bottle and took a sip.

"You would have if you hadn't left the island two days early."

"Don't rub it in. It's not like I wanted to leave as soon as Logan and Serafina said 'I do.' You know I had a race on Monday to get back to and no time to hang out." But his brothers were still waiting for a response about Vanessa. "She's joining us to celebrate."

"What kind of date is that?" Theo squeezed his half-empty water bottle. "Things—"

"She's not my date." Far from it, even if he'd pondered the concept these last two weeks. "She can't stand me."

"What?!" Wade exclaimed dramatically as if this were his next movie script. "What did you do to her?"

Nate groaned. That's what he'd like to know. "One minute, she's smiling and looking at me like I'm her dream come true, and the next minute, I'm the bane of her existence."

"She brought you food." Theo reached for the bag of nuts.

"Made with passion, not poison." Using Nate's words, Wade snatched the bag from Theo. "Is it okay if I try some?"

Nate nodded. "They're a bribe because she yelled at me last time."

Her softer tone and vulnerability tonight held a promise that warmed his chest.

"What did you do to get on her bad side?" Wade ripped open the bag.

"Women flock to you, especially when you're winning races." Theo's thick dark brows furrowed. "Not sure why they do that when you're a daredevil."

"Edge is what women want." Wade spoke with a mouthful. "These are so good. No doubt, Vanessa has a huge crush on you, bro."

There had been some kind of vibe in the air between them, hadn't there? "Well, she's been flustered when I'm around, but I'm not sure I read her right. She walked away and left me in the restaurant. Then, when I called to make amends, she hung up on me."

Theo covered his mouth, coughing, to stifle a laugh. He seemed to be choking on the nuts. "She hung up on you? And that doesn't prove she's, well, 'hung up' on you?"

"Dare I say, I like this girl?" Wade spoke over another mouthful.

Nate had to eye his brother, a slight unease tingling at the back of his neck. Was Wade interested in Vanessa?

"Not that kind of liking." Wade raised a finger as if he could read Nate's thoughts. "She could be good for your big ego."

"I still can't believe a woman walked out on you." Theo grabbed the nuts and dug out another handful, then slammed some in his mouth.

Nate never experienced that kind of rejection. He'd better explain the misunderstanding, though. "She parks her food truck in front of my restaurant, and—"

"Don't tell me you offered her a job at your restaurant." Wade grimaced.

Whoa. Nate shifted in his seat. "What's wrong with that?"

"Seriously? You have to ask?" Theo rattled his handful of nuts, then tossed one in the air and caught it. "Very insulting to a woman who has the hots for you, bro."

"You know how I feel when someone hates me." It wasn't in his nature to be at war or have someone at war with him. That only happened with his competitors who didn't like it when he held a long winning streak, but none had expressed their dislike of *him*, just of his sliding in ahead of them.

"You don't have any enemies, I know," Wade interrupted. "This would make a juicy story."

"You can't keep writing stories about my life. Nothing is interesting about it without those plot twists you added to the race car thriller two years ago."

"I want to hear the rest of this Vanessa story," Theo urged, and the leather couch cushion squeaked as he shifted in his seat. "She has a food truck?"

"Yeah. She's got the thing parked at my restaurant, and she refused to leave when Xenon asked her to. So I went to talk to her. She's a fighter, and she's putting in the energy to make it work. But, man, it looks like a tough life. We had an appointment at this hotel restaurant, and I suggested donating to her business so she wouldn't have to struggle with a rough business."

Both his brothers exchanged glances.

Seriously? What was their problem? His back stiffened. "I was just helping."

"I'll stop you right there." Wade lifted a hand. "I can already see this as my next rom-com, though."

"This is serious stuff," Theo said. "You know our family could sponsor your race, right?"

They'd offered in the early years, and Nate declined. Eventually, he was approached by the CEO of Dimclay's department stores. His first sponsors.

Theo folded his hands and unmuted the TV, so apparently, the conversation was over.

"In case you didn't understand"—Wade braced his elbows on his knees, leaning around Theo to speak to Nate—"you insulted Vanessa when you offered to pay her to quit her job. Didn't you even think about the fact that Logan and Serafina would've helped her if she'd let them?"

Wow. Since when was his kid brother, their prankster, so astute? Even though Vanessa said she was honoring her mother's memory, Nate suspected she wasn't fulfilled as a food-truck operator. When he had asked her if she wanted to do what she was doing, she'd hesitated before responding. So what were *her* dreams and aspirations? How had her mother passed away? He'd find out more once he had the chance to speak with her this evening.

CHAPTER 8

Some people were amiable in every situation. After spending the early part of the evening around Nate, Vanessa was starting to suspect he was one of them.

In a game room abuzz with deep laughter and the clatter of pool cues striking the tables, she retreated to the counter for another caffeinated beverage. After losing in shuffleboard to Doyle, Nate's crew manager, and foosball to Wade Stone, Vanessa needed a good place to take in the activities without participating. She scooted past colorful murals and game posters and beanbag chairs by the board-game section, the room emitting a comfortable and relaxing vibe. As other people played table games, her gaze kept finding Nate.

He was standing between the game tables, his hands moving as he talked to the driver who hauled his car. His broad shoulders stretched out the maroon shirt she'd had custom-made to make amends. The maroon complemented his dark hair.

Wow! She'd never met anyone with such an upbeat disposition, and he seemed mindful of others as he listened intently whenever someone spoke to him. No wonder everyone wanted to talk to him and women misinterpreted his friendliness. Forget all the reasons she wanted to not like him. How was that possible when she was now running to him for help?

His invitation had surprised her too. Not one to embrace a change in plans, she hadn't expected to be having fun, but she'd decided not to stress over business proposals and instead interact with Nate's brothers and friends.

Beneath the counter bliss lights, she refocused on her soda. The background melody inspired her to bounce her leg to dance to the music. Either the caffeine was catching up to her or the energy-infused room was affecting her, but she was ready to party all night if the hotel staff could kick up the music a bit.

After stressful days dealing with the theft aftermath, some personal shopping had never sounded better than it did when Serafina surprised her three days ago and said they were celebrating Vanessa's birthday, which Serafina missed while on her honeymoon. When Vanessa confessed her encounters with Nate, Serafina called her out on her pride.

"You need to tell him why you're running a food truck. Nate is a problem solver and always compelled to help. He may not go about it the right way sometimes, but he means well."

With Serafina's husband's help, Vanessa got a VIP seat and a hot pass, hence the surprise arrival.

"Vanessa?"

She startled, the ice jingling in her glass and her drink nearly spilling on her white dress patterned with vibrant spring-green leaves as she turned her back to the counter.

Nate's assistant held a napkin with a half-eaten cheese pizza slice. Vanessa caught up with Jae earlier—a South Korean who'd migrated with her parents to America when she was four years old.

"You're finally eating something." Vanessa smiled. Her stomach had been in nerves when she'd arrived, and after Nate introduced her to the group, she'd spent most of her time hovering by the food tables. She'd even ignored Nate's invitation to challenge him to a game of pool.

"This is my third round," Jae said. She was so petite. No doubt, she'd gobbled salad earlier and was now getting around to having a real meal. "I only eat this late when Nate throws a party."

"It's a great party." Vanessa raised the glass to Jae who'd made the arrangements. Vanessa had overheard Jae tell Nate that pizza was all the hotel could offer a big group on such short notice. It wasn't a formal meal that suited the swanky hotel, but everyone appeared pleased with pizza, salad, and a variety of cookies and brownies.

"I could do better." Jae nibbled a bite of her pizza.

Vanessa scanned the spacious room with over sixty people until she sighted Nate with a pool cue in hand, his head tossed back, shoulders shaking as he laughed with his two brothers and Doyle.

Two waitresses approached the pool table, and Theo spoke to one of them. They didn't leave until Nate recovered from laughing. He pointed his stick to the food area, perhaps telling them he didn't need to be served when it was a buffet-style dinner. Not that Vanessa was watching him the entire time, but the waitresses sure paid special attention to him—not much different from all the women who turned their heads when he entered a room or reportedly swooned over him in the racing stands. Okay, so she was in line with all the swooners.

That instant, Nate's gaze found hers, and she felt like sparks were traveling from her body to his. Trembling, she ducked her head, lifted her drink to her mouth, and downed the rest of the liquid. Good grief, she was caught. And the room felt ten degrees warmer.

"How do you and Nate know each other again?"

She winced, having almost forgotten Jae standing there. The woman had eaten the rest of her pizza and was now scrolling through her phone.

"We met..." Vanessa stammered. She and Nate weren't even friends, but one of Jae's jobs was probably to ward off swooning females. "It's a long story. Nate should tell you."

"You're the first woman, who's not family or team member, he's invited to a postrace celebration."

Really? A thrill rushed through her veins. But maybe he'd invited her because he wasn't worried anything could happen between them.

Without permission from her brain, her gaze flitted across the room. This time, he was staring at her, and their gazes lingered on each other. Her breath caught as an overwhelming need to wrap her arms around him swept her up.

He brought his hand to his head, saluting her, before one of his brothers poked his side with a pool cue.

"Well, Vanessa."

She shook her head, snapping out of her daze. "I'm sorry, Jae. What?"

"Let's play some games."

"Good idea." She put her glass on the counter. Anything to keep her from gawking at Nate.

As they walked past the arcade basketball, Jae stopped and snatched the tokens from the wooden bowl on the tall stool. "Would you like to play basketball?"

"It's been a while since I played." Vanessa moved closer as Jae inserted the tokens into the machine. Jae had probably paid a decent sum for the hotel to give the group unlimited tokens for the night.

The machine deposited the balls, and Vanessa snatched one of them. The skirt of her dress flounced around her knees while Jae suggested Vanessa go first.

Primed to score as many points as she could within thirty seconds, Vanessa aimed for the basket before shooting at it and grabbing another ball without waiting to see if she scored. The ball went right in. She tossed another, then snatched up the first on the rebound, tossing it and seizing another ball in quick one-two tempo again and again, missing a couple but making hoops with most of her shots.

"Did you play basketball in high school?" Jae asked after throwing three balls into the basket and missing on her set.

"I'm sure you're better than I am," Vanessa said. "I only played the game noncompetitively on the church coed team before life got busy. I'd be terrible at real basketball."

"I challenge Spitfire to a game of basketball." Warm and deep, Nate's voice rumbled close to her ear as he stepped in beside her, sending her nerves into a tailspin.

"You have names for each other, and I'm just meeting Vanessa now?" Jae stepped back to let him take her place.

"Spitfire and I go way back." He spoke as if they'd been friends forever. His hands brushed against Vanessa's while he retrieved two balls from the lever, then handed her one. "No timer this time. We'll trade off. One after the other. Take the first shot. I'll take the second."

She trembled at his proximity, feeling the heat of his presence on her skin. He had that unique scent of fancy cologne wafting off him, a eucalyptus base mixed with whatever spicy scent teased her senses. Although she'd changed into a summer dress with short sleeves and the air-conditioning kept the room cool, she felt thirty degrees hotter.

"I love the challenge." Jae clapped as Vanessa positioned herself. Her hands were too shaky to toss the ball where it needed to go, so it didn't even make it to the rim.

Nate was the opposite, steady and confident. His ball went straight into the hoop.

"What a show-off." She mumbled under her breath.

"With you"—he winked—"I can't help but show off."

With her arms like limp noodles, her performance stayed the same, and Jae groaned when Nate won. "I was so rooting for you, Vanessa."

"Traitor." Nate gazed at Jae, then Vanessa. He flashed that boyish grin before touching her shoulder and squeezing it. "Good game."

No, it wasn't. She'd never played so poorly. But she couldn't tell him how unfair the game was while battling an erratic heartbeat.

"Ready for our meeting?" he asked.

Meeting? Oh right. She was here for a business meeting, not just for fun. Since she'd left her new phone in her handbag behind the counter, she had no idea what time it was.

As people started leaving the game room, she said goodbye to some of the crew she'd connected with, then to Jae with hopes to run into each other again.

Vanessa hurried behind the counter for her handbag, pausing when Nate teased his manager as they said their goodbyes. They must be good friends rather than Doyle being just the manager. Then Nate gave a wave. "See you in Texas in a few."

"Get some rest before Wednesday now." Doyle saluted and made his exit.

Nate's two brothers were still playing air hockey as if each one of them expected to be the winner.

Vanessa started toward the beanbag chairs, the perfect place for their meeting.

"Ready to go?" Nate's voice sent a paradox of shivery warmth through her spine. He called out to his brothers to meet them upstairs, and they acknowledged him with a quick response, their attention focused on their game. The clack of the puck hitting the striker was the only noise in the room.

The restaurant workers were busy removing the linen from the tables and storing away the utensils. Vanessa trailed Nate as he led her out. Then he stepped back, letting her go first, and his warm hand rested on her lower back. It was a simple gesture, but it made her feel an inexplicable sense of belonging and comfort.

CHAPTER 9

If Vanessa had known she'd end up sitting across from Nate at a swanky hotel at midnight, she wouldn't have bothered paying for accommodations. By the time she made it to her hotel now, it would be at least two a.m. Though Nate's eyes seemed tired, he didn't appear to be in a hurry to leave. In the presidential suite's expansive seating area, she lounged on a sofa while he occupied one of the armchairs. Their water bottles awaited them on the glass table next to a pastel floral arrangement—fluffy hydrangeas and peonies offset by delicate orchids and roses.

"This is nice." She nodded to the immaculate rock chimney, preferring to look at everything around her, including the city lights, rather than Nate. Did he realize how nervous he made her? "I had a good time—probably the most fun I've had since the wedding."

He winked, settling back and resting his arms on the armrests. "You're welcome to join us anytime I win."

She couldn't afford the tickets, but she still asked, "Is that an invitation?"

He shrugged. "With the way my season has been going, I could use all the support I can get."

"Just because you're not winning every race doesn't mean you're doing that poorly."

He crossed his legs, amusement teasing up the left side of his lips. "How would you know how I've been doing?"

I literally watch all your races. "It's not really a secret."

"Lucky for me." He brushed his hands over his navy pants. "Since you know all about me through the public's eye, tell me about you."

Through the public's eye and through his sister-in-law. But where could she start? Presenting her request was humiliating after her outburst last time.

But today was a new day. Claiming a sudden surge of confidence, she sat up straighter in her seat, ready to take on whatever challenge he had in store for her. She planted both feet firmly on the floor, never mind that her head was in the clouds where he was concerned.

"Let me see if you can solve this riddle." Nate bent forward, his expression more serious, his voice low and intense.

"Okay." She tried to match his serious tone as a thrill prickled the little hairs on her nape and arms. "I love a good challenge."

Narrowing his eyes, he leaned in even closer. "You have to go through one of three doors. One has assassins, two"—he mock-shivered—"flames, and three, a lion that hasn't eaten in ninety days." He twisted his lips and fixed his eyes on her. "Which door would you choose?"

Her heart began to race. She wasn't good at riddles, but she'd better choose wisely. She looked up at Nate, searching for any hint of what he might be thinking.

No way would she go through fire, unless God told her to. Assassins were terrifying. She wouldn't stand a chance against them. A lion seemed like a better alternative, especially if it had gone without food for that many days. Ninety days was a long time, even for a hungry lion.

"Lion." She slapped her knee. "It would be dead after going three months without food."

Nate beamed. "Impressive, quick thinking."

A warm glow spread through her chest, and she settled back in her chair. "Next question, please?"

"What's your favorite ice cream?"

Huh? She blinked. Had she heard him right?

His eyes sparkled as he raised a hand. "I want to know how different we are from each other."

Okay. She thought before answering. "Vanilla. You?"

"Vanilla for me too. It's simple." He touched his flat stomach and sighed. "I wish I could eat it whenever I want to."

She nodded, understanding the sacrifices someone in his line of work had to make. But now was her turn to ask the next question. "Do you like street food?"

"Absolutely!" He sat up straighter. "I love trying new foods, especially when they're made with love and passion like yours. My brothers ate most of those sweet almonds you brought, but the ones I managed to snag were something else."

She shook a finger at him, infusing a teasing note into her voice. "For someone who keeps a strict diet, you're not picky."

"I have an entire week before my next race." He raised both hands this time. "I can pull off light sweets."

Who could help but smile at his easygoing nature? But then he surprised her with his next question. "You have a boyfriend?"

Her heart jittered an extra beat. This was a personal question, and she cocked her head at him to read his reaction.

He shrugged. "Our picture could appear in the press, online, or on gossip pages. If you have a boyfriend, that could—"

"I don't date," she interrupted, although it would surely be fun to date someone like Nate.

"Any specific reason why?"

She shrugged. "I've tried a few times, but my previous dates disapproved of the food-truck business." But truthfully, she hadn't been deeply invested in any of those relationships, which made it easier to let go. "Besides, I don't need distractions at the moment."

"You and I have a few things in common." He settled back with a smile. "I'm not interested in pursuing a relationship either."

She slid her feet from her white sandals, tucked her legs up beside her on the couch, and smoothed her dress over them. His was an odd response, considering how many dates she'd seen him on at the parties or wherever he paused for magazine photos.

As if sensing her judgment, he cocked his head to one side, mirroring her posture, and turned things on her. "A chef who's not happy with her career? Hmm, why's that?"

Taken aback by his insight, she straightened up, sitting taller in her seat. Serafina wouldn't have told him about Vanessa's passion for food, but how else would he know she wasn't excited about her job? She rubbed her thumb into her palm. "How do you know I'm not into my career?"

His blue eyes gleamed beneath the LED lighting, their hypnotic gaze capturing hers. She tore hers away and looked down at his shirt. It hugged his broad chest and lay smooth over his lean and toned stomach muscles.

"It's a bit stressful," she admitted. "If you could live in my shoes for one day, you'd understand why I'm edgy sometimes."

Nate sat up straighter, his eyes still bright as he slapped the table. "Sign me up. One day."

"Just what does that mean?"

"I'll come and sell food, cook, and stuff."

Ha. What did he think her day was like? It wouldn't be that easy. "Do you understand what you're getting yourself into? It wouldn't be like one of those television commercials where you stand on the beach."

Just in time, she stopped herself from describing some of the advertisements he'd appeared in. She didn't want him to wonder how she knew all the details about his commercials.

"You said I was a spoiled, self-absorbed snob." He chuckled. "I can't even remember the exact words you used, but I want to prove I can handle more than you think."

She winced at the memory of their earlier argument. "I didn't mean anything I said."

Nate raised an eyebrow. "You had to have thought about that before it came out of your mouth the instant you got upset."

He was right. If only she could go back and undo everything from that afternoon. She pressed her thumb harder against her palm and locked her other fingers around it. "Forgive me?"

"On one condition." His mouth quirked, sending his expression askew.

"Name it." She held her breath.

He sank back in his chair, a sly smile further curving up one side of his face. "I'll live a day in the life of Spitfire. Then you'll come to live a day in the life of Nate."

She sucked in a quick breath. What was she supposed to make of his odd proposal? Maybe the Geico race had messed with his brain somehow. "You're not taking me on race day."

"On practice day." He crossed his arms over his chest and gave a firm nod as if he'd settled the deal. "I'll take you through what race days look like for me."

Were these the kinds of negotiations he made with his girlfriends? She'd tried to keep track of the tabloid gossip about his love life. But when it exhausted her, she'd had to stop looking at tabloids altogether.

Letting her feet slide to the area rug, she crossed her arms to mirror his no-nonsense posture. "You're up for that challenge?"

"It's on, baby!" He gave a fist pump, and something fluttered in her stomach at the way he called her "baby."

Their gazes lingered on each other, and warmth spread through her body. She dropped her gaze and traced the leaf pattern on her dress, unsure of what to say next.

How could she not be excited about spending time with him? Although they were practically strangers, the brief moments spent in his company made her smile genuinely from deep within her heart and soul, rather than merely on the surface.

"What's your plan as a chef?"

Vanessa could feel herself blabbering, unsure of what to say. She had always talked about her dreams of becoming a teacher, but now that it seemed like that might not happen, being a chef began to seem like a dream she didn't know she had.

Still, was it too much to pursue two dreams at once? "What if this is the best the world has to offer?"

"Then you embrace each moment." He spread out his arms as if embracing the whole world.

"But..." Kinda hard to embrace something when all you could hold onto was a sense of dread over all the years you'd wasted. "But what if I spend years trying to fulfill my mom's dreams, only to fail?"

"Do you believe in God, Spitfire?"

Caught off guard, she sucked in a sharp breath, his words hitting like a sucker punch. "I believe in God. But I don't remember to lean on Him. Something in me wants to stand on my own feet, you know? And then it whines and cries when it can't stand up to things."

"If I've learned anything in my job, it is unpredictability." Nate drummed his fingers on his armrests. "Anything could strike while I'm racing—tire blowouts, mechanical conditions, *medical* conditions, weather changes, and you name it."

She could name a few unpredictable things striking her lately. "How do you handle that?"

He pointed up, obviously meaning God. "Worrying about what you can't control isn't healthy for you, but dealing with the unknown makes you stronger. There's also that peace in knowing God's in control of your future."

She plucked at an imprinted leaf again as if she could brush it and her troubles away. "Knowing is one thing, but putting that belief into action when your car gets broken into and you can't operate your business while you sort things out... makes it hard to remember what I know."

Nate's face softened. He scooted forward and rested a hand over hers, stilling her from picking at her dress. "Someone broke into your car?"

"It's not the first time." She shrugged, but she didn't want to shrug off the sense of protectiveness from Nate as it squeezed her chest.

"Did you find out who? Where?" His grip tightened over her hand. "Are you okay?"

Serafina had been right when she said Nate always wanted to help, even if he may not approach it the right way.

"Thanks for your concern," Vanessa whispered and slid her hand free, touched by his genuine caring.

He raked his hand through his hair in a short, frustrated gesture. "Were any valuables in your car?"

"Everything's under control. I already dealt with the situation last week."

"I'm sorry my thoughtlessness added to your stress that week." He shook his head, gripped his knees, and exhaled slowly. "I'd like to know more about your mother. You say you're trying to live out her dreams? I assume she's deceased?"

"It was a car wreck." Vanessa reached for the water bottle, her voice choking. She fought back tears. "My sister was running away in the busy street when my mom went after her...."

She swallowed hard, trying to compose herself. To this day, she only knew the details of the accident from the semitruck driver's testimony. It wasn't his fault—or hers. But she still carried a sense of guilt and regret. She'd been teaching her first year when she received the devastating news.

"I was always envious of my sister because my mom let her get away with so much." She'd been so young and selfish at the time. "But my sister had intense ADHD and autism, and I wanted to help kids like her."

Nate's hand brushed against hers as he slid a box of tissues toward her. She took one and blew her nose, grateful for his compassion. Self-conscious about her emotional outburst, she gestured with the soggy tissue, like a white flag. "You probably didn't want to hear all this."

"I have all night." He reached out and traced gentle circles on her hand with his thumb. "Tell me everything about your mom. What was she like?"

A wave of tears threatened to resurface before she pushed them down. "Mom always worked hard. She had a tireless work ethic and wanted to open a restaurant someday, so when death took her away suddenly..."

"You had to fulfill her dream." Nate sat back, taking his hand away from hers.

Already missing the warmth of his touch, she nodded, then puffed out a breath past the weight in her chest that always came when she remembered how she'd felt about her sister in the past. She drew a slow breath past the heaviness. Was she running her mom's business out of that same sense of guilt?

"What's your dream, Vanessa Douglas?"

As he asked the question, his voice slow and smooth, a shiver ran down her spine. She drew her knees closer to her body and sat up straight, captivated by his voice. The fact that Nate Stone knew her full name amazed her. Had he been thinking about her enough to learn it? "How do you know my last name?"

"It's been my intention to know all I could so I don't get on your bad side again."

A quiver ran through her body. He had a way of making her feel oddly uneasy yet comfortable. "I'm not Spitfire anymore?"

"It's good that you're a spitfire. You're passionate. I like that." His soft blue eyes locked onto hers. "What's your other passion?"

Her heart skipped a beat. With his eyes so mesmerizing, she found it hard to breathe. Still, the breathless confession rushed out. "I specialize in assisting parents in comprehending IEPs during annual meetings. These gatherings can be highly emotional for parents as they advocate for their children with disabilities, which is my true passion. The sooner I fulfill Mom's dream, the sooner I can pursue my own."

After nodding along, Nate sighed and lifted his hands, palms out as if expressing resignation. "I'm terrified to offer my help."

But help was why she was here, so she had to ask. "With my break-in, there's been unexpected expenses. I was wondering if you could please let me park the truck in your parking—"

"You can use the parking lot." His lips quirked to the left. "You might need to be out for a day or two when they fix the parking lot, and hopefully—"

"I will be gone by September. I promise." A thrill rushed through her. "Anytime your camera crew shows up I'll be out of the way."

She stood, resisting the urge to rush over and embrace him. Her dress hem bounced around her knees as renewed energy kept her from standing still. "Now, what can I do for you in return?"

"I don't need anything."

But she had to do something. "I could clean your house, car... whatever." What a silly suggestion. She didn't want to take advantage of his kindness, but he didn't even live in San Francisco, so cleaning his house wasn't an option.

Nate scratched the short beard accentuating his chiseled jaw. "I don't know how you can help."

She jutted up her chin, hands clenched at her sides. "Until you find something I can do, I'm not going to use your space."

He blinked and gawked at her.

Please, Lord, let him find something I can do to repay him. I need to be able to use that space. Of course, he didn't need anything. He had plenty of workers, and he could afford to pay for more.

"You're a very proud woman, Vanessa Douglas."

"I wouldn't be here if I was proud." But he was right. Her pride often caused her to choose a more difficult path. She wouldn't have flown all the way here if she'd reasoned with Nate like an adult the last time they spoke.

"But it would be prideful not to admit that you're right." And she'd better swallow that pride if it meant making amends.

Nate grinned, his brow rising in a challenge. "In that case, don't say I didn't warn you."

She couldn't deny the endearment she felt between them. She crossed her arms, ready to take on whatever challenge. "I'm all ears."

"You want to help me plan my family's Thanksgiving reunion?"

Serafina had told her about the annual Stone family reunion. They had a big house and kitchen. "How many people do I need to cook for?"

"No need to cook." He raised a finger. "Planning."

Whew! Planning was something she could handle—her forte, really. A brief silence passed as she tried to remember what Serafina's planning had entailed last summer.

"Too much to handle?" he asked.

She'd asked for it, and Serafina would be there to help her out. She reached to shake his hand. A grin stretched out her lips, the new challenge already exciting her. "It's a deal."

"It's a pleasure doing business with you, Spitfire." He stood as well and shook her hand, and her heart skipped another beat at the feel of his warm, strong grasp.

"The pleasure is all mine, Mr. Stone." She slid her hand back to her side. She may end up regretting this, but she couldn't back out now.

Nate stifled a yawn, revealing a bit of skin at his waist as his T-shirt lifted when he stretched. He must be exhausted.

She reached for her handbag. Whew, her trip here wasn't a waste! "I'm glad we came to a compromise."

"How are you getting to your hotel?" He tilted his head and eyed her as she retrieved her phone from her handbag.

"I'm getting an Uber." Wanting to keep her costs low, she'd booked a hotel out of town.

"You should stay here." He gestured to the suite. "I usually book an entire suite in case my family shows up. With only Wade and Theo in town, there's a spare bedroom."

"I wouldn't want to impose." She checked her phone. "It's almost two."

The time had flown by too fast, yet she would've enjoyed staying and talking to him longer.

"I can't let you drive with a stranger this late."

"I'll be fine."

He touched her shoulder. "You can leave first thing in the morning." The warmth of his hand seeped through her thin dress fabric even as his penetrating eyes seemed to see through her soul. "Please."

Her already jittery heart started beating faster, and when she opened her mouth to tell him she was capable of getting back to her hotel, she found herself nodding her agreement to stay in the fancy hotel.

CHAPTER 10

In an effort to avoid making an enemy and prove he wasn't a spoiled snob, Nate had taken on the challenge of operating a food truck. Winning people's approval wasn't a simple task, but necessary—at least to him. Even with more than enough media attention and not needing anyone's approval, he found himself standing in the commercial kitchen at the crack of dawn, awaiting Vanessa's instructions. The gentle hum of the refrigerators was a welcome contrast from the roaring engines he was accustomed to on the racetracks.

Something about Vanessa drew him in, something he couldn't quite explain, and a vibe between them made him want to go above and beyond. He knew she felt the same way, which was probably why he was there so soon after they had parted ways.

With gloved hands, he waited for her next move. The blade in her hand glinted beneath the bright lights as she connected it to the whole chicken on the cutting board and trimmed off the winglets. In a purple apron similar to his, she'd secured her long curly hair into a high ponytail that swished against her red top as she reached for the paste from a nearby bowl and applied it to the chicken. She was slender, with long legs and arms that came in handy as she reached for different items from the kitchen island.

Yesterday, he'd awakened to find a text from Vanessa thanking him for letting her stay in the suite. When he'd asked her to join him and his brothers for breakfast, she'd sent an apologetic emoji and a message that she was already at her hotel and needed to catch a flight back to San Francisco.

On instinct, he'd texted that he'd be walking in her shoes tomorrow. She'd surprised him by texting back the time and place to meet her. Six a.m. wasn't too early for him, and he'd even taken his morning run before showing up at the kitchen today.

Vanessa continued to work, pulling more chicken from the fridge and trimming off the winglets before seasoning the meat with a paste. So far, she'd prepared six chickens, which she lined up on a long tray. She was clearly used to working alone.

"When I said living in your shoes," he began, and she paused, using her wrist to scratch her forehead, "I meant working and not observing."

"Okay." She surveyed the space, then lifted her hand back to her forehead, and scratched the same spot with her wrist again.

He slid off one of his gloves and moved to her. "If scratching is what you need me to do..." He pulled her hand down and brought his fingers to the spot. "Is it here?"

Her eyes widened, and her breathing escalated. With her warm breath teasing his arm, he realized how intimate the action was, but he had to finish what he started. His heart was thundering, and he had to be mindful of their proximity. But he intended to follow through.

She stood still and silent as if holding her breath while he gently guided the tips of his short fingernails along her forehead. He doubted he was scratching her at all—his fingers were just trailing over her soft skin. Her temperature seemed higher than normal. When he looked down at her, she was biting her lower lip.

He lowered his hand back to his side. He couldn't give her false hope. Despite their earlier disagreements, an undeniable attraction and chemistry was brewing between them. That was why he was here and claiming he was friendly and nicer than she'd judged him to be. He'd never cooked anything in his kitchen. His chef did all the work. Yet, here he was.

"Thanks," she whispered, breaking the silence.

Their gazes locked, and an awareness he'd never felt before took up all the air between them. He rasped, "I hope that helped." Then he leaned against the sinks and looked up at the three spinning fans, grateful for the extra air since he needed it in this stifling room.

Vanessa spun around, keeping her back to him. "We can't be distracted."

"As long as you keep me occupied." *And aren't too much of a distraction.*

"Do you want to help me slide the chicken onto the skewer?"

"If you show me how." He snatched a glove from the box and slid it on before moving to her and focusing on the sterile light gleaming off spotless stainless steel appliances, countertops, and trays. Every bit of the space remained immaculate and utilitarian.

"Can you grab the skewers, please?" She motioned to the metal skewers at the end of the expansive island. When he did as asked, she put the cutting board in the sink behind them and brought a clean cutting board. "Please hold up one of the rods. You want to keep the pointed end up," she whispered.

Her soft fragrance teased his senses, and her nearness did something to his insides. But that must be because the two of them were alone in the confined space.

She carried one of the chickens from the tray and slid it onto the rod. But didn't she usually do this task alone? Why wasn't the neon-haired girl here?

"Don't you have someone working with you?"

She shrugged. "It's easier doing this part alone. The fewer people who know Mom's recipes the better."

So she'd rather drown in hard work than expose her mom's recipes.

"I haven't seen your mom's recipes since we got here."

"That's because we just started. Do you want to try to make something with a recipe?"

"That's why I'm here." After handing her a rod, he slid on the next chicken. It wasn't as difficult as he'd expected.

She winked. "Not bad for a race car driver."

"I told you I could live in your shoes." He reached for another chicken and slid it onto the same rod.

They repeated the process, loading each skewer with three chickens before positioning them in the oven. Then they worked on the prime rib she'd had marinating overnight.

"Why do you cook in a commercial kitchen?"

"All food vendors are required to have a commercial kitchen. Not everyone uses it, though." She handed him the silicone brush. "Go ahead and spread another coating of barbecue sauce."

Then she opened and closed a drawer to retrieve more skewers. "For me, getting a jump start on meals helps me not run out of food. I can't keep all the meat in my house. And I have my meat delivered here directly—in fact, the butcher already delivered everything for tomorrow so I can start marinating. I visit the farmers market to shop for produce. Ava brings most of the vegetables and bread to the truck later."

As the enticing aroma of broiling food simmered through the air, they crafted a flavorful seasoning for the potatoes destined for the grill. The kitchen hummed with activity, infused with mouthwatering spices and sizzling meat. There was no pause in their culinary dance, even as the meat cooked in the oven. Pans were washed and dried, vegetables were chopped for a kale salad, and a variety of sauces and dressings were whipped up from scratch.

As she drizzled the sauce over the vibrant salad, Nate recognized the familiar taste of kale from the charity event. With a playful flourish, she offered him a sample, and his exaggerated moan of delight elicited her giggles.

"Mind if I take a break and enjoy some of this salad?" He reached for a disposable plate. "The combination of pears and slivered almonds is just perfect."

"It's a crowd favorite." Her dark eyes twinkled as she filled his plate.

"I see why you have a reputation for winning people over with your food."

"I do not!" She feigned offense, brandishing her wooden spoon.

As he savored the salad and she assembled breakfast bowls and packed them into disposable containers, he inquired about her life in San Francisco. She shared stories of her Georgia roots, her mother, and their journey to San Francisco for a fresh start after her mother's boyfriend left to travel the world. She spoke of her mother's tireless efforts to establish a business that never quite found its footing.

Then he rejoined her to prepare the marinade for the next day. However, entrusting him with the task of making scrambled eggs was a mistake. He was aware that he'd poured too much olive oil into the pan, but as the oil heated, he went ahead and added the eggs. When he stirred the mixture, oil splashed over the pan's edge. A flame ignited and grew into a substantial blaze.

"Step back!" he shouted to Vanessa, who was at the fridge, as he tried to figure out how to handle the situation.

Her eyes widened while fear pulsed through him.

"Stay calm!" She dashed to a closet and returned with a fire extinguisher. "We can put it out."

He sprang into action, helping her direct the extinguisher at the fire. As foam sprayed onto the flames, the fire sputtered and died. Then she eyed him, covered in foam and speckled with egg remnants, and burst into laughter. Right. He must make an undeniably comical sight. He couldn't help laughing along.

As their laughter subsided, he looked deeply into her luminous brown eyes. She appeared more genuine and beautiful than ever. "You have very beautiful eyes."

"So do you." She caught her breath as they stood close, their mingled breaths creating a palpable tension.

His smile broadened. "I guess we'll need to start a new batch of eggs?"

Vanessa chuckled. "Maybe we should skip the eggs this time."

He'd always remember this day, and his chest swelled as gratitude for this time spent with her flooded him. Once they cleaned up the chemical foam and headed out, he assumed the most challenging part of her day was behind them. But he soon discovered otherwise. Three hours later, they arrived at the school where she volunteered. The children were endearing, and his chest swelled again while he observed her handling a young boy who experienced a meltdown when his father dropped him off.

The beanbag toss activity escalated when a boy, struggling with his motor skills, shifted from hurling bags to punching walls. Vanessa grasped his shoulders, maintaining a calm yet firm demeanor, and redirected him to the next activity.

As they continued their day, Nate drove her Sienna while she navigated the streets, communicating via phone. He learned of her parking woes when she insisted no spots were available, despite him spotting several parallel parking spaces. He offered to help, parking the car before assisting her with starting the food truck's generator, a skill that impressed her.

She sold breakfast bowls and sliders, and he processed credit card payments on her phone. They shared stories and laughter as she recounted the challenges she faced running the business, and the spray-painting incident left him holding his side as he chortled.

"You must have seen that coming with your smart mouth, right?" he joked, wiping the counter as they prepared to close from the morning and head to their final stop.

"How sympathetic of you," she retorted, slapping him with her towel, her face far from the serious expression he'd grown accustomed to.

He nodded to a framed photo in the corner of the truck. It depicted a dark-skinned woman and a young girl, who appeared to be around eight or nine years old. "Is that your mom?"

"Yes." Her expression softened, and her shoulders sloped. She picked up the photo and traced a finger along her mom's face. "People always thought we looked alike."

In the sunlight streaming through the window, the resemblance stood out clearly. "You have her eyes—even the way they tip up at the edges. Very beautiful."

"Thanks." She returned the photo to its place.

"How old was your sister when she passed away?"

"Nine." Vanessa wrapped her hands around her goose-bumpy shoulders. But the truck was warm.

"Are you cold?"

"I've been cold all morning."

He touched her forehead, her skin warm beneath his palm. "I hope you're not getting sick."

She winced. "I rarely get sick."

His stomach rumbled, and she giggled, placing her hand over her mouth to muffle the sound. "I guess it's almost lunchtime." She gestured to the seat by the back window. "Settle in, and I'll make something for you before we go."

"Now you're talking. Make it a kale salad, please. Double serving." He'd avoid the meat they'd prepared for her lunch customers. When she placed a plate in front of him, he grabbed her wrist. "Join me?"

"I'm not hungry, but I'll sit with you." She slid free and retrieved two water bottles. "I know you only drink water."

He raised an eyebrow. "Where did you hear that?"

"During one of your interviews."

Intrigued, he feigned ignorance. "What?"

She waved with her water bottle. "They asked how you stay healthy and such."

So she'd watched his interviews? A pleased tingle trickled down his spine as he twisted the cap off his water bottle.

"I'm not a groupie." She shook a finger at him, a teasing smile spreading out her full lips. "Or a lizard or whatever you call them."

"I'd be honored if you joined my pit lizard crew."

When he dramatically placed a hand on his chest, she rolled her eyes, looking both adorable and familiar in a way he couldn't quite pinpoint. One thing was certain: Vanessa was capturing his heart.

CHAPTER 11

The afternoon in Sausalito held an electric energy, the atmosphere in the truck charged with something new and exciting. Even with Ava now joining them, Nate's presence seemed to fill every corner, his scent mingling with the food aromas and adding an intoxicating layer to the experience.

Maybe it was Vanessa's whirlwind emotions or simply her first day back at the truck, but she felt an unshakeable chill and exhaustion, even with the oven radiating warmth. Nate's closeness should have provided a source of heat, but it did little to chase away the cold. Regardless, his mere presence cast a radiant glow over her day.

The construction site supervisor beamed as he took the plate Vanessa offered. "We missed you!" His gaze shifted to Nate. Then the poor guy's eyes widened, and his body jerked backward so hard he nearly dropped the plate. "Oh... Mr. Stone."

"Enjoy your lunch." Nate's infectious grin accompanied his easy reply. "I'll be there when we slow down." He'd formed a connection with the construction site supervisor during his recent visits. He moved with the practiced ease of someone who had done this before, as if he'd always been a part of Vanessa's life, giving the impression they were a well-oiled team. Which was something she'd never managed with anyone.

A warm, grateful feeling blossomed in her chest, making her regret her previous harsh words. "You're a pro at this."

Nate leaned in closer, his voice a low, tantalizing rumble. "Keep the compliments coming, and you've got yourself an employee every Tuesday and Wednesday." The vibrations from his voice sent delicious shivers skittering down her spine.

As someone called for their order, she relayed the message to Ava while Nate's efficiency at the register sped things up.

"I can't believe it," Ava whispered, passing the wrong plate to Vanessa, her eyes filled with excitement.

"Order Number 3," Vanessa reminded her, struggling to hold back a smile. Ava had been thrown off-balance since Nate had appeared, driving Vanessa's Sienna and donning an apron as if it were the most natural thing in the world.

Ava's voice was barely a whisper but still loud enough to make Vanessa nervous. "Hottie is in your truck."

Vanessa shot her a warning glance, heart pounding. "Let's keep it down."

Then Serafina and Logan made their way to the back of the short line, hand in hand. Wow. What were they doing here? Vanessa's chest warmed as she called out. "Serafina! Logan!"

"Vanessa!" Serafina boomed, her dark-brown hair cascading in waves, tied back in a long yellow scarf that complemented her self-tailored, yellow polka-dot dress. They stepped out of the line and approached the truck's entrance.

Nate groaned under his breath. "They're only here to give me a hard time."

"Publicity is good," Vanessa teased. "Please unlock the back door while I serve our customers."

Once the line was cleared, Vanessa asked Ava to take over at the serving window. Ava shared a warm side hug with Serafina before moving to her new post. Then Vanessa embraced her best friend, planting a kiss on each cheek. Serafina's tanned face seemed to glow even brighter since marrying Logan.

"Aren't you supposed to be at work?"

"Logan and I took an extended lunch break." Serafina beamed. "You know my diligent teacher's assistant is more than capable of handling the kids for a bit in my absence."

Meanwhile, Logan and Nate exchanged playful banter about Nate's questionable kitchen skills. "Just don't burn down the kitchen," Logan joked.

Vanessa and Nate shared a look, neither admitting he *had* started a fire. She pressed a hand to her racing heart. Did he know the blaze on the stove wasn't the only fire she feared he'd started?

Her eyes alight, Serafina hugged Vanessa's arm and leaned in to whisper in her ear. "What did you do to Nate? He looks so alive. Logan was worried he wouldn't make it through lunch."

"Nate's been amazing—a true surprise, especially given his willingness to drive my beat-up car and work in this humble food truck."

Nate removed his apron and passed it to Logan. "If you're here, get to work."

Logan tossed the apron back at Nate, smirking. "I brought my wife out on a lunch date, and I expect you to serve us."

With a nudge, Nate steered Logan toward the ovens. "How romantic does it get when you serve your wife?"

Serafina's eyes softened as she caressed Logan's cheek. "I'll do the honor of serving you, sweetheart."

"I'd be lost without you." Logan pulled his wife close and planted a tender kiss on her lips.

"Good grief." Nate rolled his eyes. "Give me a break."

Shrugging, Logan responded, "What can I say? *You've* got every right to be jealous of how close Sera and I are. However, *I'm* not a bit jealous of how close you and Ava and Vanessa are in this little space. Seriously, never mind who serves whom, I don't think we all fit in here at all."

"He's right, boss," Ava piped up. "You should get your friends out of here. I can handle things."

So Vanessa nodded toward the window. "Why don't we go sit outside by the fountain?"

Nate joined Logan and Serafina on the bench while Vanessa perched on the fountain's rim, curiously not hungry.

"If Nate's career doesn't work out"—Logan forked through his prime rib—"Vanessa, you've got yourself an employee."

Nate's gaze met hers, the warmth emanating from his eyes causing her to fidget. "She might fire me."

"I'd hire you, maybe," she admitted, her fingers tightening on the fountain's stonework edge.

He winked. "I want to prove to this lady that I'm not a snob."

Serafina raised an eyebrow. "As long as the tabloids paint you as a snob, it'll take a while to prove otherwise."

"Hey!" Nate held up both hands. "I can't control people's gossip."

Serafina nodded. "The world needs to see the real Nate."

He dropped his hands to grip his knees. "I'm always the real Nate."

"When Nate left at the crack of dawn"—Serafina shifted her gaze between Logan and Vanessa—"we thought he was joking."

Vanessa had confided in Serafina about her encounter with Nate, omitting his offer to work with her at the truck. She hadn't anticipated him taking it seriously. As she looked at him now, her chest swelled. He had followed through. "He's a man of his word, I think."

"You think?" Nate glanced down at the T-shirt she'd provided, then locked eyes with her. A sense of promise seemed to fill the air. Logan and Serafina faded into the background, the world narrowing until it felt like only Vanessa and Nate existed.

Shortly later, Logan and Serafina left, and the lunch rush subsided. Nate went to chat with the construction workers, giving Vanessa some much-needed breathing space. She took the opportunity to sit with Ava so her assistant could eat.

"I thought you were only going to talk to him so he would let us stay." Ava bounced in her seat, her purple ponytail jiggling beneath her hairnet. "I didn't expect you to have him working."

"He offered." Vanessa pressed her hand to her forehead. Despite the budding headache, she could still feel the lingering warmth of his touch from earlier when he'd grazed her skin. She craved more of that electrifying sensation.

Ava's voice pulled her back to the present. "Did you hear what I said?"

"What's that?"

"Did you know that Nate Stone... Well, I looked him up. He's had, like, the most winning streaks of the famous races in a row." Ava stabbed her shredded pork with a fork.

Vanessa knew all about Nate's impressive racing record but had only shared that knowledge with Serafina. She didn't want to be labeled a secret admirer.

"By the way..." Ava's voice lowered, her face breaking into a mischievous grin. "I think he likes you."

Having sensed that as well, Vanessa stifled the urge to nod. But what made Ava suspect it too? "What do you mean?"

"I saw him checking you out when you weren't looking."

Vanessa swallowed, attempting to conceal her excitement. However, Ava could just be trying to gauge her reaction.

"Now that we have the space to sell our food"—Vanessa shifted the conversation from Nate—"there's a high chance you'll be getting your truck before the end of this year."

Ava clapped, squealing.

"Tell me how you intend to run the food truck?" Vanessa cocked her head. "Where you'll park it, and what you'll be cooking?"

"Tacos." Ava moved her fork around her food. "It wouldn't make as much money as your meats do, but the menu would be simple. I'll assign tasks and only hire those who can cook."

A shiver ran down Vanessa's spine. The idea of trusting others with her business made her uneasy. Ava's motto of working smarter, not harder, was admirable and perhaps the best way to avoid burnout. However, Vanessa couldn't risk exposing her mom's recipes to anyone.

So how *would* she have people run her mom's restaurant without giving them the recipes? Pushing the thought away, she wrapped her arms around herself, trying to stifle the goose bumps that spread across her body. Sleep sounded incredibly appealing.

She stifled a yawn, only half listening to Ava's excitement.

"You look so tired today," Ava remarked. "Are you okay? We just had a whole week off."

"I hope I'm not getting sick. I better not be. I hugged Serafina earlier and spent time close to Nate—and he has a race coming up this weekend."

"I can close up the truck." Ava scooped the last of her pulled pork. "Maybe Nate can let you park it here tonight."

Parking the truck was always a hassle. The gas-station arrangement had fallen through, leaving her needing a new solution.

"You know I can cook too, right?" Ava swallowed her last bite, then pointed her empty fork at Vanessa. "In case you need a day off."

Vanessa couldn't remember the last time she'd been sick, especially not since owning the food truck. "I'll be fine." A good night's sleep should have her back on her feet by tomorrow. "I just don't want to make anyone sick."

"I can do this," Ava insisted.

Though Vanessa did not doubt her assistant's capabilities, she couldn't bring herself to entrust Ava with the cherished recipes.

As Vanessa stood to start preparing dinner, beads of sweat formed on her forehead, and her stomach churned. She let out a moan and gripped the counter with one hand while pressing the other against her middle.

"You don't look fine." Ava came up behind her and rubbed her arm, and Vanessa had to agree when the nausea intensified. She was going to be sick.

Overwhelmed by the urge to vomit, she rushed to the door, flung it open, and stumbled down the steps. She barely made it to the trash can behind the truck before leaning over and emptying her stomach. As she retched, a hand gripped her shoulder, and someone scooped her hair back.

"Are you okay?"

It was him. Nate. The one person she didn't want to see her like this. She tried to speak, but all that came out was a groan as she vomited again. His hand on her back rubbed soothing circles, and his whispered reassurances made her heart swell as tears welled in her eyes. Nate was the kind of man who could make any woman's dreams come true.

Ava must have been nearby because Nate called for her to bring water and a napkin.

Vanessa shivered, both embarrassed and unexpectedly connected to him in this vulnerable moment. After a few minutes, she stopped throwing up, and she straightened up. "Thank you," she said when he handed her a napkin. She wiped her mouth before tossing the tissue into the trash.

"Here." He offered a disposable cup of water. "Drink some."

With shaky hands, she lifted the cup to her lips, and a sip soothed her dry throat. She looked up at him, feeling a rush of emotion. "I don't know how to..."

"No problem." He smiled down at her with warm, caring eyes. "Let's get you home."

His gaze held hers, and something in the depths of his eyes made her stomach flutter once more. When he placed a steady hand on her back and led her away from the trash can, a mix of gratitude, embarrassment, and attraction consumed her. Could this be the beginning of a deeper connection between them?

***

Sitting at the end of the bed in the small bedroom, Nate observed Vanessa under the nightstand lamp's soft glow. Her chest rose and fell, and her long eyelashes framed her closed eyes. She looked so vulnerable and peaceful, a stark contrast to the feisty chef serving street food during the day. His chest tightened.

When they arrived at her apartment, she'd rushed to the bathroom to throw up again. He'd followed her, holding her hair back as she retched. After she cleaned up and changed, he searched her kitchen cupboards for medicine and gave her a couple of ibuprofen tablets. She didn't want to eat anything, preferring to hydrate with water instead.

His heart ached as he continued to watch her, her soft breathing filling the room. Something had shifted inside him when she vomited earlier—a protective instinct had taken over.

His gaze landed on a framed photo on her nightstand. Vanessa and her mother and sister all stood together. Vanessa's hands rested on her sister's shoulders in a protective stance. Did she have any other relatives? He couldn't fathom life without his siblings and parents.

If not for his adoption into a loving family, he could have faced a life of homelessness and loneliness. His adoptive parents, Kyle, a research analyst, and Regina, a child psychiatrist, showered Nate and his siblings with unconditional love, instilling in them the essential values in life such as faith, family, and friendships. They taught their children the importance of hard work and the rewards of pursuing a passion.

He yawned, exhausted from the day's hustle. He needed to leave, lest he catch Vanessa's sickness—disastrous before his upcoming race.

Like any venture, running a food truck demanded a great deal of effort. Before anyone committed to the street-food business, they should be mentally and physically prepared for its challenges.

The nightstand clock read eleven. While he hoped she could sleep through the night, he had to wake her to let her know he was leaving. He brushed her hair from her face. Her forehead was still warm but not as hot as earlier. Emotions welled in his chest as he touched her face. She was beautiful and fascinating. He whispered her name.

Her eyes fluttered open, and she squinted, shielding her face with her arm. "Nate?" Her voice was hoarse. "You're still here."

"I am," he whispered, wishing he could stay all night and take care of her. "I have to go, but I'll see you in the morning."

"The alarm." She tossed the covers aside, resting her chin on her hands, elbows sinking into the pillow. "I forgot to set the alarm."

"You can't work tomorrow, Spitfire."

"I have the butcher coming." She sat up, shivering in her pajamas. "I left the meat in the fridge. I can't let all that go to waste."

Now, more than ever, her assistant needed to step up. "I'll tell Ava to come and cook—"

"No," she protested through a yawn.

"If it's the recipes you're worried about, I'll be there with her." He hadn't thought through his offer, but if it gave her peace of mind, he'd do it. He helped her lie down and pulled the covers up to her chin. "Go back to sleep, okay?"

"Ava can't cook prime rib."

"I saw how you made it today." He traced his fingers along her chin, his throat tightening. "I'll work with her and get it ready for your customers."

"You're tired. I can't have you working... again." She closed her eyes, wincing as if in pain.

"I saw where you keep your recipes too." In the secure locker at the commercial kitchen. He just needed to find the key on her key ring.

"You can't drive... the truck." She was too weak to protest but didn't seem ready to give up.

"If I have to work early, I better go to bed." His muscles ached. He had texted Logan and Serafina not to wait up for him, and he wouldn't likely see them tomorrow morning. "What time does the butcher show up at the kitchen?"

"Close to six. I'll be there."

"As long as I don't make eggs, Ava and I can handle lunch and dinner." Whether dinner would be served would depend on Ava's competence in the truck.

Even with her eyes closed, a faint smile graced Vanessa's lips. "How are you going to cook?"

If she meant his skills in the kitchen, he'd gained some experience observing her follow the recipes for the sauces and spices they'd made.

"Already doubting my skills?" he teased.

"How are you going to get... the truck to the commercial kitchen?"

To transfer the grilled meats from the kitchen to the truck, he'd need to transport the truck from Sausalito to the kitchen. "I'll figure something out."

Ava better know some chefs who could help them. Otherwise, he'd mess up, and Vanessa might never talk to him again. He'd seen Ava's phone number on a sticky note by Vanessa's dining table, so he'd call her on his way to Logan's penthouse. He smiled, remembering the NASCAR schedule on Vanessa's board below the sticky notes.

"You'd be surprised by all the things you don't know about me." Her words at the Kansas Speedway rushed into his mind. Could she be a motorsports fan? He'd find out soon.

Her breathing steadied now as she succumbed to the pull of sleep. He couldn't help but place a hand on her over the blanket and say a silent prayer for her recovery.

"'Night, Vee." He fought the urge to lean in and press his lips to her cheek, but he'd wait for the right time. He couldn't shake the feeling that something monumental had changed, shifted, like the very particles in the air.

***

Not wanting to wake up Vanessa so early the next day, Nate met Ava at the commercial kitchen, where he'd instructed her to bring the truck from Sausalito. He kept Vanessa's recipes discreet as he cooked with Ava before they loaded the meats onto the truck.

While he sent Ava with an Uber to get two of her chef friends, Nate drove the truck to Sausalito. He didn't have insurance to drive Vanessa's truck, but if anything happened, he'd cover the damage. It would also be a better excuse to get Vanessa a new truck.

A few hours later, Ava showed up with the vegetables and two of her friends. Once Nate introduced himself, he stepped out of the food truck to text Vanessa.

The sky was a brilliant blue, and the water sparkled in the midmorning sunlight. Seagulls soared overhead, and the salty scent of the sea mingled with the pungent scent of freshly cut wood from the construction site.

Nate scrolled over the screen for Vanessa's number. At ten past ten, she should be awake, even though he hoped she was still curled up in bed. He sent a text.

Nate: I just wanted to check in and see how you're feeling. I also wanted to let you know we've got things under control here. (After the firefighters came to put out the fire in the truck.) But don't worry. We're using a rental truck today.

He didn't expect her to text back, and if his phone hadn't vibrated in his hand, he might not have heard it over the rumble of heavy equipment at the restaurant.

Vanessa: There's no way I'd entertain working today. If you burn down the truck, then we'll be forced to take a long-term break.

His cheeks lifted into a smile. She got his joke and didn't freak out assuming he'd actually had a fire.

Nate: I'm sorry you're not well. Is there anything I can do to help?

Vanessa: How much more can I ask you to do? I appreciate your help today.

Nate: Can I send over some soup or anything?

Vanessa: Food doesn't sound good at all.

Nate: Get some rest. Text me if you need anything.

Vanessa: Thanks. I appreciate it. You're the best!

He grinned, his chest expanding as he sent a sleepy emoji.

Before they started selling food, he'd call Jae and have her order flowers, Sprite, groceries, and soups for Vanessa. She'd need food around when she got her appetite back.

When they opened up the window to serve lunch at noon, the two workaholic helpers Ava had enlisted impressed him. It seemed they had more people today than yesterday, and some customers called him by name, which hadn't been the case yesterday. The ladies brought out food in record time while he ran the cash register.

"Where did you find our helpers again?" he asked when the lunch rush was over and the women sat down to eat.

"We used to work together on side gigs for truck events. They prefer to work on standby rather than commit to jobs long term."

Made sense. If he was in the street-food business, he'd prefer not to commit to the job full-time either. Not having your kitchen, dealing with parking, and whatnot was draining.

"You ladies enjoy your food." He moved to the sink and unearthed a serving bowl he'd seen Vanessa use yesterday. As promised, he wanted to make the barbecue sauce without exposing Vanessa's recipes. So, he headed to the desk in the corner where Vanessa had the framed photo of her mom and sister. He ignored the sticky notes on the board that Vanessa had jotted down before she knew she'd be sick.

Opening the drawer, he rummaged through a Rolodex of handwritten recipes until he found the barbecue.

"Do you need any help, Mr. Stone?" Ava asked when he swung open the cabinet labeled condiments.

"I need to pass this training." He pointed to the table where the girls sat eating in silence as if it was uncomfortable for them to talk. "You can be my witness to Vanessa that I cooked something."

The women giggled. All three of them, including Ava, seemed to be in their mid to late twenties.

"No way!" A man's deep voice sounded at the serving window, and Nate whipped his head toward it.

"Xenon." Nate closed the note cards and put them back in the drawer, locking them up before heading to the window.

"What did she feed you?" Xenon's thick brows drew together as he eyed Nate's face, then the apron. "Why are you so—"

"What's up?" Nate kept a light tone, acting as if this truck business was normal for him. "We have prime rib, pulled pork, roasted chicken.... And oh, by the way, the sauce is the boss here at Mama Dee's."

"You came to kick her off the property." Xenon lifted his hands in question, and his bushy brows rose as if to match. "And now you're *cooking* for her?"

Nate shook his head. How had he come to this? "We made a bargain."

Vanessa was turning him into putty without even knowing it. He was so busted.

"I wanna hear that kind of bargain." Xenon slid his phone from his back pocket and spun the screen to Nate. "Seems you're trending."

Nate strained his eyes, squinting beneath the afternoon light, but he couldn't see anything. "What's that?"

Good thing he didn't care much about what the gossip pages said about him anymore.

"Someone saw you driving a food truck and took your photo today."

"We have free publicity." He shrugged. "It might be good for our restaurant and now her truck."

"Yeah, well, she makes a pretty mean brisket, though." Xenon slid his phone away and jammed one hand on his hip. "Do you have any left?"

They'd run out of the food they prepared earlier. "Lucky for you. We have a fresh batch in the oven."

"Huh!" Xenon smirked, then frowned. "Is everything okay with you?"

"I have a race this weekend. I better be okay."

As Nate spent two days immersed in Vanessa's life, he hadn't lost his temper. He enjoyed spending time with her and found peace and strength whenever he set his mind on being okay, even when faced with challenges. However, her job was far from easy, and he didn't want to live in her shoes.

By the end of the day, two things had become clear. He was falling for Vanessa, and he didn't want to be anywhere near a food truck for a while.

CHAPTER 12

Early on a Friday afternoon, Vanessa sat in a retro burger joint waiting for Serafina, who'd agreed to meet despite her usual reluctance to go out on Fridays. The location halfway between their workplaces made it the perfect spot for a quick catch-up, especially since Nate insisted on keeping extra help for the truck for the week. Since her bout with the flu, Vanessa accepted the importance of delegation, something Ava always emphasized and Nate had been a natural at.

Vanessa smiled, remembering his carefree attitude and willingness to work alongside her and then his tenderness while she was sick. He'd even prepared such large batches of potato seasoning, meat paste, and barbecue sauce that had lasted since Wednesday. He'd also arranged the meat delivery and helped Ava prepare the meats before leaving for his race in Fort Worth.

What was he doing right now? Was he practicing on the track or taking a break? Her fingers twitched toward her phone at the temptation to text him, but she couldn't appear desperate. She had to be different.

With her growing feelings for him, she sensed he might feel the same. She reread their text messages from yesterday morning.

Nate: Try not to stress about work when you're not feeling well. I took the privilege of paying an advance to our two extra helpers. They're staying for the rest of the week.

Vanessa: It's not easy for me to accept help, but I'm taking baby steps.

Nate: Baby steps are better than crawling.

She cackled, barely registering the teen wiping tables around her as she scrolled on the screen to read the message he'd sent last night at eight, reminding her not to go to work just yet.

Nate: Enjoy your beauty sleep—not that you need it.

And then she'd woken up to his morning texts.

Nate: Good morning, Spitfire! I hope you had a restful night. Do me a favor today: open your window to enjoy the sunrise. Smile and engage in an activity that will make this the best day ever.

How could she not smile when thinking of him that morning as she savored the vibrant pink and orange hues of a sky partly obstructed by dingy buildings? She'd texted him a photo of it.

"Vanessa!" Serafina's voice brought her back to reality as her friend set her purse down and reached for a hug.

After returning her embrace, Vanessa held Serafina at arm's length. "Wow. That might be your cutest vintage dress."

"Just because I sometimes get puked on by sick kids doesn't mean I can't look good," Serafina joked. "Your outfit is quite chic too today."

"Thanks. I changed before leaving the food truck. I had to dress nicely after being in bed for days. With a business to run, dressing up a little and meeting you was the best I could manage today." They shared a smile. Then Vanessa looped her arm through her friend's and walked her to the counter, happy to spend time together and swap stories.

The young man behind the counter set aside his phone and grinned at them. "You ladies know what you want?"

Wow. They were the only customers in the restaurant.

Serafina eyed the menu written on the chalkboard. "Can you give us a few minutes, please?"

After a short debate, Vanessa ordered a vanilla ice cream cone, and Serafina ordered a small pineapple milkshake. "I hope it doesn't ruin my appetite for tonight's dinner," Serafina said as Vanessa handed over her credit card. It was her turn to pay since Serafina had paid last time.

As they returned to their seats and savored their treats, Serafina stirred her thick drink. "How are you coping with having someone else work in your food truck while you're on a break? You're such a control freak when it comes to that thing."

Vanessa playfully swung her ice cream cone toward her friend. "No, I'm not."

Serafina's lips flattened like she was holding back a retort before she sipped her drink. "Seriously, though, how do you expect to manage your mom's restaurant while teaching?"

"I'm not thinking that far ahead, but I guess this is good practice for when I hire people to manage it." She'd always intended the restaurant's earnings to go to a charity for autism.

Serafina's long hair danced over her shoulders as she shook her head. "I still can't believe *Nate* worked for you after all those months of you crushing on him."

A warmth spread through Vanessa's chest. "That was so nice of him."

"He texted me about five times to make sure I stopped by your house this morning." Serafina bobbed her straw in her drink. "He was worried sick about you."

Vanessa scrunched up her face at the memory of how she had acted. "Yelling at him and getting sick in front of him weren't exactly the smoothest ways to pursue him."

She twisted the cone in her hand, not focusing on licking up the drips as her shoulders sloped. "I can't even bring myself to be around the women he dated before—models, intelligent designers, and business owners."

"Which makes you the perfect candidate." Serafina brought her straw to her mouth. "Oh, this is so thick. They make the best shakes. I don't know why you'd pick ice cream here, though. Nothing's as good as Soft Swirl."

"Yeah." Vanilla trickled onto Vanessa's fingertip, and she hurried to lick up the drop. Then she scooted back against her bench ready to change the subject. "So, how does it feel being married to your bestie?"

Serafina's eyes shone. "I wouldn't want to be with anyone else. I'm so happy."

As Serafina shared the updates and renovations they were planning for their home in Tuscany, Vanessa felt happy for her friend. Still, at the same time, a deep ache and desire to have what Serafina had found grew within her. However, Vanessa couldn't settle for a relationship yet, not until her mom's business was stable. But, with Nate, maybe she could have both.

Hours later, as Vanessa lay in bed, her friend's words echoed in her mind.

"Which makes you the perfect candidate."

Was she the perfect woman for him? For Vanessa, Nate seemed to be the only man who'd captured her attention, the one man who could make her laugh and smile. But she was probably getting too ahead of herself. Thinking about him made her heart race.

Would he text her or not? Taking the initiative, she pulled out her phone and texted him. When he didn't respond, disappointment set in. Then, seconds later, her phone rang.

"Hello?" she answered breathlessly.

"Hey," he replied in a low drawl.

Her heart danced at the sound of his voice. "What did you do today?" A wistful sigh slipped loose as she cuddled back against the pillows and imagined lying there beside him and talking late into the night.

Okay, that wouldn't do! She sprang to her feet, trying to maintain her composure. She paced the bedroom, then dropped onto the edge of her bed, and focused on the bouquet he'd sent. The magnificent magnolias seemed to float in the air above the vase, the flowers supposedly like the ones in his North Carolina gardens.

"I didn't do anything fun. I mean, I love driving, but that was pretty much it. What about you?"

"I took your advice and met Serafina for ice cream. It was nice."

"Good. Do you think you could have made it any better?"

"Maybe. I don't know," Vanessa admitted, feeling out of touch with fun. "Tell me more about your day."

"I spent most of it thinking about you."

As a wave of giddiness tingled through her, her voice squealed out high-pitched. "You did?"

"You know I did. You were sick when I left."

They shared a comfortable silence until she spoke again. "I'll be praying for your race this weekend."

"Thanks, I appreciate it. Speaking of races. Why do you have a NASCAR calendar on your board?"

She shrugged, touching one of the velvety petals in the vase. "I have to cheer on my favorite racers." Even though he couldn't see her, she pouted her lower lip.

"Don't tell me you're a lizard too?" Nate teased.

"Maybe?" Her smile grew. "I have some mysteries I best keep to myself."

"Can I take you to dinner on Monday?"

He had a busy schedule, especially on Mondays after race day. "Don't you have sponsor stuff to deal with?"

"I'll eventually have to eat dinner."

"Dinner would be great." Her stomach fluttered.

"Whoo-hoo." He chortled. "It's a date, then."

A date. It sounded good coming from her crush. "I thought we were both not interested in dating or relationships."

"Exactly," he singsonged the word. "Which is why we have to test our theory. Go against what we think we know."

He was something else. He seemed to have answers for everything, but she wanted nothing more than to test her heart and see if she was capable of falling in love. Who better to test theories with than Nate, who made her feel things she'd never felt before? Nate, who had the unique ability to make her happy and relaxed.

But, more than grateful for all he'd done for her, she wanted to be the one to take him out to dinner. "As long as I pay."

"No, it's on me. I asked you out first."

She bit her lower lip, enjoying his lighthearted and almost flirtatious manner. She didn't feel like arguing now, but she'd figure out the details of their date and text him after his race on Sunday.

"I'll see you then. Good night." As much as she wanted to chat longer, Nate needed some rest before his upcoming race.

"I'll be able to sleep better if I know I'm seeing you soon," he said, his voice low and husky. "What are you doing this weekend?"

"Rooting for you, praying and watching you race virtually." Already pumped to watch it live on ESPN, she flopped back on her pillows, then blurted out without thinking. "See you in my dreams."

"See you in my dreams too."

Somehow, she pressed the End Call button, cutting the connection with this warm and affectionate version of Nate. If only date night was tomorrow instead. How was she going to survive the long wait until Monday?

***

The truck had earned extra profits on the days Nate had worked for Vanessa, and they received more customers for the rest of the week. Which made sense after Ava texted her a link to a photo of him stepping out of the driver's side of the truck. People had probably shown up expecting him to sign their autographs, but since he wasn't there, they'd had to buy the food.

Either way, he was Vanessa's for the evening, however long their mini-golf date lasted. The freshly cut grass scented the warm air, and the gentle background music added to the romantic ambience.

Nate was walking toward her with a club, grinding his teeth, and seeming bothered that it had taken him three tries to hit the ball into the hole. He'd rolled up the sleeves of his white button-down shirt, revealing toned forearms. The shirt was tucked into a pair of slim-fitting, dark-wash jeans that hugged his sculpted legs. The polished, brown-leather shoes padding against the putting mat added a sophisticated touch to his outfit.

They'd shared a pizza at the restaurant near the mini-golf course where each of the holes was set up through miniature iconic San Francisco landmarks. She'd paid in advance when she called to make their reservations. No way would Nate have let her pay, and it pleased her to have treated the billionaire to a place he clearly wouldn't have chosen.

"Would you like to tell me why you're smiling?" He stepped beside her.

"Gloating is more like it." She crouched to position the club, a mini driver, before swinging the ball at Alcatraz Island. "This is my chance to show you how it's done."

"I'm sure you're a pro at this. You probably have a secret technique or something."

Her gaze followed the ball as it arced over the pond representing the Bay. Then she scrunched her nose, unimpressed when the golf ball rolled past the hole on the famous island prison. The sun was setting, painting the sky in shades of pink and orange and casting a warm glow over the amusing course. Being a Monday night on a less popular and somewhat dilapidated course, they had the place to themselves.

"I do have a few tricks up my sleeve," she said as they crossed the course's bridge over the pond to the island. Then, with a gentle tap of her mini putter, she guided the ball into the hole before giving a victory dance. The skirt of her jean dress tickled her calves as she waved her club in triumph. She wiggled its steel head at him. "But don't worry. I'll go easy on you."

"Thanks. I appreciate that." His blue eyes sparkled in the dusky light. Laughing a deep belly laugh that warmed her to the core, he put a hand on her lower back and guided her to the next hole, this one designed to match the Golden Gate Bridge.

She putted across the bridge, her ball rolling near the hole. She wanted to know so many things about him, questions that had been building up in her mind since he'd surprised her as the owner of the restaurant where she parked her truck. "How did you get into racing?"

"I've had an obsession with cars since I was young." He smiled. "I can't even remember, but I always loved racing of any kind. Dirt races, *Mario Kart*—oh man, I got so many speeding tickets in high school."

"So you were reckless then?"

"I wouldn't call it reckless." He swung his club, and they fell silent as the ball rolled smoothly across the bridge then rimmed the hole before stopping without going in. He strolled over and tapped it, completing that hole.

At the next setup, she trundled her ball down Lombard Street, letting it roll smoothly along the crooked, but nicely slanted course, and flashed a grin before they sauntered toward Fisherman's Wharf, talking about his biological dad and grandpa he vaguely remembered.

"My parents said they were passionate about NASCAR. Probably why I was always drawn to races at a young age." His hands moved as he spoke about his adoptive parents and their support for his passion. "They wanted me to learn to race so I could go about it the right way."

She rattled her rented golf bag along, still intrigued by the event she'd catered and his connection. "I know you sponsor lots of charity events, but can you tell me about that fundraising event at the hotel? Were you just there for that day, or—"

"Autism Expression, yes." He stood, resting his club against the pad and leaning his hands on it. "Zeke and I started it two years ago."

"You started the organization?" Her golf bag bumped her legs as she stopped abruptly.

Nate nodded, his brows furrowing. "You seem surprised."

You're full of surprises. She'd thought she knew all about him from stalking him through the press. Clearly, she didn't know him as much as she'd thought.

"What does Autism Expression do? I didn't ask for details when Zeke hired me to cater for it."

"We offer support to families."

Vanessa turned, planting her ball on the tee, not wanting to show how surprised she was. As he continued explaining all the things his charity did for autism, he seemed passionate about the cause.

"That's not all." He cut one hand through the air before positioning his ball on the pad by Pier 39. "We've also partnered with other organizations for autism research and treatment."

"Why are you passionate about autism?"

He shrugged and swung at the ball. It jumped over a miniature cable car and rolled toward the wax museum. "My grandpa was autistic."

The sadness in his voice drew her closer, and she touched his shoulder, wanting to know more about his grandfather.

"I don't even know what he looked like." His gaze distant, he forked his fingers through his hair and tugged at it. "I kinda remember he smelled like mint candies and always gave me one. It bothers me that I can't remember what he or Dad looked like. Kyle and Regina did way more background research into my family tree before I was adopted. My mom died when I was three months old. Dad took care of me and his dad. Then Dad died when I was four."

His jaw twitched, and his chest rose and fell. His features contorted as he seemed to reflect on his early childhood. At least she'd had her mom alive throughout her childhood and teens. She braced her club against the three-foot-high Ghirardelli Square, stepped over the cable car, and moved to him. Wrapping her arms around his waist, she tucked her head against his chest, and he rested his chin on her hair. She squeezed him tight, emotion lodged in her throat. "I'm so sorry you had to go through that."

She listened to his breathing as they held each other and she savored his intoxicating scent.

He then cleared his throat, his breath warm over her head. "Talking about my past isn't bad if it earns me such a hug."

His lightheartedness never ceased to amaze her.

"Now, if I'm going to beat you at this game." He pulled out of the embrace and traced his fingertips along her cheek, and a trail of goose bumps scattered through her body at the warmth of his touch. "What do you say we talk about happy things for the rest of the night?"

"Deal." She grinned as a sense of promise filled her. Then she scooted back a few steps and retrieved her putter. "So, what do you do for fun, Mr. Speed?"

"Just about anything that keeps me from stress." He tapped his ball into the hole, then gestured for her to take a shot. "I like to keep active. When I'm moving, I'm not brooding, you know? So just about anything that energizes me relaxes me. Water sports like jet skiing, surfing, scuba diving or winter sports like skiing, snowboarding, snowmobiling."

He considered extreme sports relaxing? She bit her tongue as they approached Chinatown's Dragon Gate. "I take it you don't do a lot of reading by the fire?"

He chuckled and ducked through the scaled-down archway. "You've met my family. Have you counted my brothers and sisters? Do you have any idea how hard it would've been to find a quiet place to read when we were all growing up? I never did get into the habit, too much fun going on I would have missed."

As he winked, she joined in his laughter. "I can't even imagine what it must have been like." And yet she could. The thrill in his voice as he spoke of his home in the mountains and his tenderness as he talked about his big family said it all. She'd met the Stone family, and the few times she'd been in their presence, she'd admired their caring relationships and wished to be a part of a family like theirs.

The sky had grown darker. Chinese lanterns glowed around Chinatown, and colorful lights illuminated their path, making the course look like a wonderland. Nate proved to be a skilled golfer, not a surprise. She was unskilled, having played mini-golf less than five times in her life. When she missed a shot, her heart sank a little, but he just laughed it off, scooping up his ball and gesturing for her to take her turn. His encouragement and good humor always put her at ease.

The satisfying thwack of the golf balls hitting the targets or rolling along the putting mat mixed with the crickets chirping and the leaves rustling created a perfect environment for their first date. Nate had always intimidated her, both with his good looks and high financial status. But with the way he kept stealing glances at her, winking, and playfully touching her between swings, she felt anything but intimidated. Instead, undeniable chemistry charged the air. They had some things in common, enough to make their relationship work, perhaps.

On their final hole, as she lined up her shot, she felt Nate's hand on the small of her back, and a shiver ran down her spine. She took the shot over the famous pastel buildings, the Painted Ladies of Alamo Square, to the green space beyond, and to her surprise, it went straight into the hole.

"Great job!" Nate high-fived her before taking his turn.

His ball went straight into the hole, and he whooped, tossed his club, and lifted her off her feet in an embrace. She laughed and wrapped her arms around his neck, feeling his body close to hers. Her heart thundered against his, and when he lowered her back to the ground, her knees buckled. Nate was a touchy guy, and although she hadn't been as touchy-feely toward men, she loved this intimacy with him.

Much later, when he dropped her off in a sleek sports car that he usually stored at his brother's penthouse, they climbed the metal stairs, arm in arm. Laughing, she teased, "I'm glad I won the game tonight."

He shook a finger at her. "I didn't see you keeping a chart throughout the game."

"That would've taken away the fun. Mentally, I was." Not really, but what did it matter? Her heart expanded with happiness as if she was in a dream or a movie. She barely registered the people passing them in the hallway. When they approached her door, she turned to say goodbye to Nate.

She'd checked the time on the car dashboard, and it was almost eleven. Not too late, but she had to work tomorrow. She didn't want the night to end, though.

Beneath the hallway light, his smile vanished, and his gaze darkened. Her heart raced so hard, and her palms were sweaty. He must have felt her dampened palms since he was still holding one of her hands. Thankfully, she'd left her handbag at home. Otherwise, her shaky hands would've dropped it by now.

Her heart raced as she stared at him, their gazes lingering. Somehow, she fought the urge to look at his mouth, even though her mind screamed, "Kiss him!"

"Thanks for a great night," she said instead, biting her lower lip to keep from doing anything stupid, like kissing him when he might not be ready for that phase of their relationship.

Nate grinned. The slight abrasion of his stubble tickled her neck as he leaned his face next to hers to press his warm lips on her cheek. "The pleasure was all mine," he whispered, his breath hot against her ear. "You owe me another date. Wednesday. Take the day off."

A thrill ran through her as his lips brushed her cheek. She opened her mouth to say something, but the caress of his fingers tucking her hair behind her ears had her forgetting what she was supposed to say.

"I'll pick you up at nine."

She swallowed, nodding. She couldn't think of anything more important than hanging out with Nate.

"Good night, Vee." He stepped back, hands at his sides before slipping them into his pockets. It seemed like he was waiting to ensure she made it inside safely before leaving. Vee. Huh, she liked that.

Reluctantly turning her back to him, she fumbled for the key in the side pocket of her jean dress. Her credit card fell out, and she scooped it up.

Feeling Nate's lingering gaze on her, she inserted the key into the door and fought the urge to turn and look at him one last time. As she opened the door and stepped inside, emotion swelled through her heart. She couldn't deny it any longer—she was falling for Nate and falling hard. Was it possible to fall in love so soon?

CHAPTER 13

As Vanessa found herself standing beside Nate on Wednesday, the stark contrast between their personalities stood out. She played it safe and calculated her moves, while he, a thrill-seeker, embraced the unknown. But, lately, he'd been chipping away her cautious nature, one impulsive decision at a time. She'd even momentarily cast aside her commitment to work and found herself in Austin, Texas, at one of his speed tracks. She'd never envisioned taking an unplanned day off, but the intoxicating draw of his presence clouded her judgment.

Fun was a rare indulgence since she prioritized her goals. Yet, their magnetic connection made her crave every moment with him. As his affection became undeniable, each shared experience only solidified their bond.

That morning, he'd surprised her with a pastry, a hot chocolate, and a bouquet of mixed dahlias, brightening the commercial kitchen at dawn with their sunrise colors. Together, they prepared food for the truck and made an abundance of sauce so Ava and her helpers could keep their customers happy. After they parted to freshen up and gather their things, he whisked her away in a helicopter to Austin.

Embracing a "day in the life of Nate," she enjoyed a run at one of his country clubs, a delightful brunch, and a boating excursion before arriving at the speed track. Her heart raced as she slid into the passenger seat of the dual-seat race car. The helmet felt constricting, but he insisted on her safety. She suspected the thrilling ride ahead would push her boundaries even further.

In the driver's seat, he fastened his helmet and checked the controls. Then he tipped his head her way, a mischievous twinkle in his eyes. "Are you ready for the ride of your life?"

"I think so." She raised her chin, attempting to sound confident. She'd never been in a race car before, let alone driven at such high speeds.

The car roared to life, he revved the engine, and her adrenaline spiked as they pulled onto the track.

"I'll be slow on the first lap."

"Sounds good. I love slow."

During the lap, he showed her the different corners and turns on the track, but then he floored the gas pedal.

Her heart raced as they zoomed around the track, tires screeching through each high-speed turn. Clutching the seat with both hands, she felt the wind whipping past her face as they accelerated to over two hundred miles per hour. At the track's sweeping turns and high-speed straightaways, her racing heart seemed to go even faster than the car.

How could he do this for a living for ten months of the year? He took each corner with precision and pushed the car to its limits, and the g-forces he'd mentioned pressed against her body.

"Isn't this great?" he shouted.

With his excitement infectious and her adrenaline surging, she couldn't help but laugh. She relaxed, caught up in his enthusiasm and confidence. Could he convince her to try anything thrilling and dangerous? It seemed she'd willingly follow.

Nate occasionally glanced at her, his smile evident even beneath the helmet, and her heart skipped a beat. She'd never felt so alive, exhilarated, and free!

Then he guided the car back to the garage and came around to open her door. She stepped out, her hands shaking, and he removed his helmet and grinned. "So, what did you think?"

Catching her breath, she took off her helmet and shook out her hair. "It was amazing. I've *never* felt anything like it."

Nate chuckled and kissed her cheek before taking her helmet. "Glad you enjoyed it. Maybe, next time, we'll try something a little faster."

Faster? A warm shiver coursed through her at the thought of another thrilling adventure with him. His enjoyment of her company only intensified her attraction to him. "I can't wait."

"The day's not over." He lifted her hand to his lips and kissed her fingertips, raising her anticipation. "We're going out to dinner."

She smoothed a shaky hand over her rumpled blouse. "Would it be okay if we stopped at your country club to freshen up and change?"

"Sounds perfect." He winked and guided her to a street-worthy vehicle.

She'd treat the evening as a real date, and she'd packed one of her favorite dresses—a figure-hugging emerald-green number with delicately beaded straps that added a touch of glamor. Pairing it with strappy high-heeled sandals, she'd feel confident to face whatever environment he took her to.

Nate seemed to share her desire to dress up. When they reunited at the club's lobby, he had swapped his casual racing attire for dress pants and a cream-colored button-down shirt. He'd rolled up the sleeves, showing off his toned forearms. With his shiny dark hair neatly combed, he had never looked so handsome. Her heart thrilled in anticipation of a sophisticated and romantic evening.

Now, they sat across from each other on the rooftop of one of his many restaurants. The night air enveloped them, and the city skyline sparkled against the dark sky. The gentle hum of the city below created a soothing backdrop to the sophisticated music playing in the background.

With the place empty except for them, she couldn't help wondering how he'd managed to cancel all the evening's reservations to have the space ready for them.

As they enjoyed the food, which was nothing short of amazing, a cool breeze wafted the sweet scent of roses from their table. The string lights and lanterns showered them in a dizzying glow, adding to the enchanting ambience. Everything Nate did seemed to be top-notch, including his restaurants. With their dinner plates cleared, she sipped her Sprite, and he savored his water from a goblet-shaped glass.

"Is your Sausalito restaurant going to look like this one?" she asked, admiring the elegant décor.

"I try to make each restaurant harmonize with its surroundings." The flicker of LED candles cast a warm glow across his face.

Ice clinked in her glass as she lowered it. "You're so invested in racing, and I've seen you have little interest in cooking. But you're passionate about the restaurant business—why? Are you hoping to switch careers someday?"

Nate leaned back, laughing. "I'm way past that. While others can start a career at any age, I'm not wired that way."

"So why restaurants?"

"Security. In case I can't race anymore, I need some financials to bounce back to. My family alone could take care of me if it came down to me being unable to work. And then some companies could hire me to model their products. No doubt, they would cling to me until years after my retirement. But I like knowing there's more than that backing me."

"In your position, I wouldn't worry about lacking something." Funny, she'd thought she was the planner, but even though he lived life on the edge, he'd learned to look ahead and plan. "Do you ever see yourself retiring from NASCAR?"

"When and if I have a reason to." His eyes met hers with a smoldering gaze.

Her heart gave a skip, and she swallowed hard before squeaking out her question. "Like what reason?"

"I don't want to start a family with the nature of my career, but if God thinks otherwise, I'll keep the possibility open."

Wow. She wasn't in a hurry to commit to a long-term relationship, but she'd allowed herself to dream of Nate as her husband. She imagined their kids with amber skin tones. Would they have his blue eyes or her brown? Despite his initial reluctance, he seemed flexible about having a family if God led him in that direction.

He cleared his throat, pulling her from her thoughts. "Where will you take your truck when you're not in Sausalito anymore?"

Heat tingled up her neck. He probably didn't like her truck parked near his fancy restaurant, and given the appearance of his establishments, it made sense. But getting a paint job done would be an additional expense, and she couldn't afford to dig into the business savings. Maybe she could change the subject. "I'm hoping to start looking for space."

"You are?"

She explained her plans to give the truck to Ava and told him about Ava's autistic son and her reasons for continuing the street-food business.

He sank back in his seat, holding his water glass by its rim and swirling the liquid. "Do you have a business plan yet?"

"Not yet."

"When do you want to start this business?"

"Before the end of the year, if possible." But she was so far behind. "I would like to start teaching again next year too, but that's still up in the air."

"I know you don't want any help." His brow furrowed as he lowered his water glass. "But *how* are you going to be a chef and a teacher?"

She scrunched up her face. "You were right."

"About what?" He drummed his fingers on the linen tablecloth, the dance of those long fingers with well-trimmed nails somewhat hypnotic.

"Um..." What was she saying? "To hire some help at the truck. It's helping me transition to the idea of utilizing help when and if I open a restaurant someday."

Having Ava and their extra helpers was the only way Vanessa had been able to take a day off today. And she wouldn't have wanted to miss today for anything.

Nate offered suggestions and insights for her business, seeming genuinely interested in helping her but cautious not to overstep. "If you need any more help with business planning, just let me know. Since I've been driving that road of opening restaurants, I can share some insights from hurdles I've passed."

"Speaking of driving"—she shifted the conversation to his upcoming race—"are you excited about racing at home?"

He rubbed his temples, wincing. "There are high expectations when you're on home turf, but it's a great crowd to have. I'd ask you to come, but I've taken you away from your job for too many hours."

Disappointment twinged her gut, but then he continued. "There's no pressure, but if you want to come, Logan will take care of everything."

Could she do it? Be spontaneous again? Flying on short notice was an unexpected expense from her budget, but yes! She'd do it for him. "I can't make any promises."

"Things at short notice are not for you. I understand." He reached across the table and clasped her hand. "Enough about me. What do you do for fun besides your love-hate relationship with cooking, Vee?"

She smiled, her hand trembling in his. "Well, I love music and dancing." With her free hand, she gestured to the unseen speakers in the corners erupting soft background music. "I enjoy hiking and exploring new places. Shopping, reading, and watching movies whenever I have time."

Nate nodded, his thumb making a track across the back of her hand. "When you come to visit my childhood home in Pleasant View, we'll have to explore some mountain trails. And when we plan the reunion, we can hit a few trails in Hawaii while we check out vendors."

"You're doing the reunion on the island?" She cocked her head, her heart beating out a heavy thud. What would it be like to go on an adventure with him to his family's island?

"All my siblings have hosted the reunion in our hometown. This year, I'm doing it at Thanksgiving—no one's ever done our reunion then. I'd also like to change things up and have it on the island."

As the night wore on, they talked about their spiritual lives, interests, families, and uncertain future dreams. She opened up in ways she'd never done before.

Now, he scooted forward, his eyes never leaving hers. "What did you think a day in the life of Nate Stone was like?"

"I'd say it's more fun than a day in the life of Vanessa."

He beamed, and his eyes shone beneath the restaurant's twinkling lights. "I took it easy on you this time. Next time, it'll be more grueling."

There was going to be a next time? Her chest swelled. She doubted she'd experience even the easiest work while hanging out alongside him.

He stood and held out his hand. "Would you like to dance?"

When she slid her hand into his, they walked over to the open space on the rooftop. A slow song played, and he pulled her close, wrapping his arms around her waist. His breath tickled her neck. "Have I told you how stunning you look tonight?"

"More than once, yes, and you complimented my dress several times on the drive over to the restaurant."

She melted into him, her heart racing as she rested her head on his chest, feeling his heartbeat against her cheek. His warmth and the weight of his arms around her waist ignited a chain reaction in her body with one nerve firing to the next until she was ablaze with weakened knees.

He smelled so good, a mix of eucalyptus and something fancy, a scent that would linger long after they parted. They swayed together, lost in the moment and the music.

Vanessa wasn't optimistic about love, but he made her want to believe true love existed for everyone, including herself. She didn't want to ruin the moment, but she still needed to know if this was real before she got burned. She lifted her head to look at him.

"Why me?" She searched his eyes for an answer.

Confusion flickered across his face before tenderness and love softened the momentary tautness and stirred a multitude of emotions within her.

Maybe she'd better clarify. She tried to recall his previous dates but couldn't even remember their names. "I'm not a model or a remarkable figure in any way."

He moved his hand to caress her cheek, his fingers leaving a trail of warmth before sliding away. "Maybe because you're the one person who's going to tell me what I don't want to hear."

It wasn't exactly a romantic reason to be together, but with his hands resting on her bare shoulders, she shivered at his touch.

"You're honest, and you're real with me, unlike the women in my previous relationships who see me only as a celebrity NASCAR racer." A mischievous glint appeared in his eyes as his lips quirked to the left the way they did when he gave her that smoldering look. "Or maybe it's because you're crazy about me."

The desire in his eyes mirrored her feelings. He leaned in closer, their breaths mingling, their mouths almost touching. "Do I need to explain why I want to kiss you?"

Her heart pounded. Barely managing a headshake, she edged closer. Surely, he could see she'd been ready for that kiss since the day he stumbled onto her truck a month ago! Her lips parted, inviting him to kiss her since she couldn't manage to speak.

His lips brushed against hers, tender, passionate, and perfect. Sparks ignited like fireworks inside her as she melted into him. Her feet were wobbly, and her fingers grazed his bristly beard to trace his jaw. They kissed, and their lips mingled. Emotion swelled every cell of her body, and her heart soared. As he slid his hands behind her ears and raked them into her hair, she savored the feel of his strong fingers and cherished the taste of his sweet and warm lips.

They were in sync, matching the rhythm of their pounding hearts. When they separated, he kissed the top of her head and smiled, his eyes aglow. Then he rubbed his thumb on her tingling lower lip and whispered in a strained voice. "You're amazing."

She was just her. But... "*You're* amazing."

Breathless, she still clutched his shirt collar.

He chuckled and tucked her hair behind her ear, pushing back loose strands and grinning from ear to ear. "I love your hair just like this."

"I like everything about you." She patted his shirt collar. "Thank you for a wonderful evening."

"Thank you for spending it with me."

That day had been incredible, and the night was magical. Being alone on the rooftop with the entire city at their feet and the man of her dreams in her arms, she felt like she was having an out-of-body experience. Something just clicked with Nate, and all of a sudden, they'd been transported to a world made just for them.

CHAPTER 14

On the last Sunday in May, Nate woke up like he would on any race day. However, today was different. It was the Coca-Cola 600, one of the biggest races held on his home track, and it consumed his mind as he stood at the kitchen island guzzling water at five a.m.

His phone rang, and Logan's number flashed across the screen. "Hey," Logan began as soon as Nate swiped to answer. "Thought I'd check in and see how you're holding up on the big day."

"Isn't it crazy early on the West Coast?"

"A bit, but I often start my day around one thirty since I have to be up 'crazy early' to talk to Stone Enterprises' overseas teams. Even on Sunday, my internal clock is used to that. So, back to the topic, how are you doing?"

"Well, until someone so rudely interrupted my morning, I was trying to reflect on what I had read in my Bible twenty minutes ago—that, although the horse is prepared for the day of battle, victory belongs to the Lord, as stated in Proverbs 21."

Logan chuckled. "A good reading for race day, bro."

"Yeah." Nate sipped more water and wiped a drip from his chin. "Seems the race is all I can focus on, even when reading the Bible." Since Thursday, after he parted ways with Vanessa, he'd done nothing but test drive and practice for the race. Vanessa... Their shared kiss on the rooftop... Their kiss again later that night when he dropped her off... Their kiss when he stopped by the kitchen to bring her breakfast before leaving the next morning...

Those kisses still burned on his lips.

"That's not entirely accurate regarding the racing. I've been thinking about a certain someone as well." He rubbed a hand over his face. "Is this what it's like, Logan? I tell you, I hardly slept thinking about her. You can't imagine how much she's affecting me. Until now, I never allowed myself to consider a serious relationship."

"You sound like me, bro. I attempted to date, but couldn't really commit until I realized I was in love with Serafina. Once I embraced that, though, there was no turning back."

No turning back... Had he reached that point? It wasn't just about the possibility of love with Vanessa. It was as if he'd found a new best friend and something more at the same time, someone he could confide in.

Would she come to his race? She hadn't mentioned anything, and he didn't want to ask, considering how many times she had already traveled on his account.

His family would be at the race. "Are you and Serafina coming?"

He'd reserved a seat for her in the paddock area. If they flew in, they could bring Vanessa in the Stone jet.

"You can count on it. Reserve us some seats."

"Already done." Since not all his siblings could attend the same race, there were always available seats. Win or lose, he could count on his true fans, his family, to support him no matter what. But was Vanessa coming? Logan would've said so if he knew. "Look, I'm gonna head out, but thanks for checking in. I'll see you after the race."

"Sounds good. Sera and I will be there."

With contemporary gospel music throbbing in his earbuds, Nate stepped out for his morning run while visions of Vanessa's smile rolled into his mind. He wasn't dying today, and it wasn't his last day. But something about her made him feel exposed and vulnerable. Her passionate dedication to follow through with her mother's legacy proved her the kind of woman who'd love without wavering. And she'd asked him if he wanted kids, which led him to believe she wanted a family.

He shook his head to stay focused and blew out a breath. Today was race day, and he needed to clear his mind of every distraction, including Vanessa. He increased the music's volume to block out any thoughts as he jogged around the lake by his house. He took a trail into the woods, ascending further up. As he sprinted past, chipmunks scampered off the trail, and the refreshing smell of pine and wildflowers hung in the air.

After his run, he returned home and prepared to head to the track three hours later to meet with his crew and ensure everyone was ready to perform their best. With adrenaline coursing through his veins, he entered his garage where his crew huddled around the Number 62 car's open hood and Doyle gave orders. They knew Nate needed to outperform at his home track.

As Nate approached, Doyle lifted his head and saluted him. "'Sup, chief?"

Nate returned the smile and slapped Doyle's shoulder, his excitement building. Moving closer to the car, he greeted the rest of his crew. "How's *Impulse* running?"

They exchanged nods, and the jerk man flashed a thumbs-up as he wiped his greased hands with a blackened cloth. The smell of rubber from new tires mixed with the aroma of the hamburgers a crew member grilled. Beyond them, activity buzzed on the Charlotte Motor Speedway as crews rolled tires from tire-vendor tents to their designated garages.

As they tested the car, the day moved by. Closer to late afternoon, Nate and Doyle gathered the eighty-member team for a prerace strategy meeting, going over their fuel strategy and tire management and intended number of pit stops.

Nate acknowledged the team. "You're the backbone of my success, and I'm grateful for your hard work and dedication."

One crew member high-fived him. "Without you, we have no jobs."

Displaying their camaraderie and support, the others waved, nodded, or fist-bumped.

Then Nate pointed to the team and used the words he always used at the end of his meetings. "And without God?"

The responses varied, but he always emphasized that he could do nothing without God.

The track's noise level increased as the racing cars lined up, and the excited fans cheered while the media speculated and interviewers' announcements rang out. Heat radiated through his fireproof suit, and perspiration drenched his forehead before he even climbed into the compact car. With his stomach tied in knots, it was going to be one of those days when he needed his bucket.

Doyle must have noticed Nate's discomfort as he called for someone to bring a bucket and handed it to Nate. "You're okay, chief?"

"Yep." Nate managed before he vomited into the blue bucket they'd set aside for him.

Doyle handed him a tissue to wipe his mouth.

"Thanks." Nate tossed the tissue into the bucket before rinsing his mouth with water and mouthwash from one of his crew members. Feeling better, he slapped his helmet on and closed his eyes to pray for safety. "God's got this."

With a deep breath, he climbed into his car, his heart racing and nerves dancing. As the race began, he pushed his car to the limit, speeding past his competitors and jostling for position. The first few laps were a blur of flashing colors and screeching tires.

With Doyle and the spotter's help giving him heads-up guidance through the track, he felt confident at each turn. However, things got challenging as the race went on and he was boxed in or had to shove through a car crash. Then Guy Damon even shoved him to the wall.

"Patience is key." The spotter's voice sounded through the headset's speaker. "Watch out for the next opening and take it."

Approaching lap two hundred, Nate took advantage of the opening and maneuvered to take the lead. The crowd went wild, cheering him on. With a hundred more laps to go and cars shooting past him, he focused on the road, pushed the car, and held his lead. Then Doyle's voice crackled through the radio. "Guy's closing in on you."

On the final lap, Nate made a daring move, passing one car on the inside and then pulling ahead of another on the outside. Through the lit track, he saw the checkered flag waving in the distance, signaling his victory. With a final burst of speed, he crossed the line in first place, the roar of the crowd ringing in his ears.

Exhausted after almost four hours of pushing himself and his car, Nate collapsed back in his seat, and a surge of happiness expanded his chest as he celebrated his victory.

Doyle's voice rang through the headset. "We did it, chief!"

"Glory be to God!" Nate exclaimed, grateful for his team's help and support and God's grace. As the crowd continued to cheer and applaud, he let out a triumphant yell. He'd done it. He had won the Coca-Cola 600!

Breathless and with his heart still racing, he climbed out of his car and removed his helmet. Grinning from ear to ear, he waved to the cheering fans and pumped his fist in the air. His team and fans surrounded him, and elation buoyed him, victory's thrill coursing through his veins.

As he looked up into the paddock, through the speedway lights, he saw his mother waving and sighted Logan and Serafina. But Vanessa was nowhere to be seen, and his heart felt unsettled as his gaze roamed the other racers, their teams, and family members with VIP badges.

Then his heart skipped a beat. Vanessa was wading through the crowd, waving with a bright smile. His palms started sweating, and his heart thudded like it was going to rip out of his chest. No girl had ever had this effect on him.

"Vanessa!" he shouted, although he doubted she'd hear him over the crowd, but her gaze fixed on him as he made his way straight to her.

Cameras flashed, and an interviewer ran alongside him with a microphone. But Nate kept his focus on Vanessa, not wanting to lose her in the crowd. When he reached her, the crowd's cheers faded, and it was just him and her. He drew her into his arms, lowered his mouth to hers, and kissed her with all the feeling inside of him, sinking deeper into her softness and breathing in her scent.

Then the noise and cameras seemed closer, and they both pulled back. His hands were still wrapped around her waist, and her hands were still curled on the back of his neck. She looked up at him, breathless, and as the lights shone into her eyes and a longing similar to his reflected clearly in those eyes, he felt like he was on top of the world.

"Congratulations, Nate."

"I'm so glad you're here." He gripped her waist tighter. With her, he didn't need to process and strategize what needed to be done. Instead, she elevated his spontaneous and impulsive side even more.

"I'm glad too."

***

Well into the evening after the postrace interviews, Nate arrived at his three-story stone house built into the hillside to meet with his family. He showered and joined them in the kitchen, which connected to the dining room. The recessed lighting illuminated the sprawling space well, making it easy to spot everyone, including the one person he was most eager to see—Vanessa.

However, with everyone vying for his attention, it would be a while before he could make it over to her. The noise level was intense with people moving around carrying plates of the food his chefs had prepared. He'd invited his family over, regardless of whether he won or lost, so the chefs were well aware of the company they were catering to.

"You and Vanessa seem pretty serious." Theo nodded toward the sofa where Mom was sitting across from Vanessa, holding her hands as she spoke to her like one of her daughters. "Mother is welcoming her to the family. If you're not ready to take things to the next level, you'd better go set Mom straight."

"Mom will shower love on everyone, even if they're not family." Nate smiled at their mother. The way she was taking Vanessa in warmed his heart. "But I hear you, bro. Vanessa and I are taking things slow."

"You kissed her in public, and that's *slow*?" Raising a brow, Theo unlocked his phone, then turned it Nate's way. "Pictures of you guys kissing are storming the internet."

He eyed the headline: Who's Nate Stone's Mystery Girlfriend?

"It looks like the whole world knows now." Nate shrugged, a little embarrassed. Or was that solid relief to be publicly acknowledging their relationship? He slapped Theo on the back and moved to mingle with the rest of their family. They teased him about the unexpected kiss from a girlfriend he'd never mentioned. Vanessa made him feel more alive. He needed to take things slow, yet everything in him wanted to go as fast as possible—living like each day was his last.

"Great race, son." Dad broke the circle to pull him in for an embrace. Logan, Serafina, and two others stood nearby, congratulating him on his victory.

After greeting his family and crew, Nate approached his mom and Vanessa. "I hope you're not interrogating my company with difficult questions."

Mom patted the empty spot next to her for him to sit. "After today, I believe Vanessa is more than just company."

Vanessa peeped at him bashfully, and he leaned in to kiss her cheek. Then he moved to kiss his mom on the cheek and took a seat next to her on the gray leather couch that blended nicely with the stone fireplace, flagstone floor, and weathered wood ceiling. "This is Vanessa, Mom."

Mom touched his shoulder. "Vanessa and I met at your brother's wedding and Serafina's mom's funeral."

Huh. Everyone seemed to remember her except him.

"I'm so happy for you, my darling. Good job on the race." Mom squeezed his shoulder, then waved toward Vanessa. "I was telling

Vanessa how wonderful my dashing boy is. Happily, she already knows."

Vanessa fiddled with a strand of the hair she'd styled in soft waves over her silky yellow top.

"I asked Vanessa to join us for breakfast in the morning."

"Now, Mom, she has to work."

Ducking her head, Vanessa tucked her hands in her lap. "Your mom said you have ten bedrooms?"

"Yes," he confirmed. But if she stayed, who would meet the butcher in the morning? "How early do you need to get back for work?"

"Ava will be at the commercial kitchen in the morning. She'll handle everything."

Wow. "That's a huge step. I'm proud of you for delegating some responsibilities—and grateful you're willing to take that step for me."

"Now." Mom stood up. "I'll let you two catch up, and I'll go fix you a plate of food."

After Mom vacated her seat, Nate gestured for Vanessa to sit next to him, then pulled her into a side embrace, and kissed her head and ear. Overwhelmed by her presence, he couldn't get enough of her. He pressed his lips into her hair, breathing in the floral scent of her. "How early *do* you need to leave tomorrow?"

"It depends on how soon I can catch a ride on your chopper." She curled her finger in her hair, resting her face in the crook of his neck.

"Are you working tomorrow?" He cradled her closer.

"I took the day off. I'm starting to have a hard time whenever I'm away from you."

"I like hearing that." He couldn't help but kiss her again. He'd made plenty of impulsive decisions, but falling for her felt different. He had sponsorship meetings in the morning, but he'd bring her along if she didn't mind.

"As it turns out, I can't stop thinking about you either," he said, bending down to whisper in her ear, causing her to shiver. "I'm going to have to get a place in San Francisco. I want to spend more time near you."

Yep. He was in trouble because, for someone who didn't want to entangle himself in relationships, he had no idea how not to fall in love with Vanessa.

CHAPTER 15

After a day of bliss, Nate had flown back to San Francisco with her yesterday. Now, Vanessa trudged through the quiet oceanfront parking lot, where only a few early risers were ordering coffee at the café across the grass. Most of the other stores were still closed, creating a peaceful and serene atmosphere. The water lapping against the docks was more audible in the morning silence, and the fresh air was pleasant, carried by a gentle breeze from the Bay.

It was still slightly dark, with the stars and moon visible in the early dawn as she approached her food truck. It sure had been nice having a long-term parking spot she could trust to keep her truck safe overnight.

Maybe it was hard to see clearly, but the truck seemed to have something unusual. With a growing sense of unease, she quickened her steps. Her eyes narrowed as she tried to make out the small object taped to the door. Now, her steps became slower and more hesitant. The early morning light cast a soft glow, and a light breeze carried the scent of cooking oil and spices from her truck. Something wasn't right.

She squinted to make sense of what she was seeing. A padlock secured the door, and the piece of paper taped above it fluttered on the breeze. Her heart sinking, she took a deep breath and stepped closer.

The bold red font on the message almost mocked her:

> Your food truck is in violation of city regulations. It has been impounded and will be removed within 24 hours.

She couldn't be reading that right. After all her hard work on the legacy she was trying to keep alive, she couldn't lose it all now.

With trembling hands, she reached into her hoodie pouch and retrieved her phone. She struggled to steady her fingers as she fumbled with the buttons, found the flashlight option, and shone it on the paper before her. Then she read the message over and over again, hoping some

145

miraculous answer would present itself. Despite her best efforts, her
mind remained muddled and unable to formulate a clear plan.

> Notice of violation of the San Francisco municipal codes
> regarding unsafe, noncomplying structure, land, or
> occupancy.

Her gut churned, and her eyes burned like they were about to fall
out of their sockets. How was she going to get out of this situation?

The authorities must have shown up after Ava left yesterday.
Otherwise, she would've called to let Vanessa know.

What was she supposed to do with all the meat marinating in the
fridge? Or the meat delivery in less than an hour?

Had Nate been aware this was going to happen? He'd wanted to
pay her to leave his property last month. Could he still be trying to do
so by using a cowardly approach? Keep your enemies closer by making
them friends? Surely, he was better than to go behind her back after
they'd come to a resolution. Was it him or his manager?

Losing a day's business was almost too much to bear, especially
when she read the last paragraph on the notice.

> As a result of this violation, we have placed a lock on your
> truck until the violation is resolved. Any future violations
> may result in fines or other penalties.
>
> The City Parking Authority

She could lose the permit. Then what would happen to all the
months she worked so hard to finalize this part of her plan?

Panic churned into fury. The notice accused her of trespassing and
threatened Mom's legacy. If Nate had known what was going on...

While she wanted to leave him alone, her whole body heated as anger rose from her stomach, bubbling to the surface. She dialed his number.

He answered on the first ring. Which she knew because he loved morning runs.

"Hey there..." He was breathless, and cars rumbled in the background.

Since they both had no time, she'd be direct. He had to be aware of this. At least, Xenon should've told him. "Does your word mean anything?"

"Huh?"

"You could've told me you changed your mind about our agreement." Her body stiffened, and she leaned against the truck for support.

"I have so many talents, Vee, but I've never grasped riddles."

He was so annoying when he relaxed and couldn't hear the frustration in her voice.

"As it turns out, the city council locked me out of my food truck—"

"Do they want you to get a paint job?" With his voice so light, he wasn't taking her mom's business seriously.

"I knew it!"

"Knew what, Spitfire?"

Good. He was calling her Spitfire. Perhaps he sensed her irritation. "You're embarrassed by my truck, and you already made it clear you don't want it on your property." She had no idea how many words flew out of her mouth after that, but she spurted all she thought he deserved to hear. "Am I a joke to you?"

"Far from it." He fell silent, perhaps thinking before he spoke again. "You terrify me. In a good way, I mean, in one month alone, my heart and mind are consumed by you rather than my racing career."

With his heartfelt confession, her shoulders relaxed. Gripping her phone tight to her ear, she closed her eyes and took in a sharp inhale of breath.

"I feel more alive than I've felt in a long time, more spontaneous now that I know I can teach you that wild side of me. Why do you think I come here to San Francisco every week ever since you made me work at your food truck?"

"You signed up for it." The words emerged in a whisper. Something inside her softened, a tenderness melting her heart and crumbling her feet. She had to cross her legs for balance.

"I didn't know anything about the city council locking your truck. Xenon mentioned that he regretted calling the city council before we came to this resolution. I'm sure he also has no idea about any of this."

So Nate wasn't behind it, and she'd lost it on him once again. She pressed her lips together, then blurted, "I'm sorry I yelled at you."

"You want to fulfill your mom's legacy, right?"

"You know I do—desperately." The sooner the better.

"Can I let you in on a secret, how I win my races? Even the ones I don't win but intend to each time."

She nodded, then realized she was on the phone. "Yeah."

"I have almost a hundred people on my team—drivers, crew chiefs, mechanics, engineers, tire specialists, pit crew members, spotters, and team managers. Then there's administrative staff and support personnel. Each of them has a specific task, jobs I couldn't do and still drive." As a moment of silence passed between them, his breath vibrated the phone speakers as if he were struggling to let out his next words. "The most successful people rely on help and teamwork to reach their goals."

"I have two extra helpers now—thanks to you."

"And today, we'll need more than your three helpers."

Her heart warmed at his using the word *we*, including himself. She glanced at the rising sun, the sky starting to turn a beautiful mix of orange, pink, and purple, casting a soft glow over the surrounding hills and water.

"Today, we'll be working on getting the truck up and going. Which could be another week." She had to point out that reality. That was if they didn't tow the truck before she resolved this.

"Your truck will be unlocked by the end of the day or early tomorrow."

He was way too confident for his own good. "And how are you planning to do that?"

"Have you forgotten that the name Stone means something in San Francisco?"

Nate's oldest brother, Eric, founded Stone Enterprises where Logan Stone was CEO. They played a vital role in the city and community. Besides the many charities they sponsored, they offered jobs and supported a hospital for the underprivileged and anyone who couldn't afford to pay for health care. They maintained friendships with the mayor and those on the city council.

"Okay." She pushed away from the truck. She'd better get going now that the sun had risen. "I need to meet with the butcher." One missed delivery with him, and she'd be calling to pay extra to have him deliver meat to her again.

"I'll meet you in Sausalito at ten."

She had to remind him that, until the truck opened, there was no business today. "Right now, I need to figure out what to do with the food I marinated last night."

"I rephrase. Keep cooking, as usual. I'll meet you at the kitchen with a truck to transport your food."

"I don't understand."

"Today, I want the whole world to know that my girlfriend is a food-truck chef, who's yet to become a teacher. I also want them to know I fell for Vanessa Douglas, not her spray-painted food truck."

Her cheeks lifted as she smiled. Tears burned in the backs of her eyes at the tenderness and genuineness of his words, and she was unable to keep her voice from shaking. "Did you just call me your girlfriend?"

"That is, if you are not embarrassed to have me as your boyfriend?"

"It's the other way around, Nate." She let out a shuddered breath. What was happening to her? They'd only gone out for a month. He was like her wildest fantasies and dreams come true. "I'm so honored."

"On that note, Ms. Douglas, we get off work at four, and I'm taking you dancing so we can celebrate."

"Yes—yes!" Her heart expanded with a joy that surpassed all the previous emotions she'd experienced. "I'd like that so much."

"See you in a few."

She opened her mouth to respond, but her mouth hung open in silence. Nate Stone had asked her to be his girlfriend. After ending the call, she darted to the grass and outstretched her arms, letting out a happy screech and spinning around and around before she fired off a text to Serafina as she returned to her car.

Vanessa: Nate just asked me to be his girlfriend.

Serafina: What? Is that why he's on the phone with Logan this early?

Was he telling Logan about their next step in the relationship too?

Vanessa: Will explain. Going dancing tonight.

Serafina: I want to hear all the details tomorrow.

Vanessa: Totally.

She'd love nothing more than to talk about her new love life and all the mushy feelings she had for Nate.

With her heart so full, could it burst from happiness? Was that what being in love felt like? It had to be because she was in love with the most handsome man in the world. She drove her Sienna back to the kitchen, not caring if she worked that day or not. She just wanted to go shopping and plan for their date.

But when Nate said he'd wanted to make today great and let the whole world know she was his girlfriend, he hadn't been kidding. This morning, she hadn't imagined the extent to which he'd go to make this day memorable.

Now, four tents had sprung up on the parking lot, and music mingled with the chatter of people crowding the area around the food truck he'd rented and parked next to Mama Dee's BBQ truck. Not that they needed the trucks today with the four grills they had going, each with someone flipping sausages, steak, or chicken.

Ava, coming up beside her, nudged her. "You sure were in for a surprise. What did you think when you showed up and people were setting up tents and getting grills ready?"

Vanessa pressed a hand to her heart. One truck had delivered fine meats while a minivan deposited helpers, all dressed in purple T-shirts matching her apron. As if that hadn't been enough, banners with Mama Dee's BBQ and the crown symbol hung over the truck, blocking the violation notice and lock. "I have to say gratitude didn't even come close to how I felt."

She reached into the cooler and grabbed a bottle of water, taking a sip as she watched Nate. Lately, she found herself drawn to him more and more. Just thinking of him made her heart race and her face light up with a smile. Whenever he was around, energy and excitement surged through her.

Shading her eyes, Ava followed her gaze. "He sure looks content, interacting and signing autographs for those in line. Amazing how relaxed a celeb like him can be doing this."

Lean and toned in the T-shirt Vanessa had given him, he pointed people toward the tents, perhaps explaining where they could grab the menus he'd had some graphic design company print on short notice. The cameras followed him, capturing the scene. An interviewer put the microphone in front of a guy in line. It was hard to know what the interviewer was asking the customer, though.

Ava snagged a water bottle of her own and uncapped it. "I'm sorry about this morning. I can only imagine how you felt."

"I can't even remember how I felt." Waving the thought off, Vanessa snickered. "The horror vanished when Nate met me at the kitchen with a rented truck. All he insisted on was that we made plenty of barbecue sauce for the day, and I didn't know what to think."

"Makes sense since it's the best and most common recipe served with all your meats." They grinned at each other, then sang out, "The sauce is the boss!"

When Vanessa recapped her water bottle, Nate's gaze found hers, and he waved, his broad smile hers alone and leaving her knees weak and her heart beating faster.

As if to hold her up, Ava slid an arm around her waist and hugged her tight. "I guess if you had had any fears that he was embarrassed by your food truck or business, all those vanished today."

So true. Vanessa let out a contented sigh, hugged her assistant back, then slid free. "We'd better get to the tent and start serving."

They met Nate there, her handing out the sauces and manning the cash box and him handling the credit card transactions for those whose cards didn't have a touchless option. The customers didn't appear to mind waiting in line while answering the interviewer's questions. Sweat soon beaded her forehead, so she lifted her arm to swipe her forearm across it. Nate continued to chat as he accepted card transactions, answered people's questions, and sometimes leaned in to kiss her forehead and praise her talent. Vanessa basked in the warmth of his presence and savored every moment they shared together.

Not familiar with the spotlight, she felt a heat of embarrassment, but being with him in front of some stunning women who could be better suited as his dates made her squirm with excitement. She handed out change as fast as she could, the metal box clicking when she closed and opened it. And all she could do was listen to people chatting in line, whispering about Nate's love for his girlfriend.

"When did he break up with Gisele?"

The hushed voice had Vanessa observing the two women under her eyelashes. Gisele was the model Nate had posed with for *GQ* magazine in early spring.

"That's her," another woman said, but Vanessa kept her attention on her task as she thanked the man she handed the change to.

The rich smoky scent of grilled-meat filled the air as people walked toward her with their food in hand.

Vanessa and the rest of the team worked nonstop until one of the guys manning the grill came to tell Nate they were out of meat. The prime rib was almost gone too, so she turned to Ava, hoping for a solution. "Do we have any more in the truck?"

"Lina said this is the last." Ava grimaced and waved toward the truck where one of their food runners had just disappeared.

"Vanessa." The loud feminine voice in the microphone had her jerking, startled. She was expecting the media since Nate had told her about the film crew coming, but she hadn't expected to be interviewed.

"We've heard so much about your famous barbecue sauce and barbecue-infused dishes, and we'd love to have you tell us about the inspiration behind your recipes."

Beyond the woman, Nate nodded his approval, his warm smile comforting Vanessa, so she cleared her throat and spoke into the microphone. "My mom—all this is hers, her recipes and her dream. She was a single mom who always worked hard to take care of me and my sister."

A lump clogged her throat. She swallowed it to talk about her deceased mom and sister and her need to fulfill Mom's dream. "Eventually, I'd like to open a restaurant in her honor."

She paused then, overcome by the thought of the restaurant's proceeds going toward Nate's charity to support autistic families. She was far from getting the business off the ground, so she'd better not blurt that out.

"I just want to thank Nate." Her gaze flicked to him, and since he was within reach, she slid her arm around his waist and pulled him toward her in front of the camera. "He's so talented and creative. Without him, we wouldn't have been able to host all of you here."

"And, Nate"—the interviewer moved the microphone—"you're building a restaurant next door. How's that going to play out when the steakhouse opens in September?"

Nate's cheek rubbed against Vanessa's as he leaned into her, his arm snaking around her waist. "Vanessa and I aren't worried about business coming in the way of what we have."

She cringed over his genuine confession. She was the one constantly losing her mind whenever something minor happened.

As their helpers cleaned up trash after the event and loaded the grills in a pickup truck, Vanessa walked toward Nate while he waved off the guys taking the grills.

So much love for him swelled through her that she ran toward him, throwing her arms around him and kissing him with all the love radiating inside her.

He laughed, scooped her up, and swung her around. "What's that for?"

"You surprised me so much today." She'd give him the whole world if it were at her disposal, but he pretty much had everything he needed. "Doesn't look like our relationship is a secret anymore." She giggled, unable to contain her amused tones. Besides him kissing her senseless at his race, the media had now hosted an event featuring Nate and Vanessa, putting their relationship in the spotlight.

He kissed her again. "I hope you're okay with that."

"I wouldn't want it any other way."

A couple of hours later, after she washed the barbecue scent from her skin and changed, Nate picked her up from her apartment, and they stepped out on the sidewalk. With their arms around each other's waists, they walked toward the limousine. Like he'd promised, the city council had removed the lock and notices from her truck. Amazing how easily things got accomplished when you knew the right people. That applied to having the servers and cooks he pulled together today.

He helped her into the limousine, and as it joined the traffic, she tipped her head back against the plush seat, letting out any lingering tension. "I can't believe what you did today. Where'd you hire all those workers on such short notice?"

"Um, actually, everyone who worked today was a fan. They volunteered the moment I posted a need for help on my social page."

"Wow. I never imagined." She peeked at him. "I don't have social media—I never wanted it. Now, I'm tempted to join so I can check out your page."

He threaded his fingers through hers, then brought them to his mouth. "Anything you want to know—just ask."

She cuddled against his side, his warmth radiating into her, his fancy eucalyptus scent soothing her as they rode to their dinner reservations. Dancing promised to put a wonderful end to a perfect day.

Shortly later, they swayed to the music, moving in sync in a ballroom. Glittering chandeliers and the soft glow of candles bathed them. His eyes sparkled and gleamed with a silent appreciation that said she was the most beautiful woman in the room. Happiness surged through her when he tugged her closer and whispered against her hair. "You look beautiful tonight."

Her dance shoes clicked against the marble floor as she swayed with him, her heart racing against his. He looked so handsome in his black tuxedo.

"You're the most handsome man I know."

Nate laughed, the sound rumbling like a race car. He bent down and nipped a kiss against her lips, then teased, "Flattery will get you anything, Vee."

As their bodies continued to move as one, she lost herself in the moment, her mind free of any worries, any stress. All that mattered was the man in her arms, the music in her ears, and the warmth in her heart.

She lifted onto her tiptoes and trailed her hands down his face to his shoulders and chest, his heart thundering beneath her fingers.

"You know, I was thinking...." He broke the comfortable silence between them. "We should take that planning trip to Hawaii soon."

Planning involved going to his family's island to spot out vendors for the November family reunion.

She nodded. He could tell her to quit the food business, and she'd do as asked. She hadn't had time to calculate the day's earnings, but she'd never had as big a crowd as he'd accumulated today.

"I can't wait." And she couldn't. It had been fun at Serafina's wedding with all the activities the island offered and the many homes on the property. They'd each have personal space, which she needed to think about their future and what it entailed.

CHAPTER 16

Nate stood in awe, taking in the breathtaking scenery spread out beyond the great room of the secluded island's main house. The lush tropical shrubs and crystalline turquoise waters caught him with a rush of adrenaline.

"Is there anything I can get you, sir?" Hannah, one of the employees, brought him back to reality.

"I'm good. Thank you," he replied with a nod. "Don't worry about dinner. We won't need it with the short notice of our arrival."

Yesterday, he'd been thrilled to finish his race in second place, especially since Vanessa came to support him. After his obligations, they flew to Hawaii for a much-needed break. And he would make the most of their three days on the island and ensure they created lasting memories. He'd already made dinner plans, so as soon as she arrived, they could leave. That was if she wasn't facing jet lag. He stifled a yawn himself.

Fortunately, she'd agreed to stay in the seven-bedroom house he was staying in where Hannah also lived. Vanessa, thoughtful as always, didn't want to burden the employees with additional housekeeping by opening a separate house.

Footsteps echoed on the hardwood floor, and he turned in time to catch her shy smile. The sunlight danced on her brown skin, accentuating the white feather pattern on her yellow summer dress and the feathery white earrings seeming to float from her earlobes. His pulse quickened as he pulled her close, their lips meeting while he inhaled the delicate scent of her hair.

"Are you ready to go, my love?"

Her fingers traced his stubble before she bestowed another tender kiss, her gaze meeting his. "Do I need to bring my purse?"

Recalling her recent reluctance to carry it after a theft, he reassured her. "You won't need it tonight." She wouldn't need it during their upcoming island adventures either. "We're checking out some hula dancers, just like you wanted."

The excitement in her eyes enhanced his own. They left the house arm in arm, exchanging greetings with the workers maintaining the vibrant flowering shrubs.

Surrounded by the exotic blooms' aroma and the lively birds' chatter, they strolled along a path enveloped by a leafy green canopy that sprinkled dappled sunlight onto the ground.

"I love this place." She squeezed his hand. "Last time, I couldn't stop staring at you, wishing you'd notice me and end my longing."

His chest swelled. "I never caught you stealing glances. You must have been a master at it."

"You had your hands full with all the gorgeous models."

"You're the only model I want. My poor performance in the first race weighed on me then. I was preoccupied with doing better in the upcoming races." He plucked a red plumeria flower from a nearby shrub, then tucked the bloom behind her ear. Their gazes locked as she shivered from his touch. "I'm glad we're back this time as a couple."

"Me too," she whispered, her eyelids fluttering open.

Continuing their walk, he laced his fingers through hers again. "When did you first have a crush on me?"

"At Serafina's mom's funeral."

"I'm sorry I didn't see you then." He'd only attended briefly. Maybe if he'd been there longer... But no reason to dwell on the past now that he had her.

"You better be sorry for crushing my spirit," she teased, playfully shoving him before darting through the leafy canopy. She weaved between bushes to outmaneuver him.

"You should know better than to outrace me!" He chased her, her laughter mingling with the birdsong and the waves. As she darted for another palm tree, he caught her hand, spun her around, pressed her back up against the palm's trunk, and bracketed her in for a passionate kiss.

Time seemed to freeze as they lost themselves in each other's embrace. Sunlight bathed them in warmth while leaves whispered overhead. As they parted, the intensity in her eyes mirrored his feelings.

Later, they sat at a candlelit table in a restaurant overlooking the ocean. Island flowers adorned nearby tables, and music and laughter carried on the breeze.

"Do you hear that?" Her eyes widened.

Anticipating this, he'd chosen the window seat. Colorful dancers swirled and swayed on the sand, drawing a crowd.

Those now-big eyes shone, and she scooted to the edge of her seat. "Can we go down there?"

"Who's being spontaneous now?" He chuckled. "What about dinner?"

"Hannah fed us all those snacks. Surely, you're not starving."

"Being with you fills me in every single way." He stood and extended his hand. When they reached the beach, she slid off her sandals, so he removed his shoes as well. He hadn't expected to walk barefoot through the sand, but as they approached the shore, her amazement made it worth it. They sat on the cool sand, her excitement contagious.

Trying to ignore the grainy sand sticking to his legs and shorts, he snuggled Vanessa close and tucked his chin atop her head. The dancers swayed gracefully beneath the setting sun, and she leaned her head against his chest. The soft scent of her hair mingled with the salty sea air and the island's exotic aromas. Vanessa's comforting familiarity warmed his heart as the night cooled.

On Tuesday, they explored the island together, hiking through lush landscapes and marveling at breathtaking views. They went surfing and snorkeling, both new experiences for her, and his chest swelled as she beamed, exclaiming that the sea turtles were her favorite.

That evening, they investigated nearby shops, buying unique souvenirs that caught their attention. They met local business owners, sampled various dishes, and considered vendors for their upcoming reunion. Later, they discovered a venue hosting live-band performances and spent the night dancing, even collecting the band's contact information for the reunion.

On Wednesday morning, they went waterskiing, and the adrenaline-fueled adventure exhilarated Vanessa. "This is the first time I haven't thought about work in a long time," she admitted as they walked along the beach afterward.

"I'm glad." Nate drew her close. "There's one more place I want to show you." He longed to share his impulsive property purchase with her, imagining her as the woman he'd always bring to his vacation home.

That afternoon, they enjoyed lunch on *Liberation*, the four-story superyacht Nate and his siblings owned. His siblings reasoned the name implied the freedom from childhood traumas they'd found after being adopted. Now, *Liberation*'s captain sailed them toward Nate's hidden gem. As they arrived, Nate bypassed the pineapple plantation, eager to share his favorite part of the property. Her hand in his, he led her along briskly, her laughter ringing out. He tightened his grasp on her. With him growing more attached to her, he'd have trouble letting go if they realized their relationship was moving too fast.

She squeezed his hand, hurrying to keep up. "I can tell by your pace I'm going to love this place."

He showed her his oceanfront property, discussing his ideas for a vacation home that could someday become a family retreat. They strolled through canopies of green leaves where palm trees cast undulating shadows.

"When I asked Iris to draw the plans for me, I didn't know what I wanted. Still, part of me dared envision life with a family. But sometimes..." He hesitated, not ready to voice his fears just yet. "This is where the house will be built. Maybe you can give me some input when we see Iris at the reunion."

"I'm not too creative." Vanessa swung their hands, then spun around, and walked backward in front of him. "But I'd love to see what she has in mind for you."

As they stepped out of the rain forest, they entered a breathtaking stretch of white sand beach with sparkling turquoise waters. Jagged cliffs framed the secluded haven, enhancing its sense of privacy.

"This is beautiful," she whispered in evident awe.

Indeed, it was, and she was. And she was the one woman he wanted to share this scene with.

"I want to feel the sand." She let go of his hand to remove her sandals, and he followed her lead. Once they were both barefoot, they rejoined hands and strolled over stingingly hot sand to the water's edge. They waded into the clear waters, savoring the sensation of soft sand beneath their toes and gentle waves against their skin.

"Look!" Vanessa gasped, pointing into the distance.

A pod of dolphins leaped out of the water, their sleek bodies shimmering in the sunlight.

She clapped a hand over her mouth as if afraid her awestruck squeal would scare them away. Then she lowered it enough to whisper. "I've never seen them before."

"This is a first for me too," he murmured into her ear, eliciting her shivers before she spun to face him.

"I'm so glad we had a first together." Unshed tears glistened in her eyes. "Why are you not ready for a relationship?"

No reason to remind her of their shared goal. Instead, he confessed. "I lied."

Her eyes narrowed, and her full lips pinched together. So he guided her hand to his racing heart. "When I told you I didn't want a relationship, I was afraid to admit to myself that I wanted you. You ignited something in me I'd never felt before with anyone."

She lifted his other hand to her heart, which was pounding as fiercely as his own. "You ignited something in me too. I've gone on dates before, but I never let them go past the third date. With you, though, I can't seem to get enough."

Her heartfelt admission stirred a swell of emotions. But he faced so many risks as a racer. He had to warn her. "You see... I have fears when I get in that car."

"I figured as much." Her voice wavered as tears glossed her eyes.

"I'd hate for you to fall in love with me and then have to—"

"Don't say that." She pressed her fingers to his lips.

A tear rolled down her cheek. He swiped it away with his thumb, aching over her distress.

"You're not going to die. I just..." She embraced him, her chest heaving against his.

As he held her tightly, his greatest fear became reality.

"I love you, Nate," she whispered through her tears.

With his throat thick with emotion, he managed to choke out. "I love you too."

"Why does time go so fast?" she asked, likely mindful that they were leaving tomorrow. They had to since he had a race to attend that weekend.

"I know, baby." He kissed the top of her head and inhaled her scent, trying to commit it to memory for a lifetime.

"Will you ever retire from racing?" She'd asked before, so it must weigh heavily on her.

"When the time is right," he assured her, especially now that she'd given him a compelling reason to consider the importance of alleviating her worries. Just as his family had always worried about him.

She squeezed him tighter as if afraid to let go. "I'm going to come to all your races from now on."

"I'd love that."

As the sun started to set over the ocean, they stood there, arms wrapped around each other's waists. The sky showcased a stunning blend of purple, pink, and orange hues, accompanied by the gentle lapping of waves against the shore. A breeze feathered her long hair into his face, and she remained still, her breath quivering as anxiety for his career lingered.

"It's going to be okay. I've raced for over ten years, and I'm still alive." Despite the encroaching chill, her body close to his kept him warm, and he savored the rhythm of their hearts. He ran his fingers through the soft hair reaching her back. "God will protect me. He will protect us and whatever path our relationship takes."

With their time on the island drawing to a close, he'd always cherish these extraordinary three days and the memories they created together. This place would forever be their sanctuary, where time seemed to stand still beneath an everlasting sunset.

CHAPTER 17

The most glorious summer seemed to fly by as swiftly as the race cars would soon whiz across the track before Vanessa. Now, the first weekend of October, today was Nate's race day at Round 12 of the playoff. Loud chatter competed with the motor noise as people crowded the bleachers, and a gasoline scent soured the air. While the cars lined up for the race, she focused on the blue Number 62 stickers on *Impulse*, Nate's yellow car.

Walking into the bleachers, Serafina handed her a Sprite. "I know you never like to talk during the race, but other than race days—or on the tabloids when you're accompanying Nate to galas and charity events—I barely see you."

"I know, right?" Vanessa popped the can's top and sipped the tangy, tingly drink. "It's been a crazy summer." And throughout it, joy buoyed her.

Her friend smoothed her blue and yellow striped skirt—a match to Nate's Number 62 car—as she sat and mock-pouted. "I guess Nate's taking my place in your life."

"No one can take your place." Vanessa linked their arms. "Though I must admit talking to him, whether in person or via video calls, are the highlights of my days. I can't believe how freely I tell him everything, good and bad, just like he shares his highs and lows. It's like I saw with you and Logan—we laugh, we agree and disagree, and it doesn't matter what else goes on as long as we're there for each other."

"That's the way it should be. Sounds pretty serious."

Despite the heat, a shiver ran through her. It was serious. Each passing day added another image to the future she pictured with him. With her heart so light all summer and early autumn, she prayed for guidance and adapted to unforeseen events. This transformation had to come from her faith in God and her love for Nate. Merely thinking about his name elicited tender emotions.

"Well, it's wonderful to see you so happy." Serafina squeezed Vanessa's arm. "And you look great."

Vanessa laughed and gestured to her yellow camisole top and blue shorts—also Nate's colors. "Seems I spend more time conscious of my attire now. Even when going to the food truck, I'm choosing outfits with him in mind since I can't predict when he'll show up. Like when he surprised me with flowers at the truck two weeks ago."

Overwhelmed by his gesture, her body had weakened, and she'd remained motionless before the refrigerator until Nate approached. After placing the flowers on the counter, he had wrapped his hand around her waist and murmured "Hey, Spitfire" before leaning in to kiss her ear, neck, and finally lips.

"You two are like teenagers," Ava had teased, shaking her head.

Nate had then drawn back enough to eye Ava. "You think you can manage the truck for the afternoon? I want to steal Vee away."

"No problem." Ava had promised, her ponytail swinging free of her hairnet when she nodded so vehemently. "It's not just Vanessa and me anymore. Our two additional helpers are on their lunch break, exploring the charming shops across the street. But they'll be back soon, and I can text them if I need them sooner."

After they left, Nate's surprise date included dinner and an exploration of the city's art murals—something Vanessa had always wanted to do.

Vanessa blinked, refocusing. With the cars now lined up, they'd declare the start of the race soon. She leaned in closer to Serafina. "The other week, he texted and invited me to skip work and join him on another surprise date. The surprise turned out to be a bungee-jumping adventure in San Diego!" It wasn't something Vanessa ever envisioned doing, but his enthusiasm made everything manageable. "Can you picture me leaping from a cliff attached to the bungee cord?"

Serafina nudged her. "You didn't?"

"I *did!*" Vanessa squealed, jostling her friend in return. "On a whim, I agreed to try, and I had a blast. I've changed so much this summer. I've been delegating more responsibilities to Ava—oh, did I tell you I promoted her to help with morning food preparations? Everything is coming together. I'm working on renewing my teaching license, seeking a location for Mama Dee's Restaurant, refining my restaurant proposal with a business planner, *and* volunteering more hours at the special needs school." She tucked the empty Sprite can into her oversized blue purse. "I've helped Ava apply for permits, a process Nate and Logan's involvement expedited. Plus, Nate's parking-lot event raised so much funds and led to offers for catering events, but I've only accepted small events with no more than two hundred guests."

Nate continued to support her by helping out at the food truck when he was in San Francisco and taking her on lunch and dinner dates to plan the reunion. They made notes together before she called vendors on the island. Besides surprising her with diamond earrings one time and a diamond necklace another time, he also indulged her with shopping sprees and pampering sessions. He even provided her with a gold credit card to spend as much as she wanted. She, however, remained mindful not to overspend.

The green flag came out. Any minute now, the flagman would start the race by raising that flag. There! Up it went, sending cars hurtling toward the first corner.

"I'll let you focus now, but one more thing," Serafina said, her voice barely audible over the engines' roar. She patted Vanessa's arm. "Logan mentioned Nate's steakhouse was set to open in September, but he postponed it?"

"Oh, you should see it," Vanessa bounced a bit in her seat, her gaze darting between the speeding race cars and her friend. "With its breathtaking waterfront views and top-quality meats, sourced from the best farms and ranches in the region, it's going to be something else. But yes, he postponed the opening to give me time in the parking lot."

This allowed her to prepare for the future and find the ideal location for Mama Dee's Restaurant.

Serafina nodded and fell silent.

For the next hour or so, Vanessa sat on the edge of her seat, trying to focus on Number 62 as the racers reached her end of the track. Thrills coursed through her veins each time Nate expertly maneuvered *Impulse* around his competitors.

The afternoon sun now beat down on the asphalt track, and the air shimmered with heat. She removed her hat, and perspiration dripped from her hair to her forehead. She tossed the hat on the ground next to her hand fan, too anxious to focus on herself while concerned about the heat affecting track conditions, which made the surface slick and challenging. Nate had shared all the dangers when she'd asked him during an afternoon hike.

Thousands of people waved checkered flags, cheering in pure delight and no fear, while, as it had during all his other races, her heart lodged itself in her throat. She tried to take comfort from Serafina and Logan on her right side and Regina and Kyle to her left, but the roar of revving engines and the cheering of fans enhanced her nerves.

Whenever she watched the live races, she sat on the edge of her seat and preferred not to talk, so Serafina left Vanessa alone as she spoke with her husband. Now and then, however, Serafina squeezed Vanessa's shoulder, especially whenever Nate's car cornered close to the wall.

At some point, Serafina must have handed her another Sprite because Vanessa now found herself with another can of soda in her hands. She tucked it in her purse and in the process managed a glance at Regina. The woman appeared pale, and she trembled beneath the wide-leg pants that brushed against Vanessa's shorts. Nate had shared how Regina worried for his safety, yet his mom still watched his races.

The crowd erupted as Nate took the lead. Vanessa's heart raced, thrilled and counting down the minutes until the race ended so she could throw her arms around him. It didn't matter what place he finished in. As long as he came out alive, he'd won in her account. Since he'd confessed his fears, she realized the risks the racers hid from their fans when they came out of their cars beaming.

With the energy running high, she turned to Regina to see if she was okay. The woman was taking deep breaths. Her eyes were closed as she gripped her husband's arm as if only waiting for the race to be over before opening her eyes. Kyle stayed focused on the race, fanning his wife now and then with the hand fan.

Compassion for the elegant woman touched Vanessa. Nate hadn't been kidding when he said his mom had the hardest time watching his races. The season was almost over, thankfully. In one month, it would be the cup finals, and they'd have two months off from worrying. Unfortunately, in August, he'd finalized a contract for the next season—something most racers needed to secure sponsorship deals. Could she hope next year would be it for him?

Either way, Regina needed comfort now.

Vanessa touched Regina gently. "There are only three more laps."

Screeching tires and crunching metal had Vanessa whipping her neck and gaze back to the track. Nate's car slammed the rails, and she sprang to her feet.

The announcer's voice rocketed over the crowd. "That's Nate Stone in Number 62 spinning out of control, folks."

The car rammed into the wall, the impact deafening.

"My son!" Regina cried out.

"Oh no!" Serafina screeched, grabbing Vanessa's hand and holding it tight.

Sweat drenched Vanessa's body, and horror closed off her lungs, her heart sinking, her eyes filling with tears.

The crowd gasped.

Unable to see clearly, Vanessa focused on one of the giant screens while the crash unfolded. The next minutes blurred as the ambulance approached the field and she and Nate's family jogged toward the scene in a frenzy of panicked uncertainty.

"Oh dear God, please!" she cried out, her hands to her head when they neared.

Nate lay lifeless on a stretcher while medics rushed him to the ambulance. Logan ran ahead of them and spoke to one of the uniformed men.

Tears blinded Vanessa's vision.

Serafina pulled her into an embrace. "Nate is going to be okay."

"I–I hope so."

"Mother!" Logan called out.

Regina had collapsed, and Kyle shouted for medics. Since it was such a big race, they had enough medics on site. Some hurried over to tend to Regina, and she regained consciousness.

Trapped in the nightmare scene, Vanessa could scarcely breathe.

"Come on." Serafina tucked Vanessa under her arm and turned her around. "Logan's driving us to the hospital."

Somehow, her feet moved. Serafina helped her into a van and buckled her seat belt before scooting in beside her. Her hot breath pressed against Vanessa's hair as Serafina whispered "he's going to be okay" over and over again.

"Stay calm, everyone," Kyle spoke. "We don't even know the extent of Nate's injuries."

Or if he will ever wake up. Vanessa swallowed down the words. No need to torment Regina.

Soon, Serafina ushered Vanessa into the hospital waiting room. Then, while Logan answered phone calls from their siblings and her friend sat, Vanessa passed from one window to another. She had no idea how to handle duress. Perhaps because she'd been raised by a single mom and had only one sibling years younger than she was, she preferred to process her panic alone. She hugged her arms around herself as if that could somehow keep her from falling apart. Kyle stood with his wife by the door, and Regina's eyes were red and swollen, no doubt like Vanessa's.

"Hon, you need to sit," Kyle reminded his wife yet again. "We can't have you passing out again."

But Regina waved him off, not taking any of it.

Nate's manager, Doyle, stood at one of the windows, flexing and unflexing his hands. Some of the people Vanessa had met at Nate's celebration parties stood behind Doyle. Jae, Nate's assistant, had left the room earlier.

Vanessa tightened her arms around herself, stifling the cry trying to climb up her throat. If anything happened to Nate, how could she pick up the pieces to live again?

Then Serafina was at her side, rubbing her arms, easing Vanessa's tight hold. Soft hands gripped hers, and somehow, Vanessa found herself facing her friend, looking into caring brown eyes. "I can't do this," she whispered. "I survived after my mom and sister died. But... I can't handle another loss."

"You're not going to." Serafina squeezed her hands, trying to keep Vanessa's focus, but it was wandering.

"I don't care if I ever have my dreams achieved or not. I just want to start life with him—now, *today*." Vanessa let herself ramble, probably not making any sense, but what did it matter? "What's the point of careers if you have no one to share your success with at the end of the day? No one to tell about your struggles or joys."

"We're not losing Nate." Serafina gripped Vanessa's chin, forcing her to meet her gaze, but her friend's face was a blur. "I know you can hear me, Vanessa. I need you to listen, to focus. We're not losing Nate. Do you hear me? We are not losing Nate. *Say it*."

After her friend repeated her demand, Vanessa forced out the words. "We're not losing Nate?"

"Say it again," Serafina insisted.

Each time Vanessa complied, the words sounded less like a question. Soon, she let Serafina guide her to a chair. Then, they sat there, their arms entwined, Vanessa's head on Serafina's shoulder. Serafina's whispered prayers wove an invisible lifeline, even as those words she'd made Vanessa say firmed in her mind. "We're not losing Nate," Vanessa repeated every time her mind spun out of control like Number 62 had.

Hours passed, each one an eternity of waiting. Vanessa jolted with every announcement on the intercom, her panic rising as she imagined they were calling doctors to rush into Nate's room.

Finally, a doctor emerged, his furrowed gray brows doing nothing to ease her already anxious heart. "I'm Dr. Madden."

"What happened?" Regina asked, and they all gathered closer as the doctor shook Kyle's and Regina's hands.

"Nate's condition is almost critical." He spoke slowly, enunciating clearly, his tones low and somber. "He's sustained several injuries—a concussion, broken bones, and..."

As the doctor relayed the extent of Nate's injuries, all Vanessa saw were red flags and danger. She always struggled with unexpected circumstances. Now, God had gone and thrown a big one at her.

"He's been taken to the operating room for surgery to repair the broken bones. We'll address any internal injuries then.... I'll be back to let you know as soon as he's out of surgery."

Doyle stepped out with those from Nate's team as if they were going to have a meeting of some sort.

Vanessa wailed as she moved further into the room and found a corner where she sat on the hard floor with her elbows on her knees. Sobs shook her. Their time in Hawaii rushed back. The spark in his blue eyes when she learned to surf... The genuineness in his smile when they ran into the ocean... The delight in his voice when he described his plans for his property...

His affection and his vulnerability when he confessed his fears.

All of it stirred an ache so intense her head hurt.

She shuddered, hot tears searing her face.

A hand touched her.

Swiping at her tears, she looked up at Serafina, Regina, Logan, and Kyle.

"Nate will be okay, sweetheart." Regina wiped away tears from her own eyes.

"Let's pray." Kyle held out both hands. Lines etched deep around his blue eyes.

As Vanessa's tears subsided, Serafina knelt next to her again, holding her hand.

"God, You have amazing plans for Nate." Kyle bowed his head. "We trust that those plans don't involve death, not yet, at least. We're putting our trust in You and seeking Your mercy on Nate, but, Lord, we also need Your mercy on our worried hearts. Please reach out to those of us who love him—Vanessa and my family—soothe our fears, and let us come to You trusting in Your plans for Nate. Help us all rest assured in the peace You give us. Amen."

They echoed his amen. Then, like the leader of the family, Kyle motioned for them to sit in the lounge chairs.

As they gathered there, Vanessa's gaze drifted to the sky. When had daylight begun to vanish? How many hours had passed?

"Nate said you have everything set for the reunion." Kyle leaned around Regina to speak to Vanessa.

"He bought three more Jet Skis." Vanessa cleared her throat, welcoming his attempt at distracting them. "We're planning a lot of activities like beach volleyball." She could scarcely keep the shakiness from her voice because most of the activities involved movement and agility. No way would he be part of those activities if he had broken bones.

"Thank you for helping him plan." Regina, sitting beside her, patted Vanessa's knee, then nodded to Logan. "How about your brothers and sisters? Have you had any updates?"

"Yes, Mother." Like Nate and all their siblings, Logan's voice softened when he spoke to his parents. "Iris and Sabastian got on the plane. They should be here in three hours. Theo will arrive tomorrow. Wade is on his way."

As Logan continued naming their siblings, it seemed like the entire crowd would be arriving soon or sometime tomorrow. Vanessa tipped her head onto Serafina's shoulder again.

"You okay?" Serafina whispered while the others talked.

"Hmm." Vanessa closed her eyes, her face already near her bestie's ear, so she whispered back. "A bit overwhelmed. They're all so amazing. It must have been something else growing up in such a big, blended family."

"Tell me about it." Serafina, an only child, laughed. "Despite their diverse backgrounds, they all come together to support each other in times of need, creating a strong and loving bond that carries them through even the most challenging situations. It's been amazing to be grafted into their family." She nudged Vanessa. "You're going to love it when you're truly a part of the Stones."

"I had let myself daydream...." But now it may never happen. Vanessa sprang to her feet, needing a distraction. "Can I get you guys anything?"

"That's sweet, honey." Regina was shaking her head. "But I couldn't even handle a water."

"Well, whatever we're getting, I'll come with you. I need to stretch my legs." Serafina stood, even as everyone else denied wanting anything. Then she hooked her arm through Vanessa's. "Nonsense. It's past dinnertime, so we'll bring back some food for everyone. We'll force ourselves to eat. Then, when Nate wakes up, we'll be ready to give him our undivided attention."

They strolled down the sterile hospital corridors. All the hallways looked the same, so Vanessa never could've found her way back. But even two hours later, the food remained untouched. Perhaps it would get eaten sometime later.

Then Dr. Madden strode into the room. "Folks." He raised both hands as if summoning their attention. "I'm happy to announce Mr. Stone's surgery was successful. He's regaining consciousness, and we'll be allowing one person at a time in to visit him."

Regina rubbed Vanessa's back. "You go ahead and go in first, honey."

Everything in Vanessa leaped to take a step forward, but she shook her head. Nate's mom was just as eager to see her son. "I'll go after you."

When Regina returned almost fifteen minutes later, a smile softened the worry lines on her face. "Thank You, Lord." She pulled Vanessa into a hug and tweaked the words that had become the day's hopeful refrain. "Nate *is* fine."

Relief washed over Vanessa. Her knees buckled, and her heart soared. Happy tears streamed down her face as she embraced Regina, her sweet jasmine fragrance enveloping her.

When they released each other, Vanessa, desperate to see Nate, practically sprinted to his room, her steps echoing on the tile floor. She pushed open the half-open door with a trembling hand, then took a deep breath, and hesitated before stepping inside, her heart pounding.

Nate lay there with a network of wires hooked to his arm and gauze wrapped around his elevated hand. The heart monitor's steady beep and the medical equipment's gentle hum provided an odd sense of reassurance.

We're not losing Nate! Even as her heart broke at his bruised and broken body and swollen face, something inside her kicked back with a surge of gratitude for his survival. *Thank You, Lord!*

His eyelids fluttered open as he must've sensed her presence. A weak smile tugged at the left side of his mouth. Then, wincing slightly, he shifted his head on the pillows.

He whispered her name, his voice barely audible but affectionate. A lump formed in her throat as she reached for his hand, connecting with the warmth of his skin and sensing the steady pulse of life beneath her fingertips.

"I thought I smelled your lovely scent." His breathy words drew her closer, and his warm smile reassured her.

"Oh my, Nate." She pressed her free hand to her chest, then leaned in, and oh-so-carefully wrapped her arms around him, mindful of the IV. "Are you okay?"

"Hi, sweets," he murmured, planting a gentle kiss on her cheek.

She savored the warmth of his lips against her skin, then eased out of the embrace, and took a seat on the bed next to him, close enough to reach out and touch his scruffy jaw. "You gave us a scare," she whispered, hardly keeping the panic from her unsteady voice.

Silence passed as he studied her, frowning. "I don't like that you've been crying."

"How did you know?"

He caressed her cheek. His fingers trailed below her eyes, sending goose bumps across her skin. "Your eyes. They're swollen."

We're not losing Nate! She mirrored his gesture, his stubble prickling her fingertips. "I'm just glad you're going to be okay."

He pushed a lock of hair back from her face. "I'm not going anywhere," he teased. "You're stuck with me."

"You're stuck with me too." Perhaps this was God's way of ending his career.

"Doesn't look like I'm making it to Round 8," he said, his eyes downcast, the sadness evident.

"You're already a champion to me—win or lose, you survived, and that makes you a winner and my hero." *We're not losing Nate!* "I'm just so happy you're alive."

He half smiled, but disappointment dimmed his eyes. And she ached for him too. Entwining her fingers with his, she tried to distract him. "Your family is excited about the reunion."

"Oh?" His lips thinned, and his chest rose and fell in a deep breath. "We'll have to move that to Pleasant View, I guess."

The need to change the venue made sense. He'd been looking forward to the island gathering, so would he be okay with the change? "Are you sure?"

He exhaled. "Beach volleyball." He dropped his gaze to his chest where the hospital gown appeared bulky, no doubt concealing braces to support the broken ribs. Thankfully, he had one hand free from injury. "The Peak is home, though, and being there, and..."

"I understand." He'd come close to death and would rather celebrate time with his family in their hometown. "I'll come up with some Thanksgiving-themed activities."

She'd have to dig up all the ideas she could find on Pinterest and various search engines. Even if she didn't come up with the best ideas, his family would be glad to spend time with him one way or another. With that big a family, someone would surely have some creative ideas.

Nate grimaced. "I'm sorry you went through all the trouble planning."

Oh my! She wagged a finger at him. "That's my last concern right now."

She didn't even care about the money they'd lose for cancellations. No amount of money could compensate for losing him. Thanksgiving couldn't have been a better holiday for the reunion. Only God could have known how much they'd have to be thankful for this year.

"Do you know how much I love you?" He squeezed her hand and pulled her out of her thoughts. He'd shown her nothing but love and respect since he'd first noticed her.

Sure, she'd initially misinterpreted his good intentions to help, but now, she knew the real Nate. Kind and giving, her dream come true.

"Yes, I do. I love you too," she whispered, leaning in to place tender kisses along his jaw and the left corner of his mouth, the one he quirked so often, pouring her emotions into each touch.

Then he tilted his head and caught her lips with his. When he initiated a deeper kiss, pulling her closer, she savored their connection. She shifted on the bed, keeping her hand on his jaw, and continued to kiss him, feeling protected and cherished in his embrace.

They pulled apart slowly, their tired smiles reflecting each other's happiness. "I was thinking," he spoke softly. "I mean *really* thinking about us."

"You had time to think while under anesthesia?"

With their fingers entwined, he lifted her hand to his mouth and kissed her fingertips. "I don't want to wait too long. I want to start planning our future together. I know you want to get your career together—"

"I don't want to wait either," she interrupted, tears searing her eyes. "I love you so much."

"I love you." He stifled a yawn, and she didn't want to exhaust him further. "Always," he added as his eyelids fluttered closed.

But he held onto her hand while he fell asleep, and she kept their hands clasped, resting her head on the bed. No matter what the future held, they would face it together. She couldn't imagine it any other way.

CHAPTER 18

Days before Thanksgiving, Vanessa sat at the table next to Nate with a knot in her stomach, surrounded by his family. Animated conversations and strings of glittery lights filled the room with warmth and cheer. She'd met some of Nate's family members at Serafina and Logan's wedding, and she'd finally met the extended family members yesterday as they arrived for the reunion.

They'd already enjoyed a catered meal from the company Serafina and Logan used last summer. Although additional tables had been set up to accommodate over seventy people, many family members had left their seats and now congregated around Vanessa and Nate's table.

With so many people talking to him and asking her how she felt about his recent injury, she hadn't had time to appreciate the scenic mountain view through the window.

Wincing, an elderly lady patted Vanessa's shoulder. "We were all terrified when he nearly lost his life. But you, dear, were right there. It must have been awful to watch the crash and see the medics cart him away."

"You stayed to help him after his hospital discharge, didn't you?" the gentleman with Nate's aunt Sheila asked.

Vanessa nodded. "He spent the next two weeks recovering at his home in North Carolina before going to San Francisco to start physical therapy, and yes, I was there by his side—not that I made the best caregiver. We did, however, manage to keep Nate resting and following doctor's orders to avoid any activities that could aggravate his injury."

But she'd been unable to leave him and only returned to San Francisco twice to check on Ava and the business. Surprisingly—or not so surprisingly according to Nate and Serafina—the ladies had kept things running smoothly without her. Then, so she could avoid commuting between the two cities, he'd moved into his San Francisco penthouse and started physical therapy there until they flew to Pleasant View for the reunion.

"Are you still racing next year?" Julia asked.

Before Nate could answer, his youngest sister, Iris, shrugged, and as she spoke, the red highlights in her brown hair shone beneath the pendant lights. "He has to honor a contract."

"Don't tell me about honoring a contract, Iris." Julia snorted and thrust out her chin so fast her dangling pearl earrings jiggled. Getting in Iris's face, Julia slapped her own chest. "Of all people here, *I* am the one who most understands what that means, but this creates extenuating circumstances."

As Nate's family members discussed his career and plans, Vanessa pressed a hand to her tightly knotted stomach at the thought of him racing and facing another accident. Hailey, Iris, and Julia expressed their concerns until Nate raised his hand.

"As Iris said"—Nate seemed pensive, stiff even, as if he had the weight of his career on his shoulders—"I have a contract."

"What exactly are you trying to say?" Hailey waved both hands, her skin a darker brown than Vanessa's. Her question fueled the tension in the room.

"Um, maybe we should focus on the evening's activities?" Iris piped up, clearly wanting to change the topic.

Her fiancé hooked an arm around Iris's waist. "Seriously, guys, Iris is right. Let's move on before things get out of hand. The last thing we want to do is gang up on someone."

Nate, clearly done with the conversation, kissed Vanessa's cheek, neck, and ear. An embarrassed warmth revved through her as his siblings exchanged looks. Okay, a subject change was needed. She sat up straighter. "We're going to keep the reunion as simple as possible for the next few days."

Nate's hand on her waist tightened.

"That sounds great!" Iris clapped. "We've had enough excitement lately, and we all need to unwind."

But Julia arched a brow and pressed her immaculately made-up lips into a flat line, clearly holding back a retort.

So Vanessa leaned toward the older woman. "We do have plenty of plans, and if all else fails, we can always rely on movie and game nights."

"Or"—Nate piped up—"for those of you still getting around strong, enjoy some outdoor activities, like hiking, and for those of us taking it easy, maybe a bonfire?"

"*That* sounds good!" Theo victory punched the air and smacked his lips together like a kid. "Yum. Nothing beats roasting marshmallows."

Laughing at his antics, Vanessa smiled at a surge of confidence. "We've also got competitions planned for this week. We'll have teams and challenges with a grand prize for the winner."

Nate had suggested including prizes to make activities more competitive and exciting. He clamped a hand on her waist. "And that's my Vee." His blue eyes sparkled beneath the lights. "Such incredible creative skills, sweets."

Sweets, not Spitfire. Things had changed so much. Warmth spread through her chest. "Thanks." She smiled at him, savoring seeing him happy and determined to make this week unforgettable for him and his family. She stood. "Why don't we head to the family room for some charades now?"

Several minutes later, laughter filled the family room as everyone gathered to play under the bright recessed lights. Teams of four to six participants took turns acting out their chosen titles.

Although Vanessa wasn't an avid game player, the excitement swept her up. She smiled at Nate as his little niece crawled onto his lap and he lifted her despite the lingering pain from his injury.

"Okay, Vanessa, go," Logan encouraged, his arm draped over Serafina as they waited.

Vanessa took a deep breath and faced the lively group, some standing while others sat on pillows or chairs brought from other parts of the house. She gestured with her hand to make out the symbol for a TV.

"Movie." Nate blew her a kiss before taking his niece's hand to his cheek.

Vanessa gestured wildly with a charade, and her exaggerated antics elicited laughter and cheers. It mustn't have been her best act.

Several people blurted out movies as she kept trying to get the right response until Nate shouted out, "*The Greatest Showman!*"

"Yes!" She gave a fist pump and moved to sit next to him.

"Great job, babe." He rested a hand on her back.

"Great teamwork," she responded, pleased he remembered one of her favorite movies after they'd watched it during his early recovery days.

The game continued for hours so everyone could take turns acting out a movie, book, or TV show title. Even Nate's parents took turns and clearly enjoyed spending time with their kids and family, including Nate's aunts and uncles and grandparents. With the warm atmosphere of family camaraderie infectious, Vanessa settled in, growing comfortable around his relatives.

At some point during the game, soft and tiny fingers crawled on her arm, and when she looked, Nate's niece—probably three to four years old, Vanessa couldn't remember—was holding onto her.

"Hey, sweetheart." Vanessa spoke through the noise, doubting the girl could hear her. But in response, she climbed onto Vanessa's lap. The girl's amber skin tone was a mix of her mom's brown skin and her dad's light skin tones.

"You're a natural." Nate's warm breath tickled her ear as he shifted, draped his arm over her shoulder, and kissed the top of her hair.

"So are you." After all, he'd carried the girl and lovingly interacted despite his lingering pain. Holding a child with Nate sitting close,

Vanessa couldn't help but imagine a future with him and their own family. In the hospital, he'd said he wanted to make adjustments to their relationship, but they hadn't talked about what that meant since getting him better had been their priority. However, on a recent shopping trip with Serafina, Vanessa had tried on rings and daydreamed about what might lie ahead.

As the night came to an end and Logan announced the winners, Vanessa's heart felt light over getting to know Nate's family and enjoying the next days' activities with them. She could see herself becoming part of them, and Nate had said he didn't want to wait. What had he meant? When would they bring it up again?

CHAPTER 19

The next morning, Nate stepped out of the elevator into the quiet family room. White sofas and scenic mountain photos contrasted with the empty space where just last night his family had gathered for a lively game. He was about to meet Vanessa for their morning walk. While he longed to get back to his daily runs, a walk would suffice until he fully recovered.

As he took a sharp exhale, he grimaced at the pain around the rib brace. In three weeks, he should be rid of it, provided the doctor agreed. Despite the dislocated, sprained, and torn ligaments in his left hand, it had recovered well. His lower back, too, had only suffered minor injuries, allowing him to enjoy morning walks.

His heart skipped a beat when he saw Vanessa standing in the main room with her back to him as she studied the family photos along the wall. She wore a formfitting running outfit—black leggings, white tennis shoes, and a vibrant neon-pink zip-up hooded sports jacket. The outfit accentuated her muscular legs and toned arms while her dark, curly hair, pulled back into a high ponytail, would surely highlight her striking features and slim neck if she were facing him.

The morning light streamed through the kitchen windows, casting a radiant glow on her rich brown skin. He didn't want to startle her, and she must have heard him approaching.

As he neared, she spun around with a vibrant smile that warmed and melted his heart.

"Morning, sweets." He leaned in to kiss her, and her hands found his back as she returned the kiss with minty freshness.

"Did you sleep well?" she asked once they broke away. Hand in hand, they strolled down the hallway and out the front door.

"Given the circumstances, not bad." Deep sleep had eluded him since the accident, and nightmares of the crash still haunted him. The pressure of returning to racing and constant inquiries from the media compounded his stress.

A retreat to his childhood home provided a much-needed escape. Although his injuries could have been worse, he remained concerned about his family and Vanessa.

As they strolled along the sidewalk into the gardens, the morning sun rose over the mountains. The once-blossoming flowers of summer had faded away, and the shrubs lining their path stood leafless. He inhaled the crisp mountain air, wincing as his ribs twinged.

"You okay?" Vanessa touched his arm in a comforting gesture.

A smile lifted his cheeks as he gave her a sideways glance. "Yeah, just a little sore still. But the fresh air feels great." His smile widened over last night's game and how Vanessa embraced his boisterous family. "I'm glad you're here. With me."

"There's no place I'd rather be." She nestled her arm in the crook of his. Unlike others, she didn't pester him about his career or remind him of the terrifying possibility that he might never race again. Both his mom and dad were worried, but they had remained silent too, which meant a lot. "Are you having fun?"

They stepped off the sidewalk and onto the rugged trail.

"I was about to ask you the same thing." He laid his recovered hand over hers on his arm. Her touch sent a shiver down his spine. "I know I messed up our original plans. What do you think about spending the next five days with all these people?"

"God had better plans. Besides, even on the island, I expected to be around your family." She squeezed his arm, her voice cheerful. "And I love it here."

"I wish I'd brought you here last month instead." His heart swelled with the urge to share all his favorite places with her. Dry leaves crackled beneath their feet with a crisp sound. "Fall is always breathtaking here. Merely a month ago, the now-barren trees would have been a mesmerizing canvas of vivid yellows, oranges, and reds."

"I can just imagine how beautiful it is." She gestured to the snowcapped mountain peaks in the distance. "I've never been this close to big mountains before."

She'd been to his home in North Carolina, but the mountains there weren't as towering as those beyond Pleasant View. He savored the serene moment, walking with the woman he loved in one of his favorite places in the world. For the first time since his accident, he felt truly able to appreciate the moment.

"Did I ever tell you why I like it here?"

"What's not to like?" Her question emerged breathless and filled with wonder.

"This was the first stable home I can remember. No matter where I go, even in the most serene places, deep down, my heart belongs here."

"I think this is my favorite place too." She stopped to gaze at the open space beyond the vast property.

"Really?" He elbowed her in the rib cage, unable to contain his thrill. "Why?"

She faced him, her deep brown eyes meeting his so intensely that he struggled to breathe. "Wherever your home is, that's my home too."

He swallowed at the sweetness of her words.

Then she lifted her chin to the open space. "Plus, where else do I see animals in the backyard?"

A herd of deer grazed in a nearby field, and though this wasn't his first time seeing them, it was always a breathtaking sight. Standing next to him with her arm linked through his, Vanessa hugged his arm close as they remained in silent awe until the deer wandered off.

She loosened her hold on him. "What if today we visit that pumpkin patch I saw yesterday? Remember? When we went into town? Maybe we could have everyone carve pumpkins."

"A contest!" He nodded. "I like that idea. And then we could maybe do a talent show?"

"Perfect!" She leaned in to kiss his cheek, her lips warm against the chilly morning air.

As they resumed their walk, now a leisurely stroll, gratitude for her presence in his life warmed him. She had been a constant source of support since his accident, helping him through the tough moments of his recovery. And now, here they were, walking together on a beautiful late-fall morning.

Though there might still be a long road to recovery, surrounded by the beauty of nature, the presence of God, the support of family, and the love of a beautiful woman, he was confident that everything was going to be okay.

***

Somehow, Nate and Vanessa had emerged victorious in the pumpkin contest with the driver, his wife, and the two security guards serving as judges. Now, having nestled some of their carved pumpkins, lit by LED candles, at the windowsills and around common rooms throughout the house, everyone gathered in the basement game room for the talent show.

Nate, nursing sore ribs, settled onto the sofa, while Vanessa stood across the room near the foosball and pool tables, outlining the rules for the upcoming show. The room buzzed with voices, children's laughter emanated from a nearby craft table, and soft holiday music wafted through the speakers.

He chuckled as Iris, sitting beside him, grumbled about the talent show. "I'm terrible at these things."

Sabastian hugged her and kissed the top of her head. "Honey, we have talents. We don't have to sing or dance."

The show began, and their nieces and nephews performed with his oldest brother and sister-in-law directing them. Eric displayed such love for his family, taking delight in their antics, and the lighthearted silliness they all shared. Nate shifted in his seat. Could he be as good a father someday too?

"You're quiet." Iris's soft hand touched his shoulder. "Are you doing all right?"

Trust Iris, their dear little sister and the glue that held the family together, to sense his pensive thoughts amid the festivities. He patted her hand on his shoulder. "The pain's manageable. Don't worry."

But she shook her head, sending her short cherry-toned hair flicking onto her cheeks. "I didn't ask about the pain, Nate."

Right. One could never divert Iris's attention. So he shifted to face her fully. "I guess I *am* thinking about my career and the decisions I face." He often confided in Iris, knowing he could trust her to keep his confidence, even if Julia never seemed to think so. "If I continue racing, I might never provide the stable home I crave for my own family. But if I walk away, I'll be forever haunted by the fear of cars and motorsports, unable to enjoy a pastime I once loved."

She squeezed his shoulder, seeming to sense how the admission consumed him with sadness. "I can't imagine facing such a decision. Have you talked to Mom about it? I mean *really* talked to her?"

"She and Dad have been so good about giving me space on this. And you know she doesn't want me racing."

"But she's always been supportive despite her personal feelings, and she is a counselor after all. If you don't want to approach her, my advice would be to pray about it."

He nodded. Prayer was always the best way to go about things—anything.

His gaze roamed the game room, taking in the posters and pictures showcasing each family member's favorite memories, and his own prized memorabilia—a signed photo of Jim Crew, the legendary NASCAR driver who inspired him with his perseverance.

Iris must have followed his gaze because she slid her hand from his shoulder to wrap around his waist. "That must be a poignant reminder of the dilemma you face."

It was, indeed. Just how could he grapple with the balance between his dreams and the sacrifices they demanded?

Sabastian leaned in to say something to Iris, and she redirected her attention as the talent show progressed with a delightful array of talents showcased—singing, juggling, and card tricks. Then Vanessa approached, her dark eyes aglow as she stood over him and beckoned by crooking a finger his way. "Everyone, it's now Nate's and my turn to dance."

Although he'd felt fine earlier, he couldn't pinpoint why he was experiencing pain tonight. Attempting to mask his discomfort, he hoped the dance's gentle movement wouldn't strain his still-recovering body.

Perhaps sensing his unease, Vanessa reassured him with a tender smile. "Just a slow dance."

As Elvis Presley crooned "Can't Help Falling in Love," Nate rose from the couch and began swaying to the music, basking in her warm embrace. His family clapped along, their joyous energy accentuating the moment.

Nate pressed his lips to her soft hair, breathing in the sweet floral scent of her, and whispered, "I didn't realize you'd be so at ease dancing with an audience."

"I have a great teacher," she murmured, her breath tickling his neck.

As they moved together, a jolt of pain made him wince.

Vanessa drew back, and his sisters sprang from their seats, expressing their worry.

"I'm fine, guys," he assured them, masking his vulnerability.

But Vanessa frowned. "We'd better get you back to the couch."

He framed her face with his long fingers, his heart aching. "I'm sorry I can't finish our dance through such a heartfelt song." Because, deep down, he couldn't help falling in love with her.

"Let's take a break." She nestled one cheek against his palm and threaded her fingers through his other hand, then guided him to sit back down and enjoy the rest of the talent show.

"I owe you another dance," he vowed, conscious of the rigorous therapy sessions awaiting him. While he was in Pleasant View, Tessa Whitlock, a trusted family friend, had agreed to treat him. She came highly recommended by Eric, who had experienced her expertise as his physical therapist for an entire year.

The next day, while Nate couldn't partake in sports, he and Vanessa joined some of the others in the enclosed pool and hot tub. He dipped his feet in the water and watched Vanessa swim with his siblings, content to throw a beach ball for them as they played.

How could he not embrace the joy and warmth of watching her laugh alongside his family? With the love in the room infectious, he basked in gratitude for the support and closeness they all shared.

On Thanksgiving Day, the family gathered in the kitchen to prepare a homemade feast together. Sabastian, their former chef, now Iris's fiancé, handled the turkey while Vanessa added her famous prime rib. Mom, Dad, and Nate pitched in with Dad perfecting his renowned whipped cream for the pumpkin pies.

Hailey tried to bake peach pies but charred their crusts. Two of Nate's brothers attempted Grandma's green-bean casserole but added too much flour, leaving a powdery mess all over the floor and counter. Amid the activity, banter, and laughter, the kitchen became a chaotic and heartwarming scene.

Then they all sat down to enjoy the scrumptious dinner. Extra tables crammed the dining room, jack-o'-lanterns grinned and scowled on the windowsills, and a mouthwatering aroma tinted the air.

After Dad offered a prayer of thanks, Mom insisted everyone take turns sharing what they were grateful for.

Nate went first, his voice catching as he expressed his thankfulness for Vanessa. "God brought her into my life at the right time when He knew I needed her the most." When Vanessa placed a comforting hand on his back, he surveyed his family, tears burning his eyelids. "You guys, my family, you're everything."

He swallowed hard to maintain his composure. "Mom and Dad, I'll never be able to express my love and admiration for you—not only for adopting me and my siblings but also for your unwavering faith and love toward our community." He paused as Mom was wiping at her eyes with a napkin. "But most of all, for pointing me to God. For giving me a place I can call home. For standing on love and faith as living proof of God's existence."

Everyone clapped as he finished, and Vanessa stood next. "I've had so many changes this year that you'd think it would be hard to know where to start. But most of all, I am grateful for having you guys and Nate in my life and for Nate having God's protection during the race."

She sat back down to soft amens echoing around them. As they continued the heartfelt tradition, laughter erupted at the reminder that their food was getting cold. They began to eat, still taking turns to share their gratitude with nearly everyone mentioning their thankfulness for Nate's safety.

After dinner, the family gathered in the living room where board games were strewn about the floor. They played to a background of laughter and a warm reminder of their bond. Then it was time to draw names for Christmas presents. Though not everyone could make it for the holiday, their gifts still found their way to the intended recipient, some traditions stayed the same whether they were all home or not.

Theo, the organizer of next year's reunion, grinned as he announced. "High time we did something in Brazil!"

A chorus of agreement met his enthusiasm with Mom chiming in, "As long as we're together."

On their last day together, the family gathered in the upstairs theater for a Christmas-movie marathon. As the films played, Vanessa and Nate sat close, their hands entwined. With each passing movie, more family members trickled out until only the two of them remained, lit by the dim glow of the onscreen credits.

"We're the troopers," Nate whispered, pressing a gentle kiss to her fingertips.

She smiled, and her voice emerged soft. "I haven't worked in days, so I'm barely tired."

"It's been nice having a break. I'm glad I decided to delay the launch of my restaurant." He rubbed her fingers. "But what about you? How is the search going for a place to launch your restaurant?"

"You'd be the first to know if I'd found somewhere. I'm keeping you updated on all my Realtor meetings." She leaned her head on his shoulder, and he nuzzled her curly hair, loving how she included him in her life and decisions.

Then she let out a low, heavy breath. "I should be getting my teaching license in the mail within the next two weeks, which brings me to the question of applying to schools in California or seeking a license in another state."

She must be seeking clarity on their future plans.

"Where would you like to teach?" He secured her in his arms, leaving the decision to her. A silence stretched between them, filled only by their breathing.

"If the doctors clear you..."

At her cautious tone, he had a sinking feeling about where the conversation was headed.

"Are you going back to racing?"

He could pretend everything was fine and make the realistic decision to end his career now. Especially since he also had to worry about Vanessa now whenever he climbed into the compact race car. But horrific memories of his sudden finale with the motorsport would always loom in the shadows.

Afraid to look at her, he ducked his head as he responded. "I plan to go back."

"But why?" A shiver coursed through her as she kept her head resting on his shoulder. "It's dangerous."

"I'm aware of that—obviously." He gestured to his injured body. "But now is the worst time to quit. Racing is what I love to do. I can't give it up because of fear and worry."

She lifted her head from his shoulder. The credits had ended, but the home theater screen held enough light to illuminate her worried face.

"I'm not just worried about your survival." Her voice rose on the last words. She took a deep breath and steadied herself. "Every time you race, I'm terrified you're going to end up with a traumatic injury or something worse. I can't live like this, always wondering if you're going to make it through the day by the end of your race."

His heart ached. She truly cared and worried about him just like his family. He'd asked Mom to stop watching his races, but she wouldn't listen. Would Vanessa?

Taking her hand in his, he softened his voice. "That accident was unusual. The heat was too much that day." He lived for overcoming uncertainties in his career. "It's not that there's a lot of extreme accidents lately. NASCAR has made significant safety improvements over the years to reduce the risks of injury to drivers. They have energy-absorbing walls and improved seat belts and harnesses."

Not that he could downplay the inevitable risks. "Racing is a dangerous sport, and as you witnessed, injuries can occur despite these safety measures. You don't have to be a driver to face injuries, though. There are risks in everything." Including her catering and teaching jobs. "But the thrill of it all is to overcome our fear of the unknown."

"You don't understand." She yanked her hand out of his and crossed her arms on her chest. "I can barely handle the unexpected issues of where I'm parking the truck the next day or where I'm teaching or where our future lies. Now, I have to worry about your life. You're reckless, impulsive, and all those things.... How do you expect me to handle that? Or not knowing if I'm ever going to spend the rest of my life with you or not?"

Spitfire was back. Her snapping at him after he'd done his best to explain why he couldn't quit his career blew a gasket inside him. Laying out facts made more sense now.

"I understand that you're scared, Vee." He inhaled slowly to put the brakes on his anger. He'd quit soon, but... "I can't give it up right now. I'm sorry."

She shook a finger at him. "If you're going to retire, why not do it now? You have enough investments and businesses to keep you in the billionaire charts. How much is enough for you?"

"It's not about the money." Okay, that was a cool bonus to his already fun hobby.

"Then what is it?"

He blew air out of his mouth, seeking the easiest analogy for her to understand. "Ever crash on a bike?"

She nodded and held a long pause. "I fell once and never rode a bike again."

That was the problem.

"If you quit after a fall, then you always have apprehension about the task. You get bad memories of the sport you love." He reached for her hand, but she slapped his grasp away. So he tried to stay calm. "When I was ten and went skiing with my dad, I fell. It was pretty bad, and I was horrified after stumbling into a tree. Dad told me to get back onto the slopes right away if I ever wanted to ski again."

"You're not ten anymore." She pressed her curvy lips into a livid pale line. "And you don't need to race again."

"This is where you and I are different." No reason not to be honest, right? Wasn't that what a true relationship was about? "You're stressed because you spend your days cooking and selling food, something you don't enjoy. For me, I believe in enjoying what I do. Life is too short."

"You don't think I know life is too short?" She pushed further away and sprang to her feet. "Why do you think we're having this conversation?"

This conversation involved the two of them, so he'd finish what he wanted to say. His gaze rose to hers in the dim lighting.

"Do you think your mom would want you to be happy doing what you enjoy, or would she rather you were pushing yourself to the limit for a business you don't want to be running yourself?"

He didn't run any of his extra businesses so he could focus on doing the one thing he enjoyed.

"This has nothing to do with Mom!" She cut a hand through the air, defensive again.

But someone had to be honest with her. "You can't even trust anyone to see your recipes, Vee. How are you planning on having people cooking your mom's food without a recipe?"

"For your information, Ava has seen my recipes."

"For the paste, maybe? How about the other recipes you haven't used in the food truck? The meals you intend to have on the menu when your mom's restaurant opens. Are you confident to reveal them to the strangers you'll be hiring?"

"You know what? I'm done." She threw her hands in the air, confusing him until she confirmed. "I've lived in fear most of my adult life. My mom and sister died suddenly. Since then, every single day, I'm caught off guard by circumstances I didn't expect."

That was life in general, particularly his own life, but he kept that detail to himself since she was unreasonable right now.

"I choose not to live on the edge." She wiped her face, clearly crying, and he ached over causing her tears. "I can't be worried sick every single day of my life, not knowing if the love of my life is going to make it through to the next day. You can't ask that of me."

She spun around, and he reached out to take her hand, to try to assure her they could work out their differences, she just needed to stand by him until he proved he could do this again. But she snatched her hand away and stormed from the theater.

His heart sank, feeling darker than the room as he slumped into the chair and threaded his fingers through his hair.

It was going to be okay. It had to be. Was he making the wrong decision to race next season? He'd pray about it some more. But racing also depended on a doctor giving him a clean bill of health.

Tomorrow morning, they'd go for a walk and talk it through. He shouldn't have said anything about her mom's legacy as a way to support his explanation.

CHAPTER 20

Vanessa walked through the empty restaurant space with the Realtor, scanning every inch of the room as she tried to envision the place filled with food and people. Large and open with a rustic charm, the space boasted high ceilings and wide windows that let in plenty of natural light. Exposed brick walls and vintage light fixtures gave it a cozy, welcoming feel.

It didn't feel as cozy when she glanced through the window to the cloudy sky, though. Lately, there'd been fewer sunny days as clouds matched her gloom since she'd returned from Nate's family reunion.

What would Mom want her to do? And why had Vanessa thought starting a restaurant was a good idea when she wasn't going to work there?

"You can't trust anyone with your recipes." Nate's words had taunted her since she left Pleasant View two days after Thanksgiving. Almost seven weeks ago. Time went by so quickly, except for when your heart was in shambles. Every moment, every breath, every painful hour felt like an eternity.

When he'd met her downstairs for their usual walk the morning after their misunderstanding, she was dressed with her luggage in tow ready to head to the airport. She'd not even bothered to talk to Serafina when she booked an early flight. After browsing her phone for Uber, she'd found no results for a ride that early.

Nate eyed her luggage and didn't ask why she was leaving. Instead, he lifted his soulful blue gaze to hers and offered to have the chopper ready for her. But she'd just needed a ride to the airport. So, without further questions, he'd had their family driver take her. Nate had sat in the back with her for an awkwardly silent ride.

"I shouldn't have said anything about your mom." Sincere apology laced his parting words. "She would be proud of however you choose to honor her. Take care of yourself."

A lump now formed in Vanessa's throat like it did whenever she thought of that morning, the way he looked at her, and the heartbreak behind his eyes. She'd wanted to call him so many times, but she'd made things between them seem final. Now, in mid-January, she hadn't heard from him yet. She'd shipped a Christmas gift to The Peak to one of Nate's brothers and had received a necklace from his sister, part of the Christmas gift exchange they'd drawn names for on Thanksgiving. But the closest she'd seen Nate lately was on TV. She'd seen him at the NASCAR preseason for an interview. He'd been cleared and claimed he was eager to begin the race season in February.

Besides that, she browsed the internet to check his blogs and the updates Jae posted on his behalf. Vanessa needed to snap herself out of this, but how could she turn off her heart?

"This is where you and I are different."

He was right. They *were* different, but they also complemented each other.

Oh, how she craved Nate, desired to call him and ask his opinion about this building. But he was almost further out of her reach than he'd been before he stumbled into her life.

Like she'd done since her mom and sister died, she stayed busy to banish the heartbreak, but it didn't stop the darkness from rolling in.

As they walked through the dining area, Vanessa tried to imagine tables and chairs in the space and a cacophony of conversations and laughter in the air. She could see the kitchen in her mind's eye, the chefs working to prepare delicious meals and satisfy hungry diners.

"How about that open beam ceiling and the river rock chimney as the central focal point?" The Realtor continued to point out various features, highlighting its potential and offering suggestions to customize it to suit Vanessa's needs. "As soon as I saw this place with its rustic yet classy ambience, I knew this was it for you and your barbecue restaurant."

It was as Mom once imagined. Vanessa stopped by the bar area, her hand wiping at the high-polished, live-edge wood-slab surface. She wouldn't sell alcohol, but she could use this space for those who wanted a faster dining experience.

The Realtor smiled, more excited than Vanessa. "This space has so much potential."

Vanessa's mind wandered back to Ava. She didn't want a restaurant, but what if Vanessa could help her with start-ups for her food-truck business? She'd need a steady location, like a market with only a few vendors where each sold something different so she wouldn't have to worry about facing competition.

The only positive thing about Vanessa's separation from Nate was the time to think back on her life and the years she'd invested in the street-food business since Mom died. Ava had crossed her mind the last three weeks more often than not. Ava was a single mom with an autistic son who needed help. What if God had sent her into Vanessa's life for a specific reason?

Sure, Ava utilized Nate's charity organization for counseling and support for herself and her son. But she also loved cooking. Running a restaurant was a lot of work, another reason one needed to be passionate about food and hospitality in general.

Vanessa's heart stirred as she dragged her fingers over the counter until she made it to the corner and around. While the place felt right for Mama Dee's Restaurant, it didn't feel right to follow through with her plan. Her dream.

Everything about the outcome was off. It was as if everything she'd thought she wanted had shifted off-center. Nothing made sense. Mom's dream didn't make sense.

"Do you think your mom would want you to be happy doing what you enjoy, or would she rather you were pushing yourself to the limit for a business you don't want to be running yourself?"

How in the world had she expected to run two jobs at once? For the first time, she knew what she wanted.

"So?" the Realtor asked.

Vanessa nodded several times, her chest light. Then she shrugged. "It's nice."

"But?" The woman's brows furrowed. "You were so enthusiastic last month, and this place is everything—more than everything!—you described wanting."

"I'm gonna hold off."

"What do you mean?"

Not wanting to explain herself or meet resistance, Vanessa simply smiled. "Thank you for showing this to me. I'll get back to you later."

After she handed Ava all of Mom's recipes, Vanessa would write her a check for start-up costs.

As they walked out, both lost in thought, confidence in her decision buoyed Vanessa. Although she should be sad she'd spent hours and years chasing the wrong dream, it all felt right now that she had decided to help Ava. As a single mom with a son who needed help, Ava faced similar challenges to those Vanessa's mom had experienced. The last thing Vanessa's assistant needed was added stress while trying to nurture and provide for her family. Vanessa's mom would have appreciated that kind of help, and even if nobody had offered it to her, it was Vanessa's privilege to extend support to someone else.

With building anticipation, she pulled out her phone as soon as she got in her car. Nate was the first person she wanted to tell. She looked at his name in her contacts and shivered as a sudden intense emptiness made her take a sharp inhale of breath.

Instead, she called Ava and asked if they could meet in two hours at the coffee shop near the school where Ava's son attended. The location wouldn't be out of the way for Ava, who didn't currently have a vehicle. Although Ava was on Vanessa's insurance to drive the food truck, it was in the shop for a transmission and some other issues.

As Vanessa walked toward the shop, Ava approached, her hair a shade of green now, and leaned in for an embrace. "You sounded urgent on the phone."

"Sorry. I didn't mean to worry you." Vanessa eased away. "It's nothing bad. Let's get a drink while I explain. What can I get you?"

When they entered the coffee shop, it enclosed them in a warm hug of cinnamon-coffee-scented air, and beverage pictures on the windows and menu board presented a variety of options.

"I'm fine." Ava waved away her offer.

Although Vanessa didn't want anything either, it was common courtesy not to sit in someone's establishment without ordering. She ordered soft drinks, a Sprite for herself and a berry-flavored slushie for Ava.

"It's my son's favorite flavor," Ava explained with a tender smile.

Once they sat across from each other at the window seat, Vanessa braced her elbows on the wooden tabletop and grinned at her friend, unable to keep from bouncing a bit in on the cushioned chair. "Thank you so much for meeting me at such short notice."

Ava sipped her slushie through the straw. "It's been odd not working this month." She shrugged. "But as soon as the truck comes out, I'll be ready to work."

Vanessa flattened her palms on the table, the cool wood grounding her. "If I gave you my mom's recipes, do you think you could use them?"

"What?" Ava's eyes widened. "Why? I have no desire to work at a restaurant if you're hiring me as your chef."

"I mean for you to use at your food truck."

Ava blinked, her lips scrunching the way they did when she was confused.

"You heard me right." Vanessa surprised herself by acting on impulse. Nate would be so proud of her. She wasn't one for surprises, but God had a sense of humor. "You know I've always wanted to teach."

Ava nodded.

Vanessa told her what she'd decided was the best way to honor Mom. "You're hardworking like Mom used to be. And you're an amazing advocate for your son like Mom was for my sister. So, unless you don't think you'll use the recipes—"

"Are you kidding me?" Ava squealed, and the chair scraped the tile when she stood and ran to Vanessa's side, throwing her arms around her with an enthusiastic hug.

It was a tight space since Vanessa hadn't been able to stand up yet, but Ava didn't seem to worry or care that she crouched as she hugged Vanessa.

"I had just looked up the pathetic recipes online that I was going to use."

With Ava's excitement, the recipes would be put to good use. After Ava stepped out of the embrace, Vanessa pulled out the Rolodex of recipes from her handbag, and although hesitant deep down, she handed them to their new rightful owner.

Ava hugged the Rolodex to her chest as she stood, rocking the recipe cards with care.

"I'm going to cherish these babies." She then raised a brow. "But, Vanessa? Are you sure? I mean what made you change your mind after saving all the money for a restaurant?"

Nate. But talking about him now would only lead to questions about his whereabouts.

"I'll make sure to pay for you to get the truck painted, so you have a decent—"

"Not happening." Ava put out her hand. "The spray paint is staying on for the memories."

Vanessa chuckled, and Ava lifted the Rolodex cards to her. "After everything you've told me, will it be okay if I keep the same name?"

"You don't have to."

"Mama Dee's Queen of Barbecue." Ava curtsied dramatically. "Sauce is the boss, baby."

The thrill in her friend's voice had Vanessa peering to see if the cashier was concerned about the noise, but he had his face to his phone and his fingers moving as he typed.

"I tried to come up with all sorts of names, but it was so hard to come up with something better than Mama Dee's."

"It'll be honoring my mom, then." Vanessa then relayed the amount she was pitching in to get the transmission for the food truck and pay for space and a place to store it overnight for the first six months at least. "I assume you have people who will help you sell the food?"

"My friends who worked with us are going to come aboard for the ride."

As Vanessa listened to Ava's excited thrill over the food business, she had no doubt she'd done the right thing.

She left the coffeehouse with a weight lifted off her shoulders. She wanted to talk to Nate, to thank him for his unwelcome advice—advice that hadn't seemed right at the time but that, when she'd later considered it and prayed over it, had helped her make a logical decision. Being a business owner while she taught would still have meant she was running two jobs.

She called Serafina on her drive back to the apartment like she had been doing lately since she needed someone to talk to without Nate—someone to share her biggest news and accomplishments.

"Hey," Serafina answered on the first ring. "How did the showing go?"

"You were right to tell me to wait."

"I was?"

"You were," Vanessa teasingly echoed. Each time Vanessa texted her a photo or told her about the viewings, Serafina had been dismissing as if aware Vanessa wasn't capable of running a business.

"Anyway..." She needed to get back on track to why she was calling. Horns honked when she almost swerved into another lane. Rush-hour traffic hadn't even started yet, but the road was busy. Punching a button for the speakerphone, she put the phone on her lap to focus on driving. "I just gave away Mom's recipes to Ava."

"What? Wait, did you say 'gave away'? *Why?*"

"You know cooking isn't my passion."

"Have you already handed her the recipes, or have you just talked about it?"

"Why does it matter?" Vanessa had never felt lighter and happier. "I handed her the entire Rolodex."

"Oh no! I'll meet you at your place on my way from work."

Now piqued and anxious over her friend's anxiety, Vanessa almost scooped the phone from her lap. Instead, she tightened her grip on the steering wheel. "I don't know what's going on with you, but let's meet halfway at the hamburger joint so we can talk about it. I need to know what's got you so riled up." Vanessa was the one riled up, really.

Twenty minutes later, she rushed into the retro diner. Serafina was already sitting there.

"I'm so sorry. I thought waiting was a good idea." Serafina spread her hands, and the plastic yellow bangle bracelets on her wrists jiggled.

"Waiting for what?" Vanessa slapped her purse on the table as she slid into her usual seat, unable to take more, well, *waiting.* "Just say it already."

"How do you feel about giving up your mom's recipes? I can't believe you did that. Are you sure?"

"Sera." Vanessa called her by the pet name Logan used, hoping to get her full attention. "You have something to tell me, right?"

"I do." Serafina let out a breath, her chest rising and falling. "No, I have something to give you."

She slid an envelope from her handbag and handed it over. "I should've given you this before Christmas, but Nate thought you might not have been ready for it since you were mad at him."

Vanessa opened the envelope and pulled out the paper, unfolding it hastily. Then all the air rushed from her lungs. "It's the title of the Sausalito restaurant?"

In her name.

She gasped in a gulp of air, and her heart started racing. "What does this mean?"

A sad smile curved her friend's lips as Serafina reached across the table and touched Vanessa's hand. "It means your dream of owning your mom's restaurant is here. Nate thought it only felt right for you to keep Mama Dee's Restaurant at the Oceanfront."

A tight lump clogged Vanessa's throat. Somehow, she choked out the words past it. "I can't believe it."

Was that why he'd postponed the steakhouse launch date?

The paper shook in her hands as she stared at it. When a tear dropped onto it, she wiped its trail away with the edge of her blouse.

"Now..." Serafina handed her a napkin. "How about we call Ava and tell her it was a mistake?"

Vanessa shook her head. "It's not..."

She had no idea what to do with Nate's restaurant, besides handing it back to him without hurting his feelings. That was the most generous present anyone had ever given her. It meant a lot—no, it meant *everything* that he'd supported her with Mama Dee's, despite the different outcome.

"I already hurt Nate." She sniffled. "I walked away from him without even as much as a second glance. Or so it must've looked to him."

"Nate loves you." Serafina curled her fingers around Vanessa's. "The last several weeks haven't been easy for him, and he understands why you're scared. Why do you think he's never gone public about his past relationships?"

While the tabloids had labeled him as a ladies' man and snapped pictures of him with different women, whom they claimed he was dating, Nate never confirmed any of them to be his girlfriends the way he had boldly declared Vanessa to be.

A weight pressed on her chest, and she flattened her lips together. She'd failed to support him as much as he'd supported her.

"I've never had a serious boyfriend before."

"I know." Serafina squeezed Vanessa's hands. "Don't blame yourself for this. I'd be as scared as you are if Logan was a car racer. But I suspect the only reason Nate hasn't contacted you is because he doesn't want you worried when the racing season resumes."

Nate had tried to explain why he had to race again. Maybe he just needed to do it one more year or several years. But even his mom, who was petrified each race day, still showed up to support him.

Vanessa wiped away her tears. "How's he doing?" Her voice quavered.

Serafina released Vanessa's hands and held hers up in an it's-anyone's-guess gesture. "Logan doesn't think he's himself, even if he says he's fine." She relayed his whereabouts for the rest of the month and the upcoming races in February. "That's probably consuming him right now."

"You think he might be in Pleasant View?"

Serafina grabbed her phone from her vibrant yellow handbag. "I'm going to text you Regina's number. She knows everything about her kids and their whereabouts, even if she's not with them every day."

Regina wasn't a helicopter parent, but based on what Nate said, their mom chatted with them throughout the week. No doubt, they all had a close relationship with her.

In her handbag, Vanessa's phone beeped with an incoming message as Serafina tucked her phone into her own purse. "The sooner you call, the better."

"Thank you so much." Vanessa folded the title and slid it back into the envelope. She needed to seek him out. If he decided to keep things to a friendship level, so be it. She'd rather have him as a friend than not have him at all.

CHAPTER 21

In the last seven, almost eight weeks, Nate's emotions had been in a spinout, leaving him overwhelmed despite the mild activities he'd done to relax. By God's grace, he was better physically. The intense physical therapy sessions paid off, and his doctor cleared him to race come February.

His emotional state was another topic. Besides his fear of the NASCAR season starting, he didn't want to admit, even to himself, that Vanessa wounded him more than the car crash had. What had he expected when she didn't want to put up with his career and personality?

Impulsive and reckless...

Normally, he'd be taking it easy and resting in December and January, but he'd lost so much time during his recovery. After the doctor cleared him, he'd flown back for practice runs on the track. He'd then gone twice to the Talladega Superspeedway where he'd crashed. There, memories of smoke and heat all rushed back, and he'd ended up slamming into the wall.

His team was busy building *Impulse* to outperform all the others come February. He'd be in Los Angeles in the first week of February, so he was forcing himself to take the remaining month of January off to pray and rest.

While he wanted to pursue Vanessa, it was best to leave her alone until the end of the season when he retired from NASCAR. If he gave up racing today, he'd have a looming car race in the back of his head, enough to interfere with his relationship and the start of his family.

Vanessa had been worth going against his plan and pursuing a relationship, but with their separation came a deeper level of understanding of who he was. He was a racer. And they'd never work while he was still racing. She didn't want to live in suspense. She might even move on with someone who was laid back and structured.

His heart twisted.

He'd better go snowmobiling again tomorrow so he didn't have time to keep thinking about her. Yesterday's snowmobiling with three of his siblings felt refreshing.

Today, he was meeting Mom for lunch at a restaurant near the hospital where she worked. As he entered the restaurant, the greeter recognized him from the times their family met Mom here.

"Mr. Stone."

"Saul. You look younger and younger each year." Garlic and bread flavored the air, and Nate smiled as he shook the man's hand.

"That's kind of you." Saul grinned. "Your mom is already here." He led Nate to a private room, passing ornate mirrors and familiar photos of their small town.

"This place always smells so good, and it never changes." Nate spoke over the moody classical background music. The idea of things remaining unchanged held more appeal than it used to. Just like the idea of coming home to a family... "How is your family, Saul?"

"I'm a new dad." Saul beamed. "My wife and I welcomed our first baby two months ago."

"Wow!" Nate slapped the guy on the back. "That's gotta be amazing."

"Nothing like it. But there's your mom, so I'll leave you two alone. Jordan will be your server today. He'll be over later."

"Sounds great. Thanks." Nate then moved toward Mom sitting by the window with the hospital in the foreground against the mountain backdrop.

She smiled and stood, thanking Saul for guiding Nate.

"Hello, Mother." Nate leaned in to kiss her on both cheeks, and her short brown hair brushed against his cheek when she embraced him. His chest squeezed at her tenderness, and he lingered an extra moment to breathe in her jasmine aroma, a familiar scent that was always home to him.

"How are you today?" She stepped out of his embrace. Her cream suit matched the cream tablecloth and the creamy roses brushing cheeks with the crimson ones in the bouquet on their table. The flowers presented a reminder that Valentine's Day was fast approaching and he wouldn't be able to do something special for his sweetheart.

"My day's been wonderful." Not exactly the way he wanted it, but being in Mom's or Dad's company was always rewarding as he basked in their words of wisdom.

When he took his seat across the table, he sipped water from his goblet before asking about her work that morning.

"It's slow at the hospital today, and that's a good thing, by the way."

Nate nodded. If the kids Mom saw daily were anything like he'd been before his adoption, they were blessed to have her in their lives. No doubt, she'd have adopted all the orphaned and homeless kids in the entire world if she could, but he and his siblings had added more years to Mom and Dad, running them ragged. With gray highlights at her temples, she looked stunning for someone in their early sixties.

"How have you been feeling?" Her brows knit as she studied him.

Looking at those warm golden eyes, he had to be honest. Mom knew things weren't back to normal for him, even if he put on a tough shell. "You know how my impulsiveness has always been an issue." And now, the main reason Vanessa couldn't be with him. "But you and Dad somehow managed to put up with—"

"Honey." Mom took his hands in hers across the table. "Everything you are is perfect. God made you the way He wanted you to be. Your functional impulsivity is a blessing in disguise."

"Like me crashing all those cars when I drove almost two hundred miles per hour on a mountain road?" On their private property, he'd almost killed himself once when he slammed into a boulder.

"That's the reckless part, but you're older and not reckless anymore." She squeezed his hands. "Impulsiveness has allowed you to be a good decision-maker, to act swiftly, and to seize an opportunity that might otherwise pass you by."

How did she always find positives in everything?

"If your dad and I had kept you from pursuing your passion, you could have snuck around and done it the wrong way, an unsafe way." She continued talking about his childhood, the years he couldn't remember. "Your biological dad always dreamed of racing cars and spent hours watching NASCAR races on television. He just never succeeded at pursuing that dream."

Probably because he'd had to take care of Nate and Grandpa.

A half smile quirked his mouth. "Vague memories about zooming car engines still echo in the back of my mind."

"At some point, when you settle down to start a family, you should reconsider your career."

He snorted out a laugh and reached for his menu. "It'll be a long time before I start a family. When I told you and Dad my reasons to race this year, you two understood. But Vanessa..." He shrugged and forked his fingers through his hair. It was hard to make her understand, yet somehow... "I still feel I need her blessing to race this season."

"We're expecting someone to join us."

No wonder Mom hadn't ordered yet. He glanced up, setting the menu aside and almost knocking the silverware wrapped in a black cloth napkin, as he frowned at their table for two. "Who?"

"Vanessa called two days ago and wanted to know if she could come by the house to see you."

Not that he was a teenager anymore, but it bothered him that Vanessa called Mom instead of calling him.

"She didn't plan on staying the night, so I invited her to join us for lunch."

His heart started thudding. "Mom... You shouldn't be initiating our get-togethers. This isn't good for either of us. She hates that I'm racing, and her coming is—"

"She's scared for you because she cares deeply, but that doesn't mean she's not in love with you, baby." Mom cupped a hand to his cheek. "Just give her some time to adjust to the idea of dating a race car driver. I'm terrified every time you climb into that car. Your dad is too. He just doesn't talk about it."

He knew his parents' fears, but... "Vanessa met me when I was racing, yet she gave up as soon as—"

"Honey." Mom patted his cheek, and her tender gaze seeped into his. Understanding and wisdom flowed in with it. "One of your greatest strengths is that you're always able to find peace and strength from within. You rarely let anything beat you down." Admiration carried in her voice. "The reason why you have so many fans, even racers who interact with you for less than three seconds, is because you have a way of capturing their attention. God has given you the ability to be flexible and accepting no matter what the situation is."

As her words wrapped around his chest and squeezed his heart like a hug, a lump formed in his throat.

"If Vanessa had given up on you, she wouldn't be flying halfway across the country to find you. She would've called you instead."

Mom was right.

And just then, in his peripheral vision, he saw people walking toward them. She was here. Raising his head, he locked eyes with Vanessa as Saul pointed her toward them.

She clutched her red handbag to her shoulder. Her curves swayed beneath a royal-blue long-sleeved dress, and her shoes clinked against the tile.

While they stared at each other, she smiled and sent his heart into somersaults as if in slow motion. As she approached, he pushed back the upholstered chair and rose, meeting her in one long stride.

"Spitfire." He struggled to breathe.

"Hi." She rose on tiptoes and hugged him. With the way she wrapped her arms around his waist so tightly and rested her face on his chest, she'd clearly missed him as much as he'd missed her. His throat felt like he'd swallowed metal as he secured her slender figure in his arms, savored the warmth of her against him, and breathed in the subtle flowery scent of her. He'd missed her so much.

Then they pulled apart and spoke simultaneously.

"What are you—?" he started before Vanessa cut him off.

"I just came to—"

"Same."

What was he even saying?

He'd forgotten they weren't the only ones in the room until Mom walked over. "Vanessa, honey."

Vanessa bit her lower lip, clearly embarrassed as she moved into Mom's open arms.

"I'm going to leave you two to catch up." Mom kissed Vanessa's cheek, then crossed over to hug him, and whispered, "You've got this, darling."

The server showed up, but Mom told him they needed some extra time alone.

When Mom left, Nate stared at Vanessa who was staring at him. A beautiful familiarity resurfaced between them as if the weeks apart hadn't happened. He gestured to the table. "You wanna have a seat?"

"Okay."

He walked ahead and slid out the chair Mom had vacated. Then, once Vanessa sat, he fell into his seat, and nerves danced in his stomach.

Was this happening? Had she truly reappeared in his hometown?

He cleared his throat. "How have you been?"

"Been better. You?"

His eyes searched hers. He needed to remind her how he loved her and confess how he'd missed her. But now might not be the right time or place. What if she was here to confirm their breakup?

"I found out some billionaire gave me a restaurant." With her tone so light, she mustn't be bothered by his gift.

"I know you don't want charity."

She reached to touch his hand across the table. The moment was tender as her brown eyes seeped into his with a longing that reflected his own. Could this be a turning point in their relationship? He desperately wanted it to be.

A soft, almost sad smile wobbled on her lips. "Thank you."

Hmm.

Her gaze held his as the air crackled between them. Things seemed different, yet nothing had changed. He was still racing this season, and she was still a chef turning teacher who didn't want to date a reckless man.

A million things clouded his mind as he saw her now. He longed to touch her, pull her into his arms, and kiss her senseless.

Funny. He'd always thought romantic love was a fantasy. He'd never thought it was possible to care for someone this way. He'd known they couldn't be together and it would never work out. But seeing her opened a wound. Now, his heart ached for what it couldn't have.

"About the restaurant." Her voice broke through his thoughts.

Of course, she was going to turn it down. He'd known that all along. He pressed his lips together as a sentimental ballad crooned in the background.

"I was thinking we could keep the steakhouse instead."

Yep, she was turning down his gift. What a snub.

"After paying the bills and employees, we could use the proceeds for the Autism Expression."

Did she just say we?

So why wasn't she accepting his gift? "Have you found a building for your restaurant yet?"

This time, a full smile rounded out her cheeks, pressing them up by her glowing eyes. "Ava is going to carry on Mom's legacy with the truck. She's even going to keep the name Mama Dee's."

"Wait a minute." He held up a hand. "Are you trying to say you gave Ava your recipes and she's the new barbecue queen?"

Vanessa nodded, beaming.

"But..." It didn't make sense at all. "That's what you've worked for all along."

"Your words stuck with me. I was walking through the perfect restaurant when I asked myself why and what would make the most sense."

Oh no! "I didn't mean to sabotage your mom's—"

"No, Nate. You didn't, and it's okay." The bright sparkle in her eyes matched the excitement in her voice. "I became so obsessed about fulfilling a dream that I blocked out everything, even God's voice, because I was confident I had to carry on Mom's legacy. God wants us to honor Him in what we do, but I wasn't honoring Him when I was constantly on edge and getting into arguments with other vendors."

"And nonvendors?" He tried to lighten things up by referencing their first meetings.

She chuckled, biting her lower lip. "I feel peace about it." She put her hand on her chest. "Ava was so happy when I gave her the recipes. You should've seen her face."

Vanessa then mentioned the start-up costs she'd given Ava, and his heart felt lighter over the joy radiating in her eyes. "I wanted to help her get the truck painted, but she loves the neon colors sprayed on the truck."

He laughed. It would match the woman's exotic hair-color choices. "I can only imagine."

"Nate." Vanessa's face turned serious. "You giving me your steakhouse meant a lot to me."

He'd give her the world if it were at his disposal and if she'd let him.

"I can't refuse the gift, but I have no resources to run a steakhouse. Is it possible that I can pitch in a little, though?"

He shrugged. "We both believe in the cause, so it only makes sense that we pitch in."

That was the only compromise he could reach since she was self-reliant.

"I like that very much."

A moment of silence passed as she tinkered with the silverware wrapped in a black cloth napkin. Then she leaned closer, rumpling up the tablecloth. "I'm sorry I didn't want you to race when it's something you enjoy doing."

"Don't be sorry." He reached out and touched a tress of her flowy hair, pushing loose curls aside. He missed the feel of her hair running through his fingers whenever he kissed her.

Her gaze rose to his, then lowered to his mouth. "I'm glad the doctors cleared you to race again."

"Looks like I have a pit lizard following my updates."

"Old habits are hard to break."

It didn't take a pit lizard to know because news of his injury was the talk in NASCAR news, and the moment he declared he was going to race this season, word got around fast.

"I support you," she said, the words flowing like sweet honey from her lips as he rested his hand on her soft cheek. "Right now, my focus is praying. I'm going to be praying for you more than I've ever prayed before, for each race."

Tears flowed from her eyes, and he wiped them away with his thumb.

"I want you to stay alive for a long time. I can't guarantee I'll be at each and every race, but I can promise I'll be your biggest fan."

Not all his family made it to all his races, so he didn't expect her to show up at each one. He'd still save space for her in the paddock area or the pit, depending on the different tracks. He wanted her to have a decent place to view the race.

"I love you so much." She confessed so easily with such genuineness.

"Can't Help Falling in Love" started playing, a miracle since it was the song he'd attempted to dance with her when he couldn't finish.

"I owe you a dance." He stood and reached for her hand.

She beamed. "Did you arrange for this song to play?"

"No, but God knew this moment would happen." Nate had woken up that morning with plans to have lunch with Mom. Only God could have known this moment was coming for them. "Dance with me."

She stood. This was their kind of dance. Whether she came to his races or not, her blessing and approval meant everything.

The moment he enveloped her in his arms, he leaned in and brushed his lips against hers. Intending to be quick, he was caught off guard when Vanessa, with a sound that was half gasp and half sob, captured his lips and kissed him fervently with a soft and tender kiss. It felt like a reawakening of their souls, an embrace filled with hope. As their lips entwined, the weeks of separation faded, giving way to a passionate connection and a new beginning—another season of their relationship. And he had a feeling, this dance, this song, and this moment would forever be etched in their hearts.

***

Although it had been a week since Nate last saw his family and Vanessa before the start of his racing season in Los Angeles, he could sense their prayers and support. While he wasn't certain Vanessa could attend his races, she showed up at his garage before the season's first race at the LA Coliseum. Hope surged within him as they embraced and exchanged a fervent kiss in the dimly lit garage, surrounded by the scent of gasoline and the low hum of engines being prepared.

"I just wanted to wish you luck." She nuzzled against his neck.

"I don't need it." He planted a gentle kiss on her cheek. "Not when I have my best friend and God on my side."

"See you at the finish line." Her smile radiant, she playfully patted his chest, and elation pumped through his heart.

As the race began and he climbed into his newly rebuilt Chevy, he put winning aside for the day, focusing on reclaiming his confidence behind the wheel and aiming for a top-ten finish.

He was determined not to end his final year as a loser.

With the sun beaming on the track, he navigated through the one-hundred-and-fifty-lap race, following Doyle's and the spotter's leads and treating this event more as the exhilarating sport he adored than a competition.

As the race progressed, his pulse raced. Then, rounding the final turn, he opened up the throttle and unleashed the roaring engine's full power. Envisioning Vanessa at the finish line and recalling the day he'd taken her racing motivated him to push beyond his limits. Cheers erupted from the stands as he climbed out of the car, his gaze seeking Vanessa amid the ecstatic crowd.

With her beaming smile guiding him to her, he sprinted over. Their gazes met before he scooped her into his arms and kissed her with all the love that swelled in his heart. The crowd's cheers grew louder, but at that moment, they were the only two people who mattered.

As he geared up for the Daytona 500, the most-awaited race of the season, he saw Vanessa nearly every day over the next two weeks. Serafina had provided him with Vanessa's ring size, and he now carried an engagement ring in his pocket, seeking the perfect moment to propose. Although he felt certain he and Vanessa shared the same vision for their future together—marriage—he feared he might be rushing things. But, in times like these, his spontaneous nature helped him make such significant decisions without overthinking.

As he sped around the Daytona International Speedway, his nerves threatened to overwhelm him. His hands shook, and his heart raced while he struggled to keep pace with the other drivers. The injury's lingering effects weighed him down, draining his energy and confidence. His only solace was the presence of his family and the knowledge that, wherever Vanessa was, she was either praying for him or watching the race.

"You're a bit slow, chief." Doyle's voice crackled through the radio. "This is no different from the museum race last week."

"I don't know." Nate huffed, feeling the pressure not to let his team down. "It's—"

"Hey, you," a familiar feminine voice interjected, warm and reassuring. He hadn't expected her to show up since she'd been nervous about the big race. His family had been the only familiar faces before he'd addressed his team. "Doyle was kind enough to call me in."

"Vee." Nate's heart leaped. "I didn't think you'd come."

"I'm afraid I'm all in, not just halfway," she said, and somehow, he maintained his focus on the track while taking in her comforting words. "You've got this, baby. I love you."

"I love you more."

Renewed inspiration and energy coursed through him. He wouldn't waste his team's hard work on this race. He'd overcome setbacks, and if this was his final year, he'd make it count.

As the sun dipped low in the sky, casting a warm glow over the track, he drove with fierce determination, pushing his car harder and harder. His fearful discouragement dissipated, replaced by an exhilarating joy.

After hours of intense racing and rapid pit stops, he crossed the finish line, the crowd erupting into cheers and applause. Finishing first was a familiar experience, but following last year's poor performance, he felt more grateful than ever for this victory. As the winning car, *Impulse* would be displayed for a year at the Daytona 500 Experience, a museum and gallery adjacent to the Daytona International Speedway.

At sunset, he climbed out of his car, removed his helmet, and joined his team in a celebratory huddle. He scanned the nearby crowd, anticipating Vanessa's approach. Cheers swelled, checkered flags waved, and enthusiastic announcers boomed across the airwaves. Nate paid no attention to the interviewer trailing him with a microphone.

Then he spotted her sprinting toward him, beaming. He reminded himself to breathe as her name escaped his lips like the roar of an engine. The moment she was within reach, she flung her arms around him and gripped his neck tightly. "Oh, Nate!"

Her skin felt soft beneath his hands as he brushed stray strands of hair from her face, drinking in the sight of her. "We won."

"I'm so proud of you, baby," she whispered, her voice quivering.

Before he knew it, he was cradling her face and kissing her deeply. The world around them faded, leaving only the pounding of his heart and the sensation of his fingers tangled in her hair. She kissed him back, her hands gripping the sides of his fireproof suit, pulling him closer and filling his heart to the brim.

"Fantastic performance by Nate Stone today!" The announcer's voice boomed through the microphone, seemingly louder and closer than ever.

Nate pulled away from their passionate kiss, both of them breathless. Vanessa's eyelids fluttered open, her gaze met his, and he was struck by the joy welling up inside him, a feeling so intense he'd never experienced it before.

As he made his way to the podium to accept his trophy with Vanessa at his side, their arms linked, the overwhelming emotion surged through him anew. Ignoring the interviewer's questions, he patted his jumpsuit pocket and felt the small box he'd stashed away before the race.

Time to seize the moment. He grabbed the microphone to address her. His heart raced, charged with adrenaline and nerves as he prepared to do something he'd never anticipated doing so publicly—something that, less than a year ago, he'd never imagined he'd be doing at all.

"Vee, from the moment I met you, I knew you were special." He spoke over the roaring cheers, taking her hand in his. "You energize my heart and make it whole. I can't imagine life without you."

Tears glistened in her eyes under the darkening sky as he released her hand.

He wiggled the velvet box from his pocket and opened the lid to reveal a stunning solitaire diamond engagement ring, its round brilliant cut shimmering against the black velvet. Then he dropped onto one knee. "I promise to love you unconditionally, support you in all your dreams, and make every moment we spend together unforgettable. I love you more than anything, and I want to wake up each morning with you by my side."

Vanessa gasped, her hand flying to her mouth as tears streamed down her face. "Yes!" she exclaimed even as he asked, "Will you marry me?"

Although the eruption of cheers drowned out her response, he read her lips, and she confirmed her answer when she knelt in front of him. So he handed off the microphone and slid the ring onto her finger, the solitaire sparkling in the floodlights.

"I love you with all my heart." She spoke shakily, her words brimming with promise.

He took her hand, helped her up, pulled her into his arms, and kissed her with complete reverence.

Winning the Daytona 500 in his final year of racing was a bittersweet achievement, but nothing compared to Vanessa agreeing to marry him and embark on a lifetime of adventures together.

EPILOGUE

Fairy lights shimmered, casting a warm glow on the waterfront terrace where the scent of lush flowers and candle centerpieces created a romantic atmosphere. The cascading white and gold fabric swaying above them seemed to dance with the Aegean Sea beyond the wall of open windows.

As the sun dipped below the horizon, the lights of nearby islands twinkled in the distance, casting a warm, enchanting atmosphere. Nate could almost still taste the salty air from the outdoor ceremony earlier today.

With Vanessa's hand in his, they watched the couple on the dance floor. Iris and Sabastian swayed to the melody of "All of Me" by John Legend. Their connection was evident in the adoring way they looked at each other, a blush tinting Iris's cheeks, and their heartfelt vows, which had brought many to tears, lingered in the air.

Even Dad, who was known for never crying, had glistening eyes under the late evening sky.

Vanessa's sniffles echoed Serafina's beside her. Nate squeezed Vanessa's hand. She was beautiful in a one-shouldered green dress that hugged her in all the right places. The diamond studs shimmered to complement the glossy hair falling in soft waves over her shoulders.

With the day's joy infectious, he surveyed the guests at their table, all arrayed in formal attire. Theo and Wade, both sporting huge grins, seemed captivated by the dancing couple.

Nate's attention then shifted to the head table where his parents held some of their grandchildren. Among the other members of the wedding party, Sabastian's friends, Leo and Nico, sat with Iris's friends, Liberty and Tessa, the latter of whom had been Nate's physical therapist during his recovery in Pleasant View. Their laughter mingled with the celebratory atmosphere.

In the corner, Nate's two sisters shared a table with his brothers Rohan and Owen while Eric's family and friends sat nearby. So many loved ones had traveled to Athens to celebrate Iris and Sabastian's union where this nearby seaside location choice could honor Sabastian's Greek heritage.

Nate's thoughts turned to his racing team that weekend. As it wasn't a qualifying race, he'd entrusted the six drivers from his team to represent them on the track. Comic most likely had a chance to finish in the top ten.

The DJ announced the father-daughter dance, and Nate refocused on the festivities. Iris and Sabastian chose to have their first dance before dinner, and while that was unusual, nobody seemed to mind, especially since trays of delectable appetizers had been circulating throughout the photo shoot following the ceremony. No wonder the couple had decided to hold off on dinner.

As the evening unfolded, conversation and laughter mingled with the lingering aromas from their feast of fresh seafood, grilled meats, and vibrant salads. The newlyweds moved from table to table, making time for each guest.

"What a serene setting for a romantic scene," Wade commented. His gaze flickered to the window, and excitement for his upcoming film in Greece lit up his eyes.

Vanessa waved to the scene. "I couldn't agree more! The historic buildings overlooking the ocean..." Her voice trailed off, her hand finding Nate's as he drew her closer.

Thoughts of their wedding plans lingered between them as they stared at each other. Even though they hadn't discussed their plans, it topped his priorities—Vanessa's too since she'd hinted each time she pointed out her favorite honeymoon destinations.

Logan tilted his chin toward Theo. "Speaking of buildings and hotels, did you confirm about your uncle?"

A tick twitched in Theo's jaw. His recent discovery of a deceased blood relative must be weighing on him. "What am I supposed to do with a sinking hotel?"

"Maybe you could sell it?" Serafina leaned forward to sniff the irises, lilies, and gladiolus creating a vibrant centerpiece.

"I like Sera's idea." Logan draped a hand over his wife's shoulder. "But, Theo, before you make any decisions, you should find out why a formerly five-star hotel and resort is failing."

"I've seen pictures of that resort online," Nate chimed in. "From a business perspective, investing in it and bringing it back on the map would be a good move."

"What do you think, Vanessa?" Theo included her, seeming genuinely interested in her opinion.

"It was your uncle's, so I'd keep it." She chuckled to herself. "But you're asking someone who spent years chasing the wrong dream for the sake of carrying on someone else's legacy."

Nate cupped a comforting hand on her shoulder. "Which makes your opinion the most important one."

Back to teaching part-time, Vanessa appeared to be loving every moment of it. When his racing career crossed the finish line at the end of the season, she wanted to make North Carolina their home where she could teach. She'd already researched the requirements for getting her teaching license for that state. They would retire in Pleasant View someday and have a house built there. For now, she was staying at her San Francisco apartment, and he was living in his penthouse whenever he wasn't traveling. He'd keep the lease until the end of the racing season.

Living close to the track in Charlotte, he might consider mentoring or becoming a consultant. But he was far from committing to anything other than spending time with his girl and taking her on the adventures he'd been dreaming of, but had no time for.

As they talked about their plans, Wade slapped Theo's shoulder. "Take two weeks off and work virtually. It's the twenty-first century. You don't have to be physically present to work. If you want to learn about your dead uncle and revive this hotel, what better way than to go undercover?"

"You mean I go like a private investigator?"

"Like an undercover boss," Vanessa and Serafina spoke simultaneously.

Nate had seen the show with Vanessa during his recovery days. He chuckled. "Means you go clean the bathrooms, take out trash, and do all the messy work."

Theo grimaced and eyed Logan then Wade to confirm Nate's words.

Logan nodded, and Wade grinned. "Now that would make a great TV show!"

"It is a TV show." Vanessa wagged a finger at them.

"Theo doesn't know that." Wade struck the table. "But you should totally do it."

"Seriously, bro. They're right," Nate encouraged him. "For the sake of wanting to know what your relative was like."

Theo rubbed his well-trimmed beard. "You guys really think I should do it?"

After their brief silence, Vanessa spoke up. "On a serious note, you should consider it. You might uncover some important information about your family and potentially save a failing business."

Theo took a deep breath before a slow nod dipped his chin. "Okay, I'll do it. But I'll sell it if it's not worth it. I don't want to waste time and resources on something that's not going to work."

Nate smiled, proud of Theo's bold decision. "We'll support you every step of the way."

Logan braced his elbows on the table and rested his chin on his clasped hands, eyes bright. "And I can help you with the business aspect. We'll make sure it's a success."

Wade raised his glass in a toast. "To Theo's new adventure! And to my new TV show." Wade must be teasing about turning Theo's uncertain adventure into a reality TV show. However, an undercover mission involving a media mogul and a potential TV show in the making promised excitement.

Later, after a night of dancing, the bouquet toss took center stage. Nate's gaze followed Vanessa as she leaped for Iris's bouquet the moment it was tossed. The radiant happiness illuminating her face as she scooped up the bouquet signaled their wedding was just around the corner. It was an enchanting night filled with love and laughter. His tender gaze met Vanessa's, and his heart swelled with adoration for the woman of his dreams.

The promise of their future together seemed to shimmer in the air as they lost themselves in the magic of the night.

-THE END-

Next in the Billionaires' Reunion!

A Genuine Disguise

When love blossoms between a hotel maid and a billionaire in disguise, will the unveiling of his secret identity unite them or break them apart?

Whitney never imagined working at a hotel would be her dream job, but it helps her support her recovering addict mother and sister while saving for her much-needed heart valve replacement. Her mundane routine takes an unexpected turn when a charming new employee joins her team, bringing fresh enthusiasm to her days.

Theo Stone, a self-made billionaire, has come a long way since his humble beginnings as a South American baby adopted by a family in the States. When he unexpectedly inherits a struggling hotel from a long-lost uncle, selling the property seems like the logical choice. However, his brother persuades him to go undercover as an employee to better understand the hotel's issues. Theo agrees, not expecting to fall for the captivating team leader, Whitney.

As Whitney and Theo grow closer with each room they clean, the secret he's concealing begins to feel more like a betrayal. But when the truth about Theo is finally revealed, can their love survive the shock, and will they both find the strength to overcome the challenges that lie ahead?

A Genuine Disguise is Book 4 in the standalone series.

Fall in love with The Billionaires' Reunion Christian Romance series while catching up with the big Stone Family as they reunite in their scenic small-town. There's several seasons of love and adventure in this spin off series following Eric Stone's siblings from The CEO's companion in the caregiver series. With each family member taking a turn to coordinate a family gathering, there's plenty of laughter, tears and Happily Ever Afters. (You don't need to have read The Caregiver series first to enjoy this series.)

ABOUT THE AUTHOR

Rose Fresquez is the author of the Buchanan -Firefighter series, Romance in the Rockies, The caregiver series, two short stories and two family devotionals. She also writes in a multi-author project: Chapel Cove Series.

Rose is married and is the proud mother of four amazing kids. She loves to sing praises to God. When she's not busy taking care of her family, she's writing.

OTHER BOOKS BY ROSE

Checkout the Rest of Rose's Books
THE BUCHANAN SERIES

1. *First Site*
2. *Something right*
3. *Bright Side*
4. *Short Sighted*
5. *New Light (A Christmas Novella)*

ROMANCE IN THE ROCKIES SERIES

1. *Complex*
2. *Choices*
3. *Beyond Repair*
4. *Stand Out*
5. *Crystal Clear*

THE CAREGIVER SERIES

1. *The Doctor's Nanny*
2. *The Entrepreneur's Nurse*
3. *The Physician's Helper*
4. *The CEO's Companion*
5. *The Investor's Wife*
6. *The Soldier's Trainer*
7. *The Realtor's Attendant*

THE BILLIONAIRE REUNION SERIES

1. *A legitimate Date*
2. *A Sudden Romance*